Rolling In The Deep

Evelyn C. Fortson

ISBN: 979-8-35098-463-7 (printed)

ISBN: 979-8-35098-464-4 (eBook)

For my grandsons, Omariell and Aseer, my creative muses,
thank you for bringing joy into my life
when it was in short supply.
Love, Gram Gram!

Also, by Evelyn C. Fortson

Bittersweet

Finally, Doing Me!

Acknowledgment

I want to thank Mrs. Honey Obeng for her selfless act of kindness and generosity in reading, rereading, and editing my manuscript. Mrs. Obeng graduated from New York City Public Schools, The City University of New York, and Bard College. She taught English as a Second Language in the Republic of China, Abu Dhabi, and conducts Socratic Seminars in English Language Art classes in Hesperia, California. The self-proclaimed bibliophile's education and vast experience are inspiring, and her generous spirit is humbling. Thank you, Mrs. Obeng, for being you.

Table of Contents

"Blessed is he whose transgression is forgiven, whose sin is covered."
Psalm 32:1

Chapter 1

Clouds the color of tarnished silver blanketed the sky all day. The only hint that it was indeed day was the weak glow of the sun that backlit an occasional cloud or two. Despite the dreary sky that promised rain, the church overflowed with mourners. Morning Star Baptist Church's congregation had filled the sanctuary with Dinah Mae's friends. Indigo, her granddaughter, was the only family member there. Big Momma had outlived or lost contact with the family she left back home in Coushatta, Louisiana. The usherettes were dressed in all white, including the white-gloved hands that directed the mourners to their seats. The pastor acknowledged Sister Dinah's faithful years of service, fifty years of membership, and fifteen years on the usher board. Indigo was presented with a scroll that acknowledged her grandmother's kingdom work. Pastor Banks announced the service as a celebration of Sister Dinah's life, but Indigo thought of it as an ending. She didn't feel much like celebrating and concluded that God didn't either. That's why the day had been so bleak.

The last of the mourners, except for Mr. Ambrose, had finally left Big Momma's house just as the sun gave up its efforts and night arrived. The day's gloom had turned into a tenebrous night that hid the moon. Indigo stood before the picture window in her grandmother's living room, looking at the night sky. She shivered as she saw a massive black cloud looming over the house across the street. *Someone just walked over my*

1

grave, she thought. A faint smile flickered across her face because that was something her grandmother would say.

Big Momma was more than her grandmother. She was the one who kissed her boo-boos, looked for the bogeyman in the closet and under the bed, and wiped away tears. The callous hands that scratched Indigo's cheeks when she was young had been mottled with age spots, (smooth and paper-thin) the last time Big Momma had wiped away her tears. Those hands had aged quicker than the rest of her because of too much time in hot, soapy water that had molded her into the woman she was today. The hands that scraped her soft, young flesh in loving embraces also whipped her behind when deemed necessary. Big Momma showered pearls of wisdom on her from childhood to adulthood, but they meant nothing to her back then. Now, she understood how wise her grandmother had been. Sayings that she thought were silly then, are profound now that the messenger is gone. *A hard head makes a soft behind, God willing, and the creek don't rise; a watched pot never boils, and If you lay down with dogs, you'll get up with fleas,* flowed from Big Momma's mouth like the gospel songs she sang around the house.

When Indigo was seven years old, her mother, Wanda, abandoned her. Memories of her mother were like looking at fuzzy photographs whose images were almost unrecognizable. No matter how hard she concentrated, she couldn't conjure up a feeling associated with her mother. She must have been twelve or thirteen when she last asked Big Momma about her mother. Her grandmother had flinched when she asked, and Indigo had thought the question, seemingly coming out of nowhere, must have caught her by surprise. She showed Indigo old pictures of her mother and answered her questions with a hollow-sounding voice. Big Momma didn't elaborate on her answers or segue into other stories about her mother. Instead, her voice lacked warmth and became more brittle with each question asked. Indigo never asked about her mother after that day because a distance had developed between her and Big Momma. She thought maybe she had hurt her grandmother's feelings by asking about her mother. She had revealed to her grandmother that she still loved the woman who hadn't cared enough to raise her. Indigo had never felt a limit to her grandmother's love; she thought it had no boundaries, until that day. The need to have her grandmother's boundless love stopped her from asking more questions. After Big Momma's death, an old loneliness she hadn't felt in years crept into her soul, and old questions that needed to be answered, resurfaced.

The smile that lit up her face a second ago when she heard herself reciting one of her grandmother's sayings was replaced with a look of despair. A feeling of utter hopelessness coursed through her body so strongly that she had to grip the top of the rocking chair to keep from falling.

"You all right?" asked Ambrose.

"Yeah, I'm fine," said Indigo, deciding to sit down before she fell. She sat, rocking back and forth, and continued to look out the window. "I can't believe she's gone. What am I supposed to do without her?"

The question hung in the air between them because neither she nor Ambrose had an answer. The question she asked out loud was the same one Ambrose had been asking since Dinah died.

Ambrose had been in love with Dinah for more years than he had been married to his wife, Lucinda. He had buried his wife thirty years ago, so he was no stranger to grief, but losing Dinah had taken everything out of him. Maybe grief got harder as you got older, or perhaps he loved Dinah more. He had loved Lucinda and had sent for her to join him in Los Angeles, the promised land. They raised their children here in a city that didn't quite live up to its promise. The same southern hatred lived up North, except it didn't reveal itself all at once. It lived behind smiling faces and disguised itself behind mannerisms that white folks labeled as

"Tolerance." As he raised his kids, made love to his wife, and became good friends with Delray, he fell in love with his friend's wife, Dinah. Ambrose glanced at Indigo as he tried to stay in the present, not wanting to wander into the past where the dead lived. Indigo sat rocking, lost in thought, no longer seeing the dark sky or the falling rain, while Ambrose lost his battle and relived the past.

Ambrose had come to Los Angeles in 1953, about a year after Delray and Dinah. He would never forget his buddy Delray. He was walking down Alameda Street looking for work. Earlier that day, he had taken the bus to the Firestone Tire and Rubber Company in South Gate. South Gate was a Sundown town. Negros could cross the tracks and mow white folk's lawns and clean their homes, but they best be back on their side of the tracks come sundown. Instead of the vigilante justice meted out by *The good ol' boys* in the South, the police kept *niggas* in line in the North. Ambrose had followed the stream of white men up to the huge building that looked like a mission. The men stared at him with undisguised hostility as he walked alongside them to the massive plant.

He headed west after leaving the tire plant, deciding his chances were better on the Alameda Street corridor, rumored to have plenty of jobs. Although he had no experience in paper and plastic production, chemical manufacturing, food processing, or any other trade, he needed a job. He was on the verge of giving up and walking to the bus stop to go home. Suddenly, the desire to walk down Central Avenue, where he would be shrouded in the blackness of his neighborhood, became an overwhelming desire. He walked swiftly down the street, the muscles in his neck and shoulders relaxing at the thought of going home. Ambrose stopped abruptly when he heard a man screaming. He had heard a scream like that back South. His heart was pounding so hard that he grabbed his chest. Fear gripped him, keeping him glued to the sidewalk. Two men bustled out of the building he stood in front of. A short, muscular Black man held his hand to his chest, where blood blossomed all over his shirt. A fat White man who was more accustomed to walking at a leisurely pace struggled to keep up with the bleeding man. A tall, burly Black man ran out of the building, removed the rubber apron he was wearing, and threw it on the ground. He also pulled off his shirt and wrapped it around the bleeding man's bloodied hand.

"Come on, man. I'll take you to the hospital, said the tall Black man.

The two Black men walked down the loading dock steps and got into a car.

"Goddammit, Delray, he can drive himself!" yelled the fat White man, who pulled a handkerchief out of his breast pocket and dabbed at the sweat that rolled down his forehead and the back of his neck.

Ambrose watched the car drive away before finally regaining the use of his legs.

"You...hey, you there!" shouted the White man.

Ambrose turned to look at the man and pointed to himself.

"Yeah, you. Are you looking for work?"

"Yes sir, I am," answered Ambrose.

"Well, come on in," said the man, gesturing for Ambrose to follow him.

That was how Ambrose got his first job in Los Angeles, where he first saw the man who would become his good friend.

While Ambrose relived the past, so did Indigo. She was getting dressed to see Big Momma when Treyvon decided to come home after staying out all night. She heard the front door open and close, and she heard him walking down the hall. She had just fastened her bra and was sliding it around to the front so she could place her breasts inside the cups and pull the straps on her shoulders when he walked into the bedroom.

He looked tired, like something the cat had dragged in. Indigo found herself trying to think of the saying she had heard her Grandmother say. She glanced at Treyvon and smirked when she remembered it; he looked like he had been *rode hard and put away wet.* He sat on the edge of the bed and watched her as she finished getting dressed.

"Where you think you going?" he asked.

Indigo heard him, but she didn't answer because a man who stayed out all night didn't deserve an answer, and besides, she didn't have time to discuss the status of their relationship.

"I said, where you think you're going?" After a few seconds passed without an answer, Treyvon repeated the question and added a warning. "I'm not going to ask you again."

"Fuck you, Treyvon. I didn't hear you tell me where you've been all night, so don't worry about where I'm going!" Indigo slipped her t-shirt over her head and slid one arm into the sleeve. She was putting her other arm into the other sleeve when Treyvon jumped up, grabbed her, and threw her on the bed.

"Where you going, huh?" hissed Treyvon as he lay on top of her.

"Get the fuck off me!" screamed Indigo, bucking her body in an attempt to dislodge him.

Treyvon's smooth brown face, usually smiling or on the verge of a smile, was contorted almost beyond recognition. His face was so close to hers that turning her head to the side was difficult. She was trapped under his body and began to understand what was happening to her.

"Baby, what's wrong?" she asked softly, hoping to reach the man she knew.

He either didn't hear her or chose not to answer. He yanked the t-shirt over her head and shoved her bra above her breasts. Indigo lay still, trying to decide whether she should fight or try to reason with him.

"Treyvon, baby…. What's wrong? You can tell me…and we can talk it out. What's wrong, baby?"

"What's wrong is your fucked up attitude! You're mad because I've been out all night, but did you wonder if something happened last night?" said Treyvon. "You and your girls go out all the time."

"Yeah, but I don't stay out all night."

"You guys go on girls' trips, and I don't trip. But the one night I don't come home, you think you don't have to answer me?

"You're right, Treyvon. I'm sorry. What happened? Are you all right?"

Treyvon pushed off the bed as if doing a push-up, freeing Indigo. He stood up and began taking off his shirt.

"It got a little weird last night," he said as he sat beside her. "After the club, we ended up at Keon's place. He wanted to show everybody his new spot. After a while, some girls came by, and I was gonna leave." He stopped and looked at her.

Indigo was sitting next to him, having already placed her breasts back in her bra and pulled down her t-shirt. She looked into his eyes, fearing what his confession would do to them.

"We were sitting out around the pool bullshitting and listening to music. Jaheem was making the drinks, and Craig was rolling the joints. I must have grabbed the wrong drink because before I knew it, I was stumbling around and almost fell into the pool. Eddie took me inside and dropped me in a chair. I woke up this morning and got the hell out of there."

Indigo looked away from him before she chuckled dryly. "You expect me to believe some shit like that? Huh?"

"It's the truth."

"I'm not some punk ass bitch that you can play," she said, standing up.

Punk Ass Bitch slapped Treyvon in his face and slammed him back into his childhood. He had been a scrawny little kid with glasses from elementary school until his junior year of high school. He had heard the words punk, sissy, lil bitch, gay, and even faggot once or twice whispered about him. All because he had been different from most of the other boys in the neighborhood. He loved to read and draw and got good grades in school. He remembered being eleven years old when his mother stopped hugging him because his father thought that her smothering him was going to make him into a sissy. One day, a bully had beaten him up after school simply because it was Friday. When he got home, his mother hugged him, and he began to cry. That night, his father asked him if he had fought back, and when he said he had, his father proudly slapped his back. Treyvon's chest swelled as his father instructed him on how to handle bullies in the future and how to fight. In the backyard, he and his father sparred into the night until his mother called him in to get ready for bed. Later that night, he had gotten out of bed to use the bathroom. Walking down the dark hallway, he heard his parents talking at the dining table.

"You know he ain't hard like other boys," whispered his mother.

"I know, and you're gonna make him into a sissy, Ruthie. You baby him too much."

"But he's my baby boy."

"He ain't no baby. Besides, I don't want no punk ass bitch for a son," hissed his father.

Treyvon had turned around and quietly went back to his room. He lay in his bed as hot tears ran down his face. How could his mother and father think such a thing about him?

"Who's a bitch, Indigo?" he asked, watching her walk away from him.

"Well, it ain't me," she said, flippantly.

Treyvon got off the bed and stood in front of Indigo so close that she had to back up to look at him. Looking up at him, she didn't see the man she had lived with for a year; instead, looking down at her was an angry stranger.

"Move out of my way," said Indigo.

Treyvon bumped into her with his chest, causing her to tumble back on the bed, which was when he hit her on the jaw with his fist. When she regained consciousness, she was lying face down on their bed with him on top of her, violating her in an area of her body that she would never have allowed. The pain was searing hot. She felt like he was ripping her apart and setting her on fire all at the same time. Treyvon pushed her head down into the mattress so that her screams were muffled. The screaming stopped as Indigo struggled to turn her head so she could breathe. After he pulled himself out of the place where he had never been invited, he held on to her. She didn't know how long she lay there, listening to his breathing. She shifted her head to look at him when she thought he was asleep. His eyes were open, and he stared back at her. Then he abused her in a familiar part of her, a place where he had been received warmly before any number of times. After a few painful thrusts, her body betrayed her and began to involuntarily move in sync with his, as it had always done. Captured in his gaze, Treyvon smiled widely and pounded harder because he knew she was losing control. He caressed her with the softness that she knew and loved, and then he pulled and pinched, which caused her to whimper. This feeling was not the pleasure that came from lovemaking. It wasn't the beautiful connection of body and soul. This was something different, something wild that clawed, ripped, and debased. She fought the urge to let go and take part fully, but in the end, she lost the battle. If he had stopped, she would have begged him to continue and finish what he had started. He lifted her body in the air, with only her shoulders on the mattress. He was kneeling in bed, metering out pleasure, pain, and shame.

When he was done, he fell asleep, and Indigo limped like a wounded animal out of the bed. She tiptoed out of the room, went to the bathroom down the hall, and gingerly cleaned herself. Indigo had to return to the bedroom for clothes, but she went into the kitchen first and got a butcher knife. She entered the bedroom and grabbed clothes from the drawer with trembling hands. Indigo walked naked to the bed where Treyvon lay and stood over him with her clothing in one hand and the knife in another. She stood poised to plunge it into him for so long that she had to lower her arm because it ached.

"Do it," he said without opening his eyes.

Indigo jumped when she heard him speak.

"Do it," said Treyvon, sitting up and opening his eyes.

She walked backward away from him, arm raised, clenching the knife. He rose from the bed slowly, assuring her that he wasn't going to hurt her. The man that she thought she knew was back. The slight upturn of his lips softened the features of his face, and the cooing sound of his voice calmed her somewhat. He sauntered toward her as she continued to walk backward out of the bedroom and down the hall. Indigo backpedaled down the hallway until Treyvon disappeared into the bathroom and closed the door. She stood frozen like Lot's wife, who had looked back at Sodom, to the place she called home. Maybe that was part of the confusion; the man she called home had vanished before her, and she didn't know where her home was anymore. It was at that moment that she thought of Big Momma. Big Momma was home; she needed her grandmother to hold her and tell her everything would be all right. She needed her to reassure her that the bogeyman wasn't there. Standing in the hallway, before she lowered the knife, Indigo tried to reconcile who she thought Treyvon was to who he was just minutes ago. The before and after pictures were too disparate for her to make sense of. When she heard the shower running, she knew she had to leave there quickly. She threw her clothes on, found her purse and keys, and left without looking back.

Indigo frantically wiped at tears as she drove recklessly to Big Momma's house. She almost ran into the car in front of her as it stopped at a yellow light. She parked her car in her grandmother's driveway but couldn't get out. Shame kept her in the car. She didn't want Big Momma to know; she didn't want anyone to know. The savagery of the sodomy, the one thing that he knew she would never consent to, filled her with shame. She had agreed to every other sexual desire that Treyvon asked for except —--that. They both had asked for and gave each other what they needed in bed. Making love wasn't the only thing that they did. Sometimes, they desired a quick release or something less gentle. But never this brutal taking. She had never been so afraid before. Treyvon had sole control over what happened to her. She had lost everything at that moment, even her self-control. She sat in the car until she thought she had composed herself enough to fool her grandmother's gaze. Before getting out and walking up the walkway she took a few deep breaths. After waiting a few seconds for her grandmother to answer the door, Indigo unlocked it and went inside.

"Big Momma, it's me."

The house was quiet, and the T.V. was off; no gospel music played on the boom box that Big Momma had bought in the 1980s. She went to the kitchen first, then to her grandmother's bedroom, the bathroom, and then to her old bedroom. She retraced her steps back to the kitchen and opened the back door to see if her grandmother was in the backyard.

"Huh…" escaped from behind her pursed lips.

Indigo walked to the front of the house and looked out the window, half expecting to see Big Momma walking up the sidewalk. *She's probably next door mad because it took so long for me to get here. She'll come home when she thinks she's taught me a lesson.*

In the bathroom, Indigo splashed water on her face. The cool water felt good, so she decided to take a bath to soak away the filthy residue of Treyvon that had oozed out and dried on her. While the tub filled with water, she removed her clothes and looked for physical wounds on her body in the full-length mirror that hung on the back of the bathroom door. There were no wounds that she could see, but she knew her soul had been scarred. When she finished examining her body, Indigo stepped into the tub, leaned back, and let the water run until it reached the overflow drain.

"He raped me…why would he do that?" she asked out loud. She closed her eyes, took a deep breath, and exhaled loudly. "I'm not crazy… it really happened. He raped me. He's an ape, which is found in rape. I was RAPED BY AN APE," she shouted until she heard the hysteria that rose with each chorus of the song. The words caught in her throat as she feared she was going crazy. *This is what insanity feels like*, she thought. Her mind was fighting her perceived sense of reality, questioning what had happened and trying to make sense of it. Her body told her she had been raped, but her mind searched for an alternative interpretation of the event. Indigo gripped her head with both hands, drew her knees to her chest, and cried.

When she got out of the tub, the water was cold. She put the same clothes back on except for her underwear. She threw her panties with crusted bits of Treyvon on them in the trash.

Sitting on the couch in the front room, Indigo began to worry again. If Big Momma had been next door, she would have come home by now. If she had walked the few blocks to the store, she should have been back already, even considering the stops she would have made speaking to her neighbors or picking some spearmints that grew wild outside Miss Shirley's fence. She should have made it home by now. Indigo went next door, and when Mr. Ambrose didn't answer, she walked down his driveway. His backyard was empty, so she returned to the front yard. She was standing on the sidewalk in front of Mr. Ambrose's house, looking up the street toward the market.

"Indigo…is that you?" yelled Lottie from across the street. "Come here for a minute."

Indigo caught movement out of her peripheral vision and looked across the street. She saw Miss Lottie waving her arm, beckoning her to come. Miss Lottie's mouth was moving, but she couldn't hear what she was saying. She walked to the curb and looked both ways before crossing the street. Miss Lottie, who usually sat on the porch on an old chair, stood by the gate. Her annoying mutt, Roscoe, started barking and growling before Indigo reached the sidewalk.

"Shut up, now…sit," commanded Lottie. "Indigo, how's Dinah? Is she going to be okay?"

"What? Whatcha mean, Miss Lottie?" asked Indigo louder than she meant to.

"They took Dinah to the hospital."

"Who are they?"

"Ambrose got in the ambulance with her."

Every hair on the back of her neck prickled her skin. She asked which hospital before covering her mouth with her hands to stifle the mournful sounds her mouth spewed.

"Probably Killer King," Lottie gasped and stopped speaking abruptly. Everyone referred to Martin Luther King Hospital as "Killer King." The hospital received the moniker for various reasons. It was located in Watts, an underserved poor neighborhood of African Americans and Hispanic immigrants whose status was questionable. The people rushed to the emergency room were victims of gunshots and stabbings and would have died no matter which hospital they were taken to. Also, the community used the emergency room for their primary care, which caused absurd delays.

"You know they don't take us to St. Frances. Didn't Ambrose call you?" yelled Lottie.

Indigo was already running across the street. She ran into the house and grabbed her purse. She dumped the contents on the dining room table when she didn't feel the phone inside. She must have left it at the apartment. She threw everything back in her purse except for her keys. She drove to Killer King because that's where her grandmother was most likely transported. Mr. Ambrose was sitting in the emergency room, overflowing with the sick and wounded. The second she crossed the threshold, her anxiety, fear, and worry collided with those of the others in the room. She walked past crying babies, worried mothers, and the wounded, who were also angry because it was taking too damn long to receive treatment or get word of their loved one's condition. Ambrose looked up at Indigo, who stood before him. He reached for her hand and tried to stand but fell hard back into his seat, unable to stand. Indigo kneeled.

"Is Big Momma, okay?" she whispered, sounding like a frightened little girl.

"She's okay, baby girl, but you and me well…," said Ambrose, patting her hand.

"What…whatcha mean you and me?" She gripped his hand, squeezing hard as she prepared for what she knew was coming.

"Dinah's gone. She's gone home to glory, but you and me, baby girl, we're still here in hell," said Ambrose, wincing from the pain as Indigo gripped his hand tighter.

Chapter 2

Lightning lit the sky for a nanosecond, like a kid flicking a light switch on and off, only to be thrown instantly back into darkness. It was the boom of thunder that shook the house and brought both Ambrose and Indigo back to the present.

"You need to get away from that window. That was close," warned Ambrose.

"I know." Indigo closed the curtains. "Did you eat anything today?" she asked, turning to look at him.

"I wasn't hungry earlier, but I might, could, eat something now."

"I'll make you a plate."

"Make it to go. I best be getting home."

She went into the kitchen and opened the refrigerator, which was full of plasticware containing fried chicken, string beans, and potato salad. She made him a plate and wrapped it in aluminum foil.

"Thanks, baby girl. I'll see you tomorrow."

She walked with him to the door and watched him walk out of the yard from the doorway. He looked like he had aged ten years since Big Momma's death. Ambrose, who usually walked erect with long strides for a man his height, shuffled, slightly bent over, out the yard. Onyx and Zari, Ambrose's grandchildren, had tried to get him to go home earlier before they left, but he refused to leave. His daughter Tamar had attended the funeral, but his son Jonathan hadn't come. Jonathan lived in Northern California, but Indigo had thought he would come down and was disappointed that he hadn't come to pay his respects to a woman who had once watched over him.

She closed the front door and leaned against it, breathing in and out slowly. Today had been hard, but she thought everything had turned out well. She felt her grandmother would have approved. After checking that the back door was locked, she turned off the lights and went to her old bedroom. The bedroom remained frozen in the 90s. A Poster of Boyz II Men hung over one twin bed, while a poster of Jodeci hung over the other. She had put on pajamas and got into bed when her cell phone buzzed.

"Hey, girl. How're you holding up?" asked Amani.

"I'm good,"

"Are you sure you don't want me to come back over? I can spend the night."

"No…I'm so tired. I just want to go to sleep."

"Okay, then…I'll let you go. Oh, hold up! Why wasn't Treyvon standing by your side?"

"I'll tell you tomorrow."

"Uh-uh, gurl, you need to tell me now. What's going—."

"Amani, gurl, I'll tell you about it tomorrow. I'm beat. I'm hanging up now." Indigo ended the connection even though she could still hear Amani talking on the other end. She turned off the light and drifted off to sleep. She didn't know how long she had been asleep before she felt something floating stealthily into the room. Her eyes were closed, but she was wide awake and could see the thing in the room through closed eyes. It was darker than the darkness of the room. Indigo lay stiffy in the bed, barely breathing as the ethereal shape moved further into the room. Her

heart pounded wildly in her chest, making it hard to tap down the panicked voice in her head, screaming for her to turn on the light. The sweat
that had formed on her forehead was now dripping down the side of her
face. She desperately wanted to turn on the light, but her brain couldn't
make her body move. She lay in bed, immobile in the physical world,
but her spirit, which had moved outside the body, remembered what Big
Momma had told her. She began to rebuke and cast out the demon in the
name of Jesus. She commanded it to leave repeatedly until it vanished,
and her spirit reentered her body. Indigo opened her eyes, reached out
her hand, and turned on the bedside lamp. The light alleviated some fear,
but some remained in the shadows, under the bed, and behind the closet
door. She had to get out of the room. Indigo went to the bathroom before
going to the kitchen. She turned on every light as she moved from room
to room, still frightened of the dark edges just beyond the light. When
the kettle's whistle blew, she jumped, and with trembling hands, she made
herself a cup of tea. She sat in the rocking chair in the living room and
sipped her tea. It had been a long time since a witch rode her back. She
was a little girl in that very room when it first happened. She had lain in
bed, paralyzed by fear, until whatever was sitting on her bed left. When
she told her grandmother what happened, Big Momma told her that it
was a witch and that when a witch rode her back, the only way to get it off
quickly was to call on the name of Jesus.

When she finished her tea, Indigo couldn't bring herself to go back
into her bedroom, so she went into Big Momma's room instead. She looked
around the room, knowing she would have to go through her grandmother's papers and clothes and figure out what to do with the house. A
month off work would go by too fast; she needed to start discarding the
things that made up her grandmother's life. Standing by the door, she told
herself she would start tomorrow.

"This is tomorrow. It's 3:30 a.m.," said Indigo out loud, looking around the room.

The room was beautiful in its simplicity. It was a small room; the bed was covered in an old-fashioned white chenille bedspread with a large rose in the center. Wooden nightstands on each side of the bed matched the chifforobe, the only other piece of furniture in the room. Homemade curtains from white eyelet fabric covered the two windows in the room. They were not the same curtains the Big Momma made decades ago because the embroidery had unraveled from the annual washing and the bleaching. Her grandmother replaced the curtains with the same material whenever she declared they looked a little too ratty. Indigo asked her grandmother why she hadn't bought a fabric with a pretty design on it, like the big floral curtains she had made for her room. Her grandmother told her that she made the same curtains for her windows because they reminded her of when it was hers and Big Daddy's room. The room as a whole and, for that matter, every room in the house had a country vibe. Maybe it was a way of remembering the life she had left behind. Indigo wondered if she could throw away the things that meant something to her grandmother. Little trinkets and mementos, some of whose worth was priceless to her grandmother, would now be given to Goodwill because their value had died with their owner. She turned off the light and closed the bedroom door. The room had always been a sanctuary, even in the dark. She climbed into her grandmother's bed and breathed in the delicate fragrance of roses. Fresh roses were in vases scattered around the house from spring to winter except after Christmas. Big Momma cut her bushes down before January to give the bushes a chance to rest. She remembered cold winter mornings and the clotting smell of freshly turned dirt as she sprinkled bone meal around the rose bushes while Big Momma worked the fertilizer into the soil.

Indigo didn't wake up until 10:00 a.m., having tossed and turned until she finally fell asleep around 5:00 a.m. After breakfast, she took her second cup of coffee into Big Momma's room, the room she would claim as her own, to tackle sorting through the things she would keep, throw away, or donate. Undergarments were put in the trash pile, but the new nightgowns and panties were placed in the donate pile. Like other women of her generation, her grandmother stored new undergarments and night-gowns in the back of the dresser drawer for emergencies. Indigo smiled, thinking Big Momma had the same motto as the Boy Scouts: *Always Be Prepared.* The drawer of the chifforobe had t-shirts with her church wom-en's conference logo on them. She remembered how she sometimes slept in those t-shirts, so she made a new pile of clothes to keep. Sorting the clothes didn't take long, but it was emotionally draining. She took a break to make herself a cup of tea. The doorbell rang just as she put the water on to boil.

"Who is it?" shouted Indigo through the closed door.

"It's me, Amani."

She opened the wooden and iron security doors and hugged her friend before she could enter the house.

"How you doing?" Amani asked when they released each other.

"I'm okay…I was going through Big Momma's clothes."

"Why so soon? Are you sure you're up for that?"

"I took a month off, but you know how quickly that'll go. I thought I might sell or rent out the house, but now…"

"But now what?"

"But now, I need a place to live."

"What!"

Indigo stepped back to allow Amani to enter the house. "Let's go to the kitchen." She closed the doors and led the way.

"I'm making myself some tea. Would you like a cup?"

"It's hot; I need something cold."

"There are plenty of sodas left from yesterday." Indigo filled a tall glass with ice and gave it to Amani. She pointed to the liters of sodas on the kitchen counter, from which Amani could choose. After the water boiled, she prepared her tea and ushered Amani outside into the back-yard. They sat under a shade tree in rusty yellow metal patio chairs with bent U-shaped legs that allowed them to rock if they were so inclined.

"Where did Big Momma get this old country shit from?" laughed Amani.

"She probably brought it with her from Louisiana," smiled Indigo.

"So," said Amani, looking severe. "What's going on with you and Treyvon? Why do you need a place to stay?"

Surprised at how quickly the tears came, she swiped at them as they fell. Amani reached forward and patted Indigo's leg.

"It's okay…let it out. I got you."

Indigo bent forward in her chair, her hands resting in her lap as her chin touched her chest. She wept for all that had happened and for every-thing she had lost. Either one of the events in the last few weeks would have left an indelible mark and changed how she moved in the world. But both horrors happening so closely together left her feeling mentally and physically fragile.

Amani watched Indigo and thought it had more to do with the loss of her grandmother than any lover's quarrel. But she thought Treyvon should have put that aside and been there for her. She had called Treyvon last night, trying to find out what was going on, but he hadn't answered his phone. She sat quietly until Indigo was done. When Indigo sat up straight and reached for the tea, she had placed on the small table next to her chair, Amani murmured, "I got you."

"Sorry about that," said Indigo, sucking in air loudly through her nose and exhaling just as loudly out her mouth.

"You ain't got nothing to be sorry about," said Amani before taking a big gulp of her soda.

The two friends sat under the tree, enjoying the shade it offered and the silence that their relationship allowed. Amani knew she couldn't rush her friend, so she waited until she was ready to speak. The feeling that all was right with the world occurs in rare moments, and this was one of them for Amani. Sitting with her best friend surrounded by flowers, watching birds darting past, and butterflies fluttering around contributed to the feeling. Amani's eyes drooped because the sun made it impossible to keep them open. When Indigo began to speak, Amani stirred herself and sat up straighter. She wasn't expecting what Indigo had to say. Her breath caught in her throat, and her mouth hung open in disbelief. If it had been anyone else telling her this bullshit, she would have cussed them out, but this was Indigo.

"I...I can't believe Treyvon would do that," Amani said when she could speak.

"You don't believe me?"

"I didn't say that...I...I can't believe Treyvon could or would do something like that."

"Like rape me." Indigo made a sound, a sort of hiccup and cry, before she continued. "TREYVON RAPED ME, AMANI...he raped me."

"That's an awful word to throw around," admonished Amani. "Saying something like that could ruin someone's life and reputation."

"I'm not throwing it around. I'm telling you what happened."

"Give me a minute to process this shit. This is some wild shit you're saying. You're trying to tell me that my friend, whom I've known my entire life, is a rapist?"

"I'm not trying to tell you…I'm telling you that he raped me!"

"What, you guys never had rough sex before? Maybe he got carried away. Did you tell him to stop?"

Indigo gasped, unable to look into Amani's eyes because of the shame she felt and because, at one point, she wouldn't have wanted him to stop. "I'm not going to sit here and try and convince you to believe me, so I think you should leave." Indigo stood up to show her out.

"Wow, really, Indigo, so you're kicking me out because of some bull-shit you and Treyvon are going through?"

"Nah, I'm not asking you to leave because of me and Treyvon. I'm asking you to go because of you and me. We're not good. Did you forget that I'm your friend too?"

"I haven't forgotten, but I think you have. A friend wouldn't kick a friend out of her house, so FUCK YOU, INDIGO!" shouted Amani, standing up to go.

"Fuck you too, bitch," replied Indigo dryly.

Amani, noting the tone of Indigo's voice, became more enraged. She lowered her face to align it with Indigo's face before speaking. "I got you bitch." Amani poked Indigo on the shoulder with her index finger, stood up straight, and turned to leave.

"Hey, hey! What's going on over there?" Ambrose yelled from his backyard.

Ambrose and his grandson Onyx had heard the commotion from inside the house and came into the backyard to see what was happening next door. Ambrose was holding onto the chain-link fence that separated the two yards, and Onyx stood beside him with his hands folded in front of his chest. Neither of the women answered because they were stunned that they had an audience witnessing their poor behavior.

Indigo recovered first and replied, "Nothing is going on, Mr. Ambrose. Sorry about the noise." She looked at Amani when she said the noise and saw she was visibly shaken. Indigo wanted to hug her and ask her to stay so they could talk more. She wished she could explain how one act was brutal and how the other had manipulated and stripped her of her dignity. Instead, she walked toward the back door, and Amani followed. Amani retrieved her purse and walked out the front door without saying a word. Indigo returned to the backyard to pick up the cup and glass. She was surprised to see that Onyx was still standing by the fence.

"You all right?" he asked.

"I'm fine," she said, annoyed that he was there.

"What was that about?"

"Nothing." Indigo grabbed the cup and dumped the melting ice out of Amani's glass. She was heading back to the house when Onyx yelled.

"Hey, my grandpa wants to know if you have any more pound cake left."

"Yeah, I do."

"Well, I'll be over in a bit to get some, if that's okay?"

"Okay," she said, walking into the house, leaving Onyx standing by the fence, looking after her.

Indigo was putting bags of clothes she intended to donate in the trunk of her car when Onyx came out of his grandfather's front door. She waited for him by the front gate, and they walked up the pathway together.

"Come on into the kitchen," she said when they entered the house.

He walked behind her, admiring her voluptuous frame.

"Damn!" he said, not meaning to say it aloud.

"What?" she asked, turning around to look at him.

"Dang, girl, you sure have grown up. I remember you being this skinny, knock-kneed kid, and now you're all grown up."

She looked at him for a second before continuing toward the kitchen. "First off, I was never knock-kneed, and second, I'm not the only skinny kid who has grown up." She took the cake off the kitchen counter and placed it on the kitchen table. She gestured for Onyx to have a seat. Indigo cut a small piece of cake for herself and wrapped the rest of it in foil for Ambrose.

"My bad," smiled Onyx, watching her move around the kitchen. "You're slightly bowlegged. I don't know why I thought you were knock-kneed."

Looking down at her legs, Indigo caused Onyx to laugh at her. She sat across from him.

"It's not that funny."

"I know, but the look on your face is."

"Oh, so I'm funny-looking, too," she said, smiling.

"Nah, girl, you're fine as hell," said Onyx without a trace of a smile.

The banter stopped as they looked at each other, no longer seeing the children they once were. Onyx, always a skinny kid, was now 6 feet with broad shoulders that tapered down to narrow hips and long legs. Indigo stood at 5'4" with tiny breasts and a small waist that flowed into wide hips supported by nicely shaped legs. They both were blessed with beautiful dark skin, but he was slightly darker; his almond-shaped eyes were tighter, his lashes were longer, and his eyebrows were naturally arched. Like most women, she augmented her lashes and eyebrows, but they still didn't match his natural beauty.

She asked him about his grandfather to break the silence that was becoming awkward.

"He's doing all right, but I have to admit I'm a little worried about him. He's taking your grandmother's death pretty hard."

"I know. I'll check on him for you. I'll be here all the time for a while until I go back to work."

"I would appreciate that. Let me give you my number."

After they placed their numbers in each other's phones, Onyx brought up the incident in the backyard. Indigo tried to blow it off with some lame excuse about the silly things that girlfriends fight about. She took his silence as acceptance of her explanation, so she was shocked when he asked who Treyvon was.

"He's my—was. He's a guy I know."

"So, a guy you know raped you?"

A multitude of emotions ambushed her all at once. She gasped, involuntarily clamped her mouth with her hands, and began to cry.

"Hey," he said, reaching across the table to touch her elbow but stopping himself, unsure if touching her was the right thing to do. "Indigo, I promise you that motherfucker won't hurt you again."

She lowered her head to the table and sobbed. Onyx scooted his chair close to her, wanting to comfort her but unsure how to do so. He placed one arm on the back of her chair, lowered his head next to her ear, and whispered. "How do I get a hold of that nigga?"

After a short silence, she asked him to leave. She jumped from the shriek of the chair being pushed back. The tension in the room was taut with an energy that she thought was anger, but she soon identified it as violent. She kept her head on the table and closed her eyes, but in her mind's eye, she saw him hopping from one foot to the other while asking her how he could find Treyvon.

"Please Onyx…I can't right now."

Her head remained on the table, and she remained nonresponsive to his request. After a while, he took the plate with the cake but hovered for a few seconds, looking down at her before he gave up and left. She stayed seated at the table, shaken that he knew. She hadn't seen him in about seven years and had always thought of him as family until the year she developed a crush on sixteen-year-old Onyx. A crush that had faded with time and changed circumstances, but seeing him these past several days made her wonder if those feelings had ever left. Onyx's love had been a thing wished for—hoped for, and was as sweet as the young, inexperienced girl she was then. She thought her world was over when he balled up the note she left under his bike's tire and threw it in the street as he zipped down the sidewalk. She had been embarrassed when, as a girl, she confessed her unrequited love, but now she was mortified that he knew what had happened to her. Indigo saw Zari and Onyx on the weekends when their grandfather kept them because their mother worked on the weekends. She, Zari, and other girls in the neighborhood spent hours playing hopscotch or double-dutch jump rope on the sidewalk in front of Mr. Ambrose and Big Momma's house. Onyx and other neighborhood boys loved buzzing down the sidewalk on their bikes, scattering the girls off the sidewalk, screaming and shrieking. The girls yelled at the backs of the boys, whose legs pumped as fast as they could, to stop interrupting their games. By the time Indigo was in middle school, Onyx's mother had gotten married, so Mr. Ambrose didn't watch his grandkids as much as he used to. Onyx and his sister only spent a few weeks in the summer with their grandfather. By that time, she and Zari were not as close as they once were. During those summer weeks, she would catch glimpses of Onyx in the backyard with his grandfather doing yard work. She would spy on him from the top of the book she was reading on the front porch as he hung out in the front yard with his boys, trying to be cool.

She rose from the table, thinking it was a long time ago. Onyx wasn't a boy, and she wasn't a little girl anymore. His knowing that she had been raped made her feel dirty like he would always see her that way. She wanted to go to the backyard and trim and water the rose bushes that lined the back fence, but she didn't want to run into Onyx again, so she decided to lie down in her room and read.

Chapter 3

"What was that about?" asked Ambrose the minute Onyx entered the house.

"I don't know, Grandpa, she wouldn't say. She gave you a big old hunk of cake you wanted," he said, handing the plate to his grandfather.

"Thanks, grandson," said Ambrose, taking the plate. "I'm gonna heat up some coffee to go with this cake. You want some?"

"Nah, I'm good."

Onyx sat on the couch in front of the TV, staring at it but not watching what was on it. Meanwhile, his grandfather had gone to the kitchen. He returned to the living room with his cake on a small plate and a cup of coffee. He placed them both on the TV tray, permanently stationed next to his recliner. Ambrose was flipping the channel with the remote. Once he found a show to watch, he pushed back in the chair and sighed as his feet rose.

"Onyx, Onyx—boy, do you hear me calling you?" yelled Ambrose, pulling himself up in the chair.

"Huh," said Onyx, shaking his head. "Sorry, I must have been daydreaming or something."

"Boy, I've been calling your name for the longest," complained Ambrose. "I wanna know if she told you what she's gonna do with the house."

"I forgot to ask, but I'll find out the next time I see her."

"That's all right, I'll ask her."

"Looks like she's packing up some stuff. She has trash bags scattered around the house, and she was putting bags in the trunk of her car when I went over there."

"Huh…It could mean she's getting ready to sell. If it comes to that, I'm gonna need you to get rid of that situation," he said, looking at his grandson with a raised eyebrow.

"Why? Why don't you just let it be?"

"Because Indigo doesn't know, and Dinah didn't want her to know," said Ambrose, leaning forward with both feet planted on the floor.

Onyx saw how upset his grandfather was becoming, so he dropped the subject, but he hoped to God that it wouldn't come to that.

"Grandpa, you know I got you."

Ambrose brought the fork with a large hunk of cake to his mouth, but because his hand shook, the cake fell back on the plate. He looked up at his grandson, hoping he hadn't seen his trembling hand. He laid down the fork and nibbled at the cake with his hand even though he no longer had an appetite.

"I'm going to get going. I'll see you this weekend. Call me if you need me." Onyx got up from the sofa and squeezed Ambrose's shoulder before walking out the door. He opened the driver's side door, then closed it before walking over to see Indigo. He knocked on the door and waited for her to answer. He started to ring the doorbell but thought, what was the use? She obviously didn't want to talk to him. He reluctantly left the yard. He saw Miss Lottie waving and shouting something he couldn't make out, so he walked across the street.

"How you doing, Miss Lottie?" Onyx asked from the sidewalk next to her front gate.

"I'm good, baby. How you?"

"I'm good, Miss Lottie. Did you need something?"

"I just wanted to know how Ambrose was doing. I know he loved him some, Dinah."

"He's fine. A lot of people around here loved Miss Dinah."

"They sho' did, chile. I'm gonna miss her too," stated Lottie.

As Lottie finished her statement, Roscoe woke up and began yelping because Onyx was standing in front of his gate. The dog leaped off the porch and ran to the gate, jumping and barking at Onyx.

"Roscoe. Roscoe, be quiet!" commanded Lottie.

"I'll let my grandpa know you asked about him," he said, taking the opportunity to make his escape.

"Okay, well, take care, baby. Come here, Roscoe—be quiet."

Onyx smiled as he walked back to his car. Still smiling, he pulled out of the driveway, got out of the car again, and rolled the gate across the driveway. He counted himself lucky to have escaped Miss Lottie's interrogation before she could start. The silly smile on his face disappeared when he looked at Miss Dinah's house. A solemn expression etched his face at the thought of dealing with the situation that his grandfather needed his help with.

I need to know what that girl is gonna do with Dinah's house. Ambrose thought to himself as he sat in front of the TV. He was determined to keep the promise that he made Dinah all those years ago. He stood up slowly, stiff from sitting too long. Ambrose placed his dirty dishes in the kitchen sink and looked out the window. A memory of his wife Lucinda flashed across his mind. He remembered how happy she was when they bought this house. The neighborhood was so different then. Small wood-framed houses with detached garages. Some of the homes had garages and granny flats. They had been in California for five years before they were able to buy their home. Jonathan was three years old, and Lucinda was pregnant with Tamar. Delray and Dinah were already living in the neighborhood where the few remaining whites were leaving. Ambrose smiled at recalling how quickly White folks were leaving the area. They were getting out of the Florence Firestone area so fast and any other area that Negros moved to that the term "White Flight" was coined. Despite redlining, restrictive covenants, and discriminatory loan practices, he and Lucinda managed to buy this house. Mainly because it only took one Negro family to move in to cause the stampede of skittish White folks afraid of declining property values to sell. Realtors and Loan Officers conveniently devised ways to sell to Negros when it became apparent that no one else would be buying into these once-all-White neighborhoods. He had to admit that if it wasn't for Delray, they wouldn't have bought this house, and maybe if he hadn't lived next door to Dinah, he wouldn't have fallen in love with her. He and Delray were sitting in the alley in the back of the loading dock where the Negros had gathered empty wooden crates to sit and eat on. Sitting on crates and eating the lunch that their wives had packed for them, Delray told Ambrose that the White man next door to him had just put his house up for sale. After work that day, he rode with his friend to see the house. When they pulled into his driveway, the man whose house was for sale was outside watering his grass. Delray waved to his neighbor, who looked directly at him and didn't acknowledge his greeting.

"That old cracker never speaks to anybody," Delray muttered before he got out of the car.

Ambrose followed him to the man's yard.

"Hey neighbor, I brought my friend from work to see your house. Can we take a look at the inside?" asked Delray.

"He needs to contact the realtor," the neighbor grudgingly responded, moving to the side of the house to shut off the water.

"Well, sir, he works during the day, so he would be obliged to you if you would let him have a quick look tonight," said Delray, walking up the walkway.

"Sir, I sho'nuff would be obliged to you iffen you would see fit to let me see the house tonight," said Ambrose, skinning and grinning.

"Well," said the White man, appeased by the show of deference. "You all need to be quick. I got better things to do than give a house tour to two nig—" The neighbor caught himself before he said the n-word. He cleared his throat before continuing, "Well, come on then."

He gave them a quick tour of the house and ushered them back outside.

"Sir, I believe my wife would love the house. What do I need to do to buy it?"

"Call the realtor; wait here, and I'll get you a card."

They looked at each other, trying not to laugh until they were inside Delray's house. Delray fell onto the couch laughing, and Ambrose was bent over laughing in the middle of the room when Dinah entered the living room with her hands on her hips.

"What's going on?" she asked. When there was no response, she asked again. "What's so funny?"

"This nigga—--sorry negro was skinning and grinning so hard I thought I was back in the land of Dixie," laughed Delray.

"You started it, man, with your sho'nuff, and I would be obliged to you. After you said that, I figured you were trying to tell me it was time for the minstrel show," Ambrose replied, wiping tears from his eyes.

"I was, and it worked, too," Delray said, getting up from the couch and kissing Dinah on her lips.

Dinah swiped at him with the dish rag she pulled off her shoulder. The more she hit him with the rag, the more he tried to kiss her.

"Now, you know you wouldn't be hitting me if we didn't have company," he said, looking mischievously. "Now, give me some sugar, girl," he begged.

Dinah clicked her tongue and rolled her eyes before pecking him on the lips and telling him to behave himself.

Wanda ran out of the kitchen and hugged her dad before telling her mother the cornbread was burning. Dinah ran into the kitchen with Wanda trailing behind her.

"I better be getting home, man. See you tomorrow," said Ambrose, moving toward the front door.

"Hold on, man, I'll take you home. Dinah, baby. I'm gonna take Ambrose home. I'll be back in a minute," yelled Delray.

Good old Delray, thought Ambrose, still looking out the kitchen window and forcing himself back into the present.

Chapter 4

"Hey, Ambrose, how you doing?" asked Lottie when he opened her gate. She was sitting in her chair on the porch, watching the people in the neighborhood come and go, waiting for something worth talking about to happen. Roscoe met Ambrose at the gate, wagging his tail so hard that his backside swayed.

"I'm doing all right. How about you?"

"I can't complain. It wouldn't do any good anyway. Are you taking Roscoe for his walk?"

"Same as I always do; why?"

"Oh, I just thought maybe you weren't up to it."

"Why wouldn't I be up to it?"

"I dunno, it's only been a coupla of days since Dinah's funeral. I thought maybe—"

"Well, you thought wrong," Ambrose interrupted. "You coming?"

"Maybe next time."

"Uh-huh, you say that every time, and you ain't came for a walk yet."

"I'm gonna walk one of these days. Here," she said, getting up from the chair and walking down the steps to hand him the leash.

Their walk was slow because Roscoe marked trees and got petted by the kids in the neighborhood. Ambrose waved or stopped briefly to speak to his neighbors. He noted that there were more Mexicans than Blacks in the neighborhood, which was almost unrecognizable from the neighborhood that he moved into fifty-five years ago. There were no fences back then. He could stand in his yard, look in any direction, and see an unobstructed sea of well-kept green lawns. Nowadays, almost every yard is fenced off. The first fences erected were quaint, white-washed picket fences. Now, the fences were wire fences or stucco and wrought-iron ones. The wire fences usually denoted a Black household, and the stucco and wrought-iron ones signified a Mexican household. He put up a wire fence in the 1980s as another layer of protection from stray dogs and the crackheads that roamed the neighborhood. *It's funny how things have changed; now, Blacks are leaving Black neighborhoods because of the droves of Spanish-speaking people moving in. South Central Los Angeles looked more like Tijuana than the white-flight neighborhood he had moved into, Ambrose* thought as he walked west on Firestone Boulevard. He walked past the liquor store that had been there longer than he had. The store looked old and grimy, and it wore a patchwork of colors that covered the graffiti the taggers sprayed on the walls. Young men and old addicts stood around the parking lot, intimidating to some but not to Ambrose. They greeted him as he and Roscoe passed them on their way to the blue line. Sometimes, they walked beyond the overpass to the park before returning home, but not today. Since Dinah's death, everything had been a struggle. He wondered if it was worth living anymore. His children and grand-kids would miss him for a while, but they would be all right. On the walk back, he stopped at the market, once owned by an old Jewish man but was now a Mexican market, where he got pan dulce to go with his coffee. Just before entering the market, he remembered he had cake at home, so he rounded the corner instead. He delivered Roscoe back to Lottie, who had gone inside.

"You got something to eat over there?" she asked, opening the screen door, letting Roscoe in, and taking the leash that Ambrose handed her.

"Yeah, I've got something to eat, woman," Ambrose responded indignantly. What, you think I don't know how to take care of myself?"

"Now, Ambrose, I didn't say all that. I know Dinah used to cook enough food for both of you. I just wanted to let you know I can cook, too."

"Oh…well…what you got?" he asked contritely.

"Beef stew and cornbread. It's ready; I was waiting for you and Roscoe to get back. Come on in and help me eat some of this food," she ordered, opening the screen door wider.

He didn't hesitate to accept her invitation because his mouth was already watering at the thought of beef stew. Lottie had set the table because she was sure he wouldn't turn down a home-cooked meal. When he came from the bathroom, she was seated at the table waiting for him. They said grace before enjoying their meal. She remembered how much her late husband loved her cooking as she watched him digging into her beef stew. Cooking was one of the ways she loved. She thought how good it felt to have someone to cook for again.

The phone was ringing when Ambrose unlocked his front door.

"Grandpa, where've you been?" asked Onyx without bothering to say hello.

"I've been minding my own business."

"I've been calling you all night and was about to come over there."

"Why is everybody treating me like I'm some senile old man who can't take care of himself?"

"It's not that; I know you can take care of yourself, but when you don't answer your phone, how am I supposed to know if you're okay?"

"Sorry, I didn't mean to worry you."

"That's why you need a cell phone."

"Don't start with me again. I done told you that I don't want no cell phone."

"Okay, okay. But where were you?"

"I had dinner with Lottie. She made a beef stew, and man, it was good. I haven't—"

Before he could finish, Onyx laughed, thinking his grandfather had gotten trapped at Miss Lottie's house.

"What's so funny?"

"The thought of you and Miss Lottie having dinner is hilarious. How did you get trapped over there—Gramps, you must be slipping."

"Onyx."

Onyx was prepared to continue his banter, but he noticed the tone in his grandfather's voice that always caused him to stop short and consider the wisdom of proceeding further. "I was just making sure you were okay because you were upset when I left."

"Well, I'm okay now."

"All right then. I'll talk to you later. Goodnight, Grandpa."

"Goodnight, grandson, and thanks for checking on me."

Chapter 5

Indigo woke up in a dark room, disorientated and frightened, not knowing where she was or if it was early morning or night. She sat straight up in her bed because someone shouted her name. Her heart was beating fast, so fast that it was hard to catch her breath. Pinpricks of sweat dotted her forehead. She sat in bed, trying to calm down. When her eyes adjusted to the darkness, she saw she was in her old bedroom. She told herself that she must have been dreaming, and the screaming of her name must have been part of the dream. She reached out to turn on the bedside lamp and picked up her cell phone. It was 9:30 p.m.; she had fallen asleep in the afternoon and slept into the evening. She couldn't remember why she was sleeping in her old room when Big Momma's room was now hers. She got out of bed with more bravado than she felt and went into the kitchen to see what she could scrounge up to eat. It was too late to thaw anything, so Indigo decided to have breakfast for dinner like her grandmother did when the first of the month took too long to come around. She loved having breakfast for dinner when she was little. She hadn't known then that it meant that money was in short supply. Big Momma was a country woman who kept her kitchen stocked with flour, sugar, baking soda, baking powder, cornmeal, rice, and beans. She kept eggs and milk in the refrigerator and grew collard greens alongside her roses in the backyard. There were plenty of times her grandmother would cook cornbread and crumble a large hunk of it in a bowl, pour milk over it, sprinkle a liberal helping of sugar, and they would eat that for dinner. She loved corn mush, and to this day, whenever she cooked cornbread, she always cut a small piece fresh from the oven to eat with milk and sugar. Indigo ate scrambled eggs and bacon. She opted for milk instead of coffee because it was late, and she would never fall asleep if she had coffee now. After washing the dishes, she went into the living room to watch TV. Her grandmother had a basic cable package on an old Console TV encased inside a chunky wooden cabinet that sat directly on the floor. She returned to the kitchen and looked in the junk drawer for paper and pen. Once she found what she was looking for, she plopped back on the couch in the living room and began making a list. She had left everything she owned at the apartment, returning once for her clothes and cell phone. The first items on the list were two flat-screen TVs because she couldn't stand looking at the 1980s throwback she had been watching. The list was long, from curtains and pictures to rugs and towels. The house was in good condition. It had good bones with everything that people were putting back into old houses. The kitchen had a long white enamel sink with an attached drainboard and a wall-mounted faucet. The cabinets were solid wood, and the scarred cutting board pulled out with a slight tug. Big Momma had removed the drop-down ironing board in the kitchen but left the cabinet and installed shelves to house her spices. The only bathroom was big, with a linen cabinet and built-in drawers. The pink tiles in the bathroom went halfway up the walls, except in the shower stall, where the pink tiles were divided by a pencil-thin black tile before going up to the ceiling. Black hexagon tiles created small flowers on the white hexagon tiles on the bathroom floor. It was 2 a.m. when Indigo completed her list and had decided to live there until she could save enough money to rent something nice on the Westside. Selling the house would have been the simplest solution, but selling the house that her grandmother loved would be difficult. A decision that, once made, there would be no turning back from. A few minutes later, she turned off the TV and checked the front and back doors. The earlier uneasiness fell away as she slipped into her grandmother's bed. This was the bed she snuck into whenever she had a bad dream. Big Momma would be so tired that she would roll over to make room for her, but in the morning, she would tell her that big girls slept in their own beds. When Indigo laid her head on the pillow, the scent of roses was released, and she inhaled deeply. She felt like the little girl who had snuck into bed, and Big Momma was there with her. She pulled a pillow close, hugging it, wishing she could go back in time. Tears began to fall out of her closed eyes. They fell from eyes that were tired of crying and should have been dry. Indigo felt like a motherless child, all alone in the world. She wondered who would love her as her grandmother had. Who would care about what happened to her, and who would pray for her? She had hoped that her mother would have somehow found out that Big Momma had died and would have come back. Indigo had never given up hope that her mother would return one day. She remembered hearing her grandmother telling someone in a hushed tone that it wasn't unusual for Wanda to leave Indigo with her when she was running around with a man, but she would be back when he got tired of her. Hearing those words gave her renewed hope that her mother would come home one day. Days turned into weeks, maybe even a month or two of anticipation, as she waited for her mother to walk through the door. Some days, she would run to the front door and open it, thinking she had heard a light knocking. The joy she felt as she floated to the door matched the overwhelming sadness when she opened it and found her mother wasn't there. When Indigo graduated from middle school, she wanted her mother to return so she could show her that she didn't give a damn about her either. Now, lying in Big Momma's bed, she wanted her mother just as badly as she had as a child. She wondered if she would recognize her if she passed her on the street. Pictures of her mother were of a young woman with a lot of hair, creamy caramel skin, and red upturned lips forming a slick smile. But what would she look like now? Had life been kind to her, or had it ravaged her? She fell asleep, thinking about her mother.

The scent of roses perfumed the air as she drifted in and out of REM sleep. She dreamt she was a little girl asleep in her room at Big Momma's house. She was sleeping with a small stuffed giraffe when a loud noise and people yelling awakened her. She squeezed her giraffe, too afraid to see what all the commotion was about. When she felt brave enough, she opened her eyes. The nightlight illuminated a small circle, but it was enough. Hugging the giraffe tightly against her chest, she walked to the bedroom door. The voices were louder now, and she opened the door because it was her mother's voice she heard.

"Momma," Indigo murmured as she transitioned from her dream to fully awake in Big Momma's bed.

The room was flooded with sunlight; the curtains had not been drawn the night before. She sat in bed, trying to process the strange feeling the dream had left in its wake. *Was she dreaming or remembering?* Goosebumps rippled down her forearms, and the hair on the back of her neck bristled, shooting a pin prickle of uneasiness through her body. She closed her eyes, trying to remember the dream that was already slipping away from her. The feeling that it was important filled her, so she laid back, closed her eyes, and tried to reenter her dream. She jumped when her cell phone rang.

"Hello…hello." Indigo lowered the phone from her ear when no one answered and looked to see who was calling. It was Treyvon. She placed the phone up to her ear again; the line was silent except for his soft breathing, so she hung up. The phone was in her hand when he called twice more, but she didn't answer. She answered the third time it rang, pissed at his audacity.

"Treyvon, don't call my motherfucking phone again."

"Has that motherfucker been calling you? Onyx asked.

"What, who is this?"

"It's me, Onyx. Has that punk ass motherfucker been calling you?"

"What, no—yeah. No, not really."

"Indigo, has he been calling you or not?"

She took a deep breath, trying to answer his question coherently. "Treyvon called my phone a couple of times just now, but he didn't say anything, so when you called, I assumed you were him. Sorry about that."

"I told you I would handle homie for you."

"You don't have to do that."

"I know I don't have to but trust and believe I want to. How long have you been fucking around with that nigga?"

"Look, Onyx, you need to stop all that cussing, and I don't use the n-word, so I would appreciate it if you didn't use that word in my presence," reprimanded Indigo.

"What the fuck, Indigo," he snorted. "You cuss more than I do."

"No…I do not," she said, enunciating each word slowly.

"Yeah, okay. I will refrain from using any words you may find offensive, even if such words should roll off your tongue and pass through your delicate lips."

"Negro, please," Indigo interrupted.

"And, because I have promised to undertake such an endeavor, I hope your ladyship will allow me to check on you tonight."

"Onyx, you trying to holler at me."

"I said check on you, not checking for you."

"Okay, Rico Suave, you can come check on me," she replied coyly.

"What time is good?" he asked in a monotone voice.

"Any time after five," she replied, oblivious to his irritation. He hung up without saying goodbye, so she looked at the phone to see if he was still on the line when it rang again.

"Hey, girl," greeted Destiny.

"Hey," Indigo responded.

"What's going on with you and Amani?"

"Why? What did she say?"

"She said you got mad at her for not believing something about Treyvon."

"She *didn't tell you?*"

"No, she told me to ask you if I wanted to know, so wassup?"

"I told Amani why Treyvon wasn't at Big Momma's funeral…I told her that…Treyvon raped me the day my grandmother died." Indigo heard herself say the words coldly and dispassionately, hardly recognizing her voice.

"Oh my God—Indigo, are you okay?"

Destiny's concern and belief in what she said tore down the wall she attempted to build around her heart, and she began to cry. After she was able to speak, she thanked her friend for believing her.

"Of course, I believe you— why wouldn't I? Everybody knows that you wouldn't lie about something like that."

"Everybody but Amani."

"Give her some time, Indigo. Treyvon is like a brother to her."

Indigo didn't say anything because she knew Destiny was right. She wasn't angry with Amani because she couldn't instantly wrap her head around the rape. She was hurt, and if she was being honest with herself, she was upset because Amani had chosen Treyvon's friendship over hers.

"Was he high or drunk? Why would he do something like that?" Destiny asked as she grappled with what she had heard.

"No, he wasn't high or drunk. I've never seen him like that. He was mad because I was ignoring him. He hadn't come home the night before." She stopped speaking, trying to collect herself.

"Aw…Indigo, I'm so sorry."

"I was getting dressed to go see Big Momma when he hit me across my face. When I woke up, he was on top of me—raping me."

"Oh my God. Did you call the police?"

"No. I got out of there as soon as I could. Then, when I found out about Big Momma…I didn't want to think about it. I just wanted it to go away." She hadn't told Destiny or anyone about that day's dirty, lurid details except for Amani. And she hadn't told Amani everything. She didn't want to explain that after the sodomy, the part that she considered to be rape, her own body had betrayed her and actively participated in the sexual act. She didn't want to speak out loud about the degradation that she felt while Treyvon's skillful manipulation caused a schism between her body and mind.

"I'll come over after work. I'll pick up sushi. Text me what you want."

"You don't have to. I'm okay; besides, Onyx is coming over."

"That was fast."

"What?"

"I'm just saying."

"Are you serious?" Indigo asked, "I've gotta go." She spit out the words so fast that she slurred them together. She hung up before Destiny could say anything else. When Destiny called back, she didn't answer.

After breakfast, she went shopping, only stopping to grab something to eat. She had got everything on the list except for the TVs. She felt good; the shopping had taken her mind off everything: Big Momma, Treyvon, Amani, and Destiny. But now that she was back home, she knew it had only been a fleeting reprieve. Opening the front door while juggling bags, her spirits lifted as she recalled the saying, *"Trouble don't last always."* While she was unloading her car, Onyx pulled into his grandfather's driveway.

"Hey, let me check on my grandfather for a second, and I'll be right over to help you," he said, before walking to Ambrose's door.

"Thanks!" shouted Indigo before taking a load into the house. When she returned to her car, he was still standing on his grandfather's porch.

"Have you seen my grandfather today?"

"No, I've been gone all day."

He unlocked the door with his key and went inside. Indigo was loading her arms with more bags when Onyx returned to the porch and looked across the street.

"What's wrong?" she asked.

"Nothing, he's not here, but I think I know where he is." He closed and locked the door.

They quickly unpacked the car. She got the last items, two large woven baskets, out of the car while Onyx hauled a couple of area rugs into the house.

"Just drop them over there. Thanks," she said, smiling. "So, where do you think he is?"

"He's probably at Miss Lottie's house."

Indigo looked out the window. "Nobody is on the porch, so he's probably walking Roscoe," she said, turning around to look at him.

"It's too late for him to be walking Roscoe. He's inside having dinner with Miss Lottie."

"Say what! Come on; we got to go save him," she said, her laughter becoming more intense as a mental picture of Mr. Ambrose tied to a chair while being forced-fed by Ms. Lottie crystallized. She tugged at his arm playfully, encouraging him to follow her, but stopped when she saw the stern set of his jaw and the fold of his skin between his eyebrows.

Indigo grabbed a couple of bags and started pulling the tags off the towel before throwing them into a pile on the floor. Onyx walked over to the window, looking toward Miss Lottie's house. The happy feeling that she had earlier was gone entirely. An awkward silence invaded the room, and she didn't know what to say to him. She was suddenly aware of how big he was. She sat on the couch and got still, not wanting to bring attention to herself. *What was wrong with two old people having dinner?* She thought as she watched his silhouette in front of the window.

"What's going on here?" he asked, looking around at the bags littering the room.

"I'm going to stay here until I can afford to move."

"So, you're not going to sell it?"

"I thought about it, but I don't think I can sell my grandmother's house. Besides, I need a place until I can get myself together. I'll rent it out when the time is right."

"That's wassup."

The mood in the room changed again, less ominous because he had softened into himself again. She switched on a large ceramic lamp, which was so dated that it was back in fashion.

"I meant to pick up something to eat, but I forgot. What do you feel like eating? Mexican, Chinese?" she asked.

"Mexican. Come on, I know a spot."

A few minutes later, Onyx pulled up in front of a taco stand close to the middle school she had attended.

"This place is still here?" she asked, getting out of the car.

"Yep, and the food is still banging."

The front of the place had two windows, one to order and one to pick up your food. Three small round metal tables with four metal stools for each table were cemented in the ground in front of the building. The building looked weathered and in need of a fresh coat of paint. The sides of the building were graffitied, and the metal tables were scarred with etching of foul words, gang affiliations, and declarations of love. They stood close to the pick-up window with other people, waiting for their number to be called. She turned away from the taco stand and told him how she and her friends would get chili cheese Fritos after school from the makeshift shack across the street. He laughed and told her everybody got chili-cheese Fritos from that hole in the wall. She looked further up the street to the middle school she attended and wished she could go back in time, thinking they were the good old days. When she got into the car, holding the greasy food bag away from her lap, she looked at the school again and knew those days weren't all good, but she would relive it again if she could because Big Momma would be there.

They sat in the living room, eating with the TV on to fill the quiet spaces. When they finished, Indigo threw the wrapping in the kitchen trash can and returned to the living room. She sat beside Onyx, surrounded by bags, baskets, and rugs.

"Are you going to be okay here by yourself?" he asked, looking into her eyes.

"Yeah, I'll be fine," she answered, looking away, afraid to gaze too long into his eyes. Destiny's words resonated with her, but they weren't true. It wasn't too fast at all. She had been crushing on him since middle school. She had brushed her lips across his and confessed her love one summer afternoon when he was in the garage pumping air into his bike's tire. Onyx pulled her off him so hard that she stumbled back and almost fell. He told her he was too big to kiss a kid in middle school. That was when she stopped going next door; that was why she and Zari grew apart. Onyx's next question startled her back to the present.

"Seriously, is this Treyvon fool going to be a problem?"

"No...he probably just wants to get back together," she answered, looking down at the floor. He lifted her chin with his hand, and she looked into his eyes briefly before lowering them. He held her chin firmly, wanting her to look at him, until he realized she might be frightened.

"Indigo, you know you're safe with me. I would never hurt you. You know that, right?

"I know," she whispered, looking at her feet.

"I better see if my grandfather made it back from Miss Lottie's house." He stood up. "I'll catch you later."

Ambrose had made it back home while Onyx was next door. He was sleeping in the recliner with the TV on when Onyx unlocked the door. He closed and locked the door again before sitting on the couch, unaware that his grandfather had been asleep.

"Hey, grandson!"

"Hey."

"What you doing coming over here this late?"

"I've been next door. I came by earlier, but..." Onyx cleared his throat. "You weren't here. She's not selling the house. She said she couldn't see herself selling her grandmother's house. She's going to live there for a while, then rent it out when she moves."

"How long is a while?"

"I don't know. She said she needed to save money before she could get a place."

"Well, that's good news, grandson. It looks like everything is going to be okay."

"Yeah, looks like it," he concurred, relieved that he wouldn't have to do that sick shit his grandfather wanted him to do.

The next morning, Indigo was up early washing the sheets and towels she bought. She put her grandmother's bedding and towels in black trash bags, planning to take them to the Salvation Army's donation center later that day. By late afternoon, Indigo had finished hanging new curtains in the living room and bedrooms. She had changed the sheets and put new comforters on the beds. Decorative pillows adorned the couch and beds. Eating a chicken salad sandwich while watching TV was the last thing she remembered before being startled awake by Ambrose banging on the iron security door.

"Hey, wake up," Ambrose shouted, peering through the iron mesh of the door.

"I'm up." Indigo jumped up and unlocked the door. "How you doing, Mr. Ambrose?"

"I'm good; how about you, baby girl? You been doing okay?"

"Yeah, I'm fine. Come in, have a seat," she said, pointing to the couch.

"I see you've been decorating in here. It looks good," he said before taking a seat.

"Thank you."

"Onyx told me you'll be living here now. I'm glad you're not going to sell Dinah's house."

"I hope I never have to sell it."

"That's good. I remember how hard it was for her to keep this house after your grandfather died. She nearly worked herself to death. Do you remember me watching you and my grandkids on the weekends?"

"I remember you always feeding us Spam or deviled ham sandwiches. Just the thought of a Spam sandwich makes me gag," she said, pretending to gag.

"I don't know what you're talking about; Spam is good eating. I still eat me some Spam. Well, baby girl, I just came over to see how you were doing. I won't keep you from it," he said, hoisting himself from the couch. "You take care and let me know if you need anything, you hear."

"I will, Mr. Ambrose. Thanks."

She followed him to the door and stood on the porch, watching him walk home. This time was very different from the day of the funeral. On that day, he had looked older and was stooped over from the grief of losing a dear friend. Today, he was walking straighter. He was halfway to the gate when she thought about asking him about her mother.

"Mr. Ambrose!" she shouted with an urgency that surprised both of them.

"Yeah," said Ambrose, turning around quickly.

She walked down the pathway to him. "Do you know where my mother is?"

He was visibly shaken by the question and paused before repeating it. "Do I know where your mother is?"

"I thought maybe Big Momma knew where she was, and maybe she told you."

"Nah, she never said anything to me."

The words tumbled out of Ambrose's mouth so fast that Indigo had difficulty understanding what he said. While it took her a second to decipher what he said, Ambrose hurried out of the gate as if she was chasing him. She turned her body to watch him as he almost ran from her. She remained glued in place even after he slammed his front door.

Chapter 6

A week later, Indigo hadn't seen Mr. Ambrose. His reaction to her question about her mother was strange and didn't make sense to her. *Why run away if you didn't know anything,* she thought. Indigo was still in her pajamas even though it was late afternoon. She thought about Mr. Ambrose's reaction all week; she also found it strange that not only had she not seen him, but she hadn't heard from Onyx either. Her heart and body hurt, and no matter how much sleep she got, she was always tired. The world was moving too fast for her, and she wanted it to slow down so she could get her bearings. She couldn't shake the feeling that she was all alone in the world; she felt untethered, like she was aimlessly drifting in a place where nothing existed. The sensation of slowly disappearing wasn't unpleasant, but knowing she was alone in the world was frightening. The loss of her grandmother and the relationship she thought would lead to marriage made it difficult to cope with even the basic things in life. After paying the bills, changing her mailing address, and completing the necessary notifications when a soul left its body, made getting out of bed an arduous task. She debated daily with herself the merits of getting out of bed, going back to work, or taking one more breath. Indigo's waking moments consisted of reliving the rape and her grandmother's death. Death and rape became intertwined in her thoughts. If she hadn't been raped, then she would have gotten one last chance to see her grandmother. She hated that Big Momma had died alone because she didn't deserve that, and she hated Treyvon for robbing her of those precious moments she could have spent with her grandmother. When she slept, her dreams were reenactments of the rape and of her waiting at Big Momma's house, then walking around the neighborhood looking for both her mother and grandmother. Two emotions dominated her being: listless despondency and hatred for Treyvon. She had been taught that hate was not only an ugly word but was also an emotion that corrupted one's soul. She was careful with the word and the emotion. If she disliked someone intensely, she would look for some redeeming quality, and when that didn't work, her grandmother's warning *God don't like ugly* would chasten her. But no other word or feeling could best describe how she felt toward Treyvon. She woke one morning with a thought that was better than any affirmation she remembered, so she wrote it down and taped it up on the lamp next to the bed. SURVIVAL IS VICTORY was scribbled in all caps and was the first thing she saw in the morning and the last thing she saw at night. Those words helped her with the grief that threatened to overtake her, and hate was replaced by a determination to live a victorious life.

Although she wasn't hungry most mornings, she forced herself to eat something for breakfast, even if it was only toast with her coffee. After a week of struggling to get out of bed, Indigo had, in the course of the last two days, discarded a mountain of her grandmother's trinkets collected over a lifetime, but there were still a couple of boxes in the closet she needed to go through. After she finished her coffee and before she got dressed for the day, she looked inside the bedroom closet where the boxes were. Indigo saw the boxes every time she opened the closet to hastily yank clothes off hangers or retrieve or toss in a pair of shoes, but she ignored them because she knew the boxes contained things that would pull off the thin scab over her heart. But time was running out, and she would return to work soon, so the boxes could no longer be ignored. The boxes seemed twice the size as before, beckoning her to look inside. She stumbled backward when she picked up the first one because it was lighter than she imagined. The second box was the same size as the first one but heavier. She placed both on the bed and sat next to them. No wonder the first box was light; it only held a manilla envelope and a shoebox inside. The shoebox was filled with photographs. The first photo she picked up was a black-and-white picture of Big Momma as a young woman. Her grandmother was laughing with her head tossed back, sitting cross-legged on the hood of a black convertible. The car looked heavy, and the back of it looked like it was trying to sprout wings. She couldn't believe how young her grandmother was in the picture. She was pretty and looked as if there were endless possibilities just waiting for her to pick one. Her grandmother was a fashionista: every photo showed her dressed to the nines. The fresh-faced woman in the pictures wore lipstick, earrings, a hat, gloves, and a brooch pinned on her dress, blouse, or jacket. There was a beautiful picture of her grandparents; he had an arm around her shoulders as they smiled at the camera. Indigo gasped when she picked up the picture of Big Momma and her mother, Wanda, planting a tree in the front yard of this house. Her grandmother wore black pedal pushers and a striped blouse; she was smiling at her mother, who had her little foot on a shovel inserted in the ground. Her mother must have been nine or ten years old in the picture; maybe younger, it was hard to tell. One of the pictures that she loved was of her mother and grandmother dressed alike in their Christmas outfits in front of a silver tinsel Christmas tree. That photo showed how much mother and daughter looked alike. Both had the same light brown coloring, with brown eyes and hair. Their faces had broad foreheads and defined cheekbones that tapered to prominent chins. Their hair was parted down the middle, hanging straight down until it flipped up at the end. But the best picture was of her mother holding her as a baby. Her mother cradled her in her arms and smiled down at her; their eyes were locked on each other. There were other pictures of her and her mother, but none captured her mother's love for her, like when she was a baby in her mother's arms. Going through the photos and seeing how happy they once were made Indigo happy and sad. As a kid, she never thought about her grandmother as a young girl with hopes and dreams, but seeing her in those pictures, she knew she must have had dreams once before she had her mother and before she came along. The person she had known had only been in the form of a grandmother, someone there for her. Indigo had viewed her grandmother as being one-dimensional instead of a multifaceted woman. But looking at those pictures through the lens of her loss, she saw, maybe for the first time, Big Momma as someone other than her grandmother; she wished she had gotten to know who she was, who she was when she wasn't her grandmother. She made a stack of pictures that she would have enlarged and placed them on the nightstand. The second box made her smile because it contained her childhood drawings, report cards, a clay ashtray, and a misshapen clay heart that looked how her heart felt. She ran her fingers across the divets that her little fingers made. Indigo placed the fugly little heart next to her stack of pictures before she returned the boxes to the closet and got ready for the day.

She spent the rest of the day preparing for next week. She cleaned the house and ironed clothes. She had fallen asleep in front of the TV and woke to a semi-dark room with only the dim light from the TV illuminating. While yawning and stretching, her stomach growled loudly, telling her it was time to feed it, like the Little Shop of Horror's plant. She retrieved her keys and purse, preparing to get something to eat. Indigo flipped the porch light on and opened the front door in one fluid motion. She screamed loud enough to wake the dead when she saw Treyvon standing in front of the security door. After what felt like minutes, instead of the few seconds it took for the screams to stop erupting from her throat, she was able to hear what he was saying.

"Indigo! It's me, Treyvon. I just want to talk."

"You scared the shit out of me."

"Sorry, I didn't mean to scare you. I just wanna talk."

"Talk about what? I don't have anything to talk to you about."

"Indigo, are you all right?" Ambrose shouted, walking down his steps with a baseball bat in his hand.

"I'm fine!" she yelled back from behind the safety of the security door.

"You're sure everything's okay?" he asked, still yelling even though he stood beside the fence dividing their properties.

"Yes, everything's okay," she answered loudly, but not as loud as before.

Ambrose stood by the fence with the bat held high, ready to strike. He hesitated before going back inside his house. Indigo and Treyvon waited for him to leave before resuming their conversation.

"Can I come in?" Treyvon asked.

"Nope, but you can get the hell off my porch."

"Indigo, we need to talk. I want to apologize for what I did." Treyvon bobbed his head up and down, trying to make eye contact with her around the metalwork of the screen door.

"You want to apologize for raping me?"

"I'm sorry if I hurt you. Come on, Indigo, I messed up. Babe, I promise you that it will never happen again. Come on back home; I miss you, baby."

She looked at him with utter disgust. A chuckle escaped her, threatening to turn into hysterical laughter if she hadn't stopped herself.

"I can't believe you're standing in front of my door, talking about you apologize if you hurt me. Yes, Treyvon, if you didn't know, it hurts when someone shoves something up your ass. So can you apologize for doing that, for raping me?"

"I don't know that I would call it rape. I admit I got a little rough with you, but I don't know if you could call it rape."

"Well, I know, and yes, it's called rape when someone knocks you out and sodomizes you. What the fuck would you call it?"

"I didn't do anything to you that we hadn't done before," he said, becoming agitated.

"That's a lie! I have never let you go up in my ass. Get off my porch; we don't have anything to talk about. And just so you know, we're done—you fucking rapist!"

"Okay—okay, we're done…. but I'm going to need you to stop telling people that I raped you!" he said as he yanked and twisted the doorknob.

"Oh, so Amani told you."

"Yeah, she told me you told her that whack shit. That's not cool, Indigo."

"Neither is rape," she said, closing the wooden door.

Treyvon refused to leave. He began pounding on the screen door, yelling to be let in. She listened to the pounding and screaming for a few minutes before she started yelling through the closed doors for him to leave. After the pounding stopped, she waited a few seconds before looking out the window to see if he had gone. At first, she was confused by what she saw. He was sparring around in the yard with someone. It took her a moment to process what she was seeing. Treyvon and Onyx were fighting. She opened the front door and the security door. She ran down the steps and grabbed Onyx's arm. Treyvon swung at Onyx; Onyx dodged the punch and bumped into Indigo. Treyvon swung again when Onyx turned his head to look at Indigo, and his fist connected with the side of Onyx's face. Onyx was stunned momentarily, but he put his hands up to block the punches he knew Treyvon would throw, hoping to finish him. Onyx backed up with his guards up as Treyvon continued to swing wildly at him. Onyx continued backing up as he waited for the right opportunity to land a blow. Treyvon lobbied punches and insults at Onyx, who was throwing tentative swings in his direction. Treyvon didn't know that Onyx was testing him and wanted Treyvon to see him as a non-threat. Treyvon had just told Onyx what part of the female organ he thought he was when Onyx smiled, threw a stiff jab with his left, and followed up with an uppercut that caught the bottom of Treyvon's chin, leaving him laid out cold on the lawn. The passage of time had slowed to a snail's pace as Indigo watched the fight suddenly return to normal, giving her a touch of vertigo. Onyx grabbed her by the waist and sat her down on the porch.

"Did you get hit?"

"No, I'm just a little dizzy. Are you okay?

"Yeah," he said, smiling.

"Is he dead?"

"No, he's just sleeping."

Ambrose approached them with his baseball bat and asked Onyx if he was hurt.

"I'm good, Grandpa. Indigo, can I get some water?"

She returned with a water bottle for Onyx and Ambrose, but Ambrose declined the offer. Onyx took a swig of water, declared its goodness to no one in particular, and walked over to where Treyvon lay. He looked down at the man on the ground for a second before he poured the rest of his water on his face.

"What the fuck?" coughed Treyvon, swatting at the water and demanding that Onyx stop.

"It's all gone anyway," said Onyx, dropping the empty bottle on Treyvon.

Treyvon got up, holding his jaw. He spat on the ground before stating, "This ain't over, motherfucker."

"You ain't said nothing but a word, let's go motherfucker," challenged Onyx, patting his chest.

"All right—all right, youngbloods. Enough is enough," Ambrose said, lifting the bat.

Indigo grabbed Onyx's arm and begged him to go inside the house. She pulled him until he let her lead him inside. When they went inside, Treyvon's blustering ceased; he looked around at Ambrose and the small group on the sidewalk. Lottie and Roscoe entered the yard and watched the stranger get into his car and drive away. Roscoe ran around in circles, and Lottie asked Ambrose if he was okay.

"You don't have to worry about me. I got more sense than to be out here trying to fight."

"I hope so," she said, patting his arm. "Who was that guy? Were they fighting over Indigo?"

When Lottie stopped talking long enough for Ambrose to answer, he told her the man Onyx was fighting was an ex-boyfriend who didn't want to take no for an answer, so he had called Onyx to come over. She continued pestering him with questions he didn't have the answers to. When she finally realized Ambrose was no longer responding, she gave up and called for Roscoe. The dog ignored her and continued to wander around the yard, sniffing and marking his territory.

"Roscoe! Go home!" Ambrose commanded.

Roscoe's head jerked up and looked at Ambrose before running through the open gate and across the street. The dog ran home and waited by the closed gate for his two favorite people to make it across the street. Ambrose stood by Lottie's gate until she and Roscoe entered the house. He walked back across the street, suddenly weary, using the bat as a cane.

His eyes filled with unshed tears, and his body shook. He had placed his grandson in danger; he should have called the police, but he didn't want the death of that young man on his hands, so he had called Onyx instead. He walked to Dinah's house to tell his grandson how sorry he was. Ambrose's fist was inches from knocking on the security door when he saw Onyx pull Indigo into his arms and kiss her.

"Well, I'll be damned," he murmured, shaking his head before turning around to go home.

Chapter 7

After the night of the fight, Ambrose noticed that his grandson's visits were shorter than usual and that he spent more time visiting Indigo than he did with him. He was okay with that because he got frequent updates on what was happening next door. He also understood why Onyx was attracted to the young lady. She was beautiful, just like her grandmother, and had a spirit similar to Dinah's. There was something about Dinah that made him happy by just being near her. She lit up the room and made everything more exciting and wonderful because she was there. He smiled and closed his eyes, giving in to the warmth of reminiscing. He remembered when Lucinda was too sick to care for the kids. Dinah came over every morning, took the kids to her house after she helped Lucinda to the bathroom, and settled her back into bed. During the day, she checked on Lucinda and made her something to eat. In the evenings, she brought the kids back home, bathed them, and got them ready for bed. After his wife had recovered, she and Dinah became close. They often talked to each other over the fence in the backyard as they hung clothes on the line, weeded their gardens, or watched the children play. Watching their friendship develop into a more profound thing made Ambrose feel guiltier about his feelings. So, he was careful around Dinah, so much so that Lucinda thought he disliked her. But, when Delray unexpectedly dropped dead from a massive heart attack at work, Ambrose was around Dinah more than was prudent. He took on the role of watching out for his best friend's widow and child. He did just what his grandson was doing now. He began to check on Dinah daily to ensure she was okay. Then he started doing things for her around the house, like fixing the toilet that kept running after you flushed it or fixing a dripping faucet. When Ambrose mowed his lawn, he cut her grass, too. Dinah showed her appreciation with cookies or brownies after he finished repairing something around the house or doing yard work. On one of those days, Lucinda was washing dishes and looking out the kitchen window. She saw her friend and her husband sitting in the backyard, drinking lemonade and laughing so hard that they both wiped tears from their eyes. Lucinda laughed as she watched them until Ambrose got up from the chair he was sitting in, pulled Dinah up, and hugged her. He was facing the window that Lucinda was looking out of, but he didn't see his wife because his eyes were closed. When he released Dinah, he looked down at her, smiling, and said something that caused Dinah to shake her head up and down in the affirmative. Dinah wiped her eyes with a napkin, and they sat back in their chairs.

"Mom! Mom, can I go outside and ride my bike? Jonathan asked from the hallway.

"Did you finish your chores? Lucinda responded without taking her eyes off her husband.

"Yes, ma'am."

"Why don't you help your Dad finish mowing Miss Dinah's yard?"

"Dad told me I didn't have to help him with Miss Dinah's yard. I finished raking the leaves and grass in our yard." Jonathan replied impatiently, shuffling from one foot to the other. "Can I go now, Mom?"

"Yeah…you can go."

Lucinda continued looking out the window long after Dinah had picked up the empty glasses and returned to the house. Lucinda watched her husband whistling as he pushed the lawnmower. She was still looking out the window when he finished mowing and watched him as he raked up the freshly cut grass. She observed him as he worked and saw that when he wasn't whistling, he was smiling. Lucinda glanced at the clock on the kitchen wall. It was 1:10 pm. Ambrose never knew the date and time that he broke his wife's heart, but Lucinda never forgot that Saturday afternoon on July 10, 1965, at 1:10 pm. It was on that date, and at that time she discovered that her dear friend made her husband happy.

Ambrose hauled himself out of the recliner. He double-checked the front door, ensuring it was locked because he forgot things when daydreaming. He walked over to Lottie's house. She was sitting on the porch as usual, and Roscoe was eagerly waiting by the gate.

"You feeling all right, Ambrose?" she asked.

"I'm a little tired, but like you're always saying, what's the use of complaining? Come on, Roscoe, let's go. Where's his leash?"

"Ambrose, come and sit down while I go get Roscoe's leash."

"Why don't you have his leash? You know I always walk him around this time," he complained.

Lottie went into the house pretending to look for the leash. She had seen how Ambrose dragged himself across the street and had stuffed the leash under the pillow cushion of the chair she was sitting on. After a few minutes, she returned to the porch with two glasses of ice-cold lemonade. She handed a glass to Ambrose and plopped down into her chair, forgetting about the leash under the cushion. She let out a yelp upon contact.

"What's wrong with you, woman?"

"Nothing—I just sat down too hard, is all," said Lottie, squirming in her chair.

"Be still, woman; what's wrong with you?"

"Nothing is wrong with me. What's wrong with you?" she asked, resisting the urge to wriggle her butt.

They sat on the porch sipping their drinks. Lottie surreptitiously moved around in her chair until she found a comfortable position while Ambrose drifted back to 1965.

He missed his friend Delray, who had died a few months ago. Everything had changed when he died—Friday nights grabbing a beer or shooting craps in the back room of a barbershop on Broadway. Saturday nights going to a house party with their wives, or if one of them hit a lick shooting craps, they would treat their wives to dinner at Maurice's Snack 'N' Chat off Pico Blvd. They felt like big shots at Maurice's while their wives looked around the room, hoping to spot a celebrity. But hitting the clubs and eateries on Central Avenue was Ambrose's favorite even though the glory days of the 40s and 50s were over. The shine and luster of the building had worn off, but the people were real, and the good times were heightened because of the risk involved. But Central Avenue wasn't the same without his buddy, so Ambrose stayed home. He became the man who looked out for his deceased best friend's wife and child. He thought he had been careful not to let his feelings for Dinah show. But in Delray's absence, he was careless; he became too solicitous; he spoke her name too often or smiled too broadly when she was around. He thought no one knew how he felt about Dinah until he noticed the change in his wife, Lucinda. The one person he never wanted to know knew. Lucinda had stopped responding to his touch. She didn't withhold herself from him but didn't give herself either. She allowed him to take what he needed, which only made him feel worse. His wife cooked, cleaned, and cared for the children, but she wasn't the woman he had married. She snapped at the kids and made biting remarks to him. Her beautiful smile was replaced by a constant downward slant of her lips. Ambrose remembered how tired he had been since Lucinda's transformation. His home wasn't a peaceful place anymore. He was always trying to prove to her that he loved her. Maybe he was trying to prove to himself that he still loved her. It was mid-week, and he wondered how he would get through the rest of the week as he drove home. Lucinda had dinner ready and was waiting for him. She made his plate and placed it on the dining room table in front of him.

"Aren't the kids eating dinner?" Ambrose asked.

"They already ate."

He looked at his wife and asked if she had eaten. Her response was as dry as the lump that had formed in his throat. She left him in the room to eat dinner by himself. She went into the living room and watched TV with the kids. Alone in the room, Ambrose found it difficult to keep his eyes open. The room was too quiet without the kids' constant stream of chatter, fighting, and Tamar's whining that Jonathan was picking on her. Ambrose's head bobbed up and down, jerking him awake. He knew he was still at the dining table, but he couldn't gather enough strength to get up and go to bed.

Lucinda had bathed Tamar and put her to bed while Ambrose struggled to remain awake long enough to go to bed. Jonathan was lying in bed reading a comic book when his mother came into the room with his little sister and tucked her in the twin bed across from him. Lucinda kissed both her children before turning off the light.

"Jonathan, don't turn this light back on, or I'll take that comic book from you. Go to sleep, you hear me?"

"Yes, ma'am," he sighed.

Ambrose had fallen asleep at the table, and his head jerked up so fast that his neck made a popping sound when he realized Lucinda was shaking him awake.

"Go to bed, Ambrose."

"What?"

"You were asleep. Why don't you go to bed?" she asked.

"Yeah, I guess I will," he said, finally getting up.

Just as he went to the front door to check that it was locked, someone pounded it with loud, staccato notes. Lucinda was walking down the hall toward their bedroom, turned, and walked back to the front of the house, alarmed by the urgency of the pounding. Ambrose yanked the door open and demanded to know why his neighbor Kenny was banging on his door.

"Man, niggas then gone crazy!" Kenny cried.

"What the hell are you talkin bout?" yelled Ambrose.

"The police and niggas are going at it. Niggas are burning up shit, breaking windows and stealing shit. The police are out here shooting people, man, it's crazy out here!"

Ambrose opened the door wider and looked outside. Kenny ran to the next house to deliver the news. Lucinda came up behind Ambrose, and they watched people running up and down the sidewalk.

"Thanks, man!" he shouted to Kenny's back. Lucinda leaned against Ambrose and gripped his arm.

"What's going on?" she whispered.

"I don't know, but I better go check on Dinah," he said, stepping forward to go next door.

She grabbed his arm tighter, digging her fingernails into his skin, causing him to stop and look at her.

"What's wrong with you, woman?"

"What's wrong with me? Dinah is what's wrong with me. I'm your wife, and you kids are sleeping in their beds, but you need to check on Dinah?" she asked, releasing his arm.

He froze, barely breathing, and searched his wife's face. He knew at that moment that she knew, and a sharp pain struck his heart. Looking at the hard, shrill woman who was once the sweetest girl he ever knew made him wince because he was the reason for the transformation. He had hurt her deeply, and he was truly sorry for that. He hugged his wife and told her she was talking crazy talk. Lucinda knew the truth of what she suspected, but she clung to her husband, needing to win this battle if her marriage was worth saving. They went back into the house. He locked the door and looked in on his kids. He undressed and got into bed. He was lying on his back when Lucinda eased over to his side of the bed, reached out, and touched him. He had almost forgotten how it felt to be wanted. He responded with a hunger so wild that Lucinda laughed out loud. But shortly, her laughter turned into a husky gasping of air. They made love like they had before they were married and before they had the children. Lucinda felt like the young girl Ambrose had pursued; instead of being an obstacle to his happiness, she was the source of his joy.

The following day, Lucinda and Tamar walked Jonathan to school. Dinah and Wanda met her at the gate.

"Good morning!" said Dinah.

"Good morning," answered Lucinda.

"Do you know what happened last night?" Dinah asked. "I heard police sirens all night long."

"Kenny came by the house, talking about the police and Blacks were going crazy."

Lucinda and Tamar were holding hands and leading the way. Jonathan was in the middle of the group while Dinah, holding Wanda's hand, held up the rear. They met other women and children walking to school. Each group stopped to exchange what they knew about last night. When they reached the elementary school, they learned that the police had beaten a young man in front of his mother and kicked a pregnant woman. Lucinda and Dinah milled around outside the school with the other mothers, wondering if they should let the kids go to school. Some mothers took their kids back home, while others, like Lucinda and Dinah, let their children attend school. On the way home, both women held Tamar's hands as they walked down the sidewalk. Lucinda only gave one-word responses to Dinah's litany of questions and merely grunted at Dinah's suppositions about what happened last night. Dinah watched Lucinda and Tamar enter their house before going into her own. Dinah was not blind to the change in her friend. Lately, Lucinda had made excuses not to hang out and straight-out avoided her. If Lucinda were outside hanging clothes on the line when she came out to do the same, she would say she had to check on dinner, or she heard Tamar calling her. Dinah needed her friend because she had been sad, lonely, and scared since Delray died. It was almost a year since his death, but one year wasn't a long time to grieve for a man that she had loved since high school. Delray was the only man she had made love to. She didn't know what it was like to be with anyone else, and she didn't want to know. She wanted Lucinda to sit with her and let her cry for the man she lost, but she guessed Lucinda was tired of the gloomy, crying woman she had become. Once inside, she hurriedly made up the beds, washed the breakfast dishes, and packed her lunch before walking to the bus stop, where she traveled to the Westside to clean the houses of White women who had married well. The crowd at the bus stop was larger than usual. There was a nervous energy in the group waiting for the RTD bus to take them to the West side or Downtown. There was muttering about the lateness of the bus or whether the buses were running at all. She heard snatches of conversations and even inserted herself into them to ask questions. Thirty minutes later, she was tired of hearing the same stories about last night and considered returning home when she saw the bus coming. She wasn't the only one who saw it because people moved as if they were one unit to stand close to the stop sign where they hoped the bus would stop. The bus didn't slow down; it whizzed past the stop. She smacked her lips as the packed bus flew by. A loud protest rose from the crowd; Dinah and a few others left the bus stop to return to their homes. She went to Lucinda's house before going home to tell her she wasn't going to work. While standing outside on the porch, she told

Lucinda the latest news gathered from the crowd and about the bus, full of people, that passed them by. She left Lucinda's porch, wishing her friend had invited her in. She called the ladies of the two houses she would have cleaned that day, telling them she couldn't come to work because of the bus situation. She knew she should have waited for the next bus because she needed money to pay the bills and buy food. Instead, she went back to bed. She closed her eyes and hugged a pillow, wishing it was Delray.

That evening, Ambrose's drive home from work, the moment he turned right off Almeda onto Firestone Boulevard, he noticed more people than usual on the streets. The people clustered around the bus stops looked afraid. The expressions on their faces spooked him a little. They looked as if they knew something he didn't and were waiting for the other shoe to fall. He rolled his window up because he felt too exposed with it down. A few blocks from his street, he noticed the drugstore and the record shop windows were boarded up. When he pulled into his driveway, he glanced over at Dinah's house and then looked back at his house, where he saw Lucinda watching him from the front window. She opened the front door and met him on the porch.

"They say Black folks are still rioting." Lucinda hugged him and kissed his cheek.

"I don't know about that, but people are scared. They're boarding up the stores. They're getting ready for something."

That night, Lucinda and the kids ate dinner with him. Lucinda put the kids to bed early so they could watch the news. They could hardly believe what they saw. As they were watching the news, they heard gunshots. At first, they thought the sounds were coming from the TV, but then they realized the shots were coming from outside.

"Get down!" he shouted.

"What?"

"Get down. They're shooting outside."

Ambrose drew the curtains and turned off the lights. He hurried to the kids' room and saw that they were asleep. He went to their bedroom and got his shotgun off the top shelf of the closet. Then he went to the kitchen, looking for the flashlight in the junk drawer. He sat on the floor next to his wife and told her he needed to go next door and get Dinah and Wanda.

"Why?"

"Because it's the right thing to do. You know that," he hissed. "I'll be right back."

Ambrose turned off the porch light before he opened the front door. He told Lucinda to lock the door and left. He looked up and down the block before cutting across the lawn with the shotgun slung over his shoulder. He directed the beam of light from the flashlight low to the ground as he scurried next door.

"It's me, Ambrose, "he said, knocking loudly on the door.

Dinah opened the door wild-eyed, with Wanda clinging to her waist. "Thank God, it's you," she said.

"I came to get you and Wanda so you guys can stay with us tonight."

"Thank you, Ambrose. Let me get my purse and keys," she said, pulling Wanda off and pushing her toward him.

She went to her bedroom, got her purse, and then went down the hall to Wanda's room to get the teddy bear she slept with every night. Ambrose stood guard on the porch as she locked the door. They stood on the porch for a second, watching people running on the sidewalk or in the middle of the street. The sounds of gunshots in the distance replaced the usual sounds of a summer night. When they got to his porch, he knocked on the door and yelled for Lucinda to open up. Dinah hugged Lucinda so tightly that Lucinda joked that she couldn't breathe.

"Thank you—thank you for letting us come over."

Ambrose nudged the women out of the way and closed the door. Lucinda and Dinah took Wanda to the kids' room and untucked the foot of Tamar's bed. Once the covers were adjusted and an additional pillow was prepared for Wanda, Dinah tucked her daughter in bed. Lucinda warned Jonathan about the lights again and told him to go back to sleep. Tamar didn't even stir during the entire commotion. When they returned to the living room, Ambrose sat on the floor watching the news. Lucinda sat next to Ambrose, and Dinah sat on the floor across from them as they watched the horror on the TV screen. They stayed up long into the night, watching the news and peeping out the window as they heard car tires screeching and people yelling. Dinah slept on the couch in the clothes that she had on. The following morning, Dinah awoke to the whispered voices of Lucinda and Ambrose by the front door. Ambrose's voice had a hard edge, while Lucinda's was verging on hysteria. Dinah heard Ambrose tell Lucinda he would come home if it got too crazy.

Ambrose worked the entire day without incident; only a few guys didn't show up. Jim, the white man who hired him, stayed in the office most of the day because the tension in the slaughterhouse was stretched so taut that one misspoken word or gesture may have sparked a race riot. The White workers were the butchers, while the Blacks and Mexicans did the dangerous job of unloading cows off the truck, forcing them through a chute, where they shot the cows in the head or slit their throats. By the end of the day, Ambrose was exhausted, and all he wanted to do was go home. On the drive home, he saw people throwing rocks and bricks at the cars with White drivers. The White drivers started running red lights and driving on the wrong side of the street to get around other cars. The words "Black Owned" were sprayed on the plywood that covered the storefront windows. If he wasn't so tired, he might have laughed at the blatant lie sprayed across businesses that wanted Black folk's money but didn't want

70

to touch their hands. As he carefully made his way home, he thought about what he had given up by going up North. Up North was supposed to be better, but looking at the people on the street burning down their own communities revealed the truth. The truth is that things weren't necessarily better. They were just different. Mr. Charlie still controls where you live and work. Here a man could hold his head up, but if he got too uppity, the police would happily beat it back down. Up North, White folks preferred more subtle forms of racism. Systemic and institutional racism allowed decent White folks to plaster smiles on their faces and advise Blacks to be patient. While they professed to be tolerant, up to a point, things continued to operate as usual. They didn't dirty their hands like Mr. Charlie and the good ol' boys down South because it wasn't necessary here. The police, like the overseers and patty rollers during slavery, kept niggers in line. Anger boiled up in him as he thought about his mother, siblings, cousins, uncles, and aunts, whom he left behind and hardly saw. Weekly phone calls and occasional trips to Louisiana couldn't replace what he was missing by not being there. He wondered if he had given up too much to be here, and now this was happening. He was mentally fatigued by the time he made it home. Lucinda and Dinah had made dinner together and were setting the table when he came through the front door. He ate dinner with his family and with Dinah and Wanda as if it was an ordinary day. The adults in the room pretended everything was fine so the children wouldn't be frightened. Tamar and Wanda played in the bedroom, which was safer, while Jonathan ran up and down the hall with his toy gun, which made a popping sound when he pulled the trigger. Lucinda tried to ignore the sounds, but her nerves got the best of her, and she yelled for Jonathan to stop shooting the gun. Jonathan, bored from being kept in the house all day, continued running up and down the hall, pretending to shoot the gun while quietly mouthing the words, "Pow, pow."

When the kids were asleep, Ambrose told the women about his drive home and how some people were throwing rocks and bricks at the

White drivers. Sitting on the floor discussing when this might end, they heard someone outside screaming. He looked out the window and saw a woman in the middle of the street, holding someone in her arms. She was screaming at the top of her lungs that the police had killed her baby. A young White officer stood in front of the woman with his gun drawn while his partner was in the patrol car, calling for backup. People came out of their homes to see what the commotion was about. Soon, there was a large crowd standing uncertainly around the life-sized diorama. Ambrose, Lucinda, and Dinah came onto the porch for a closer look. The crowd began to murmur until it sounded like an animal growling. The throng of people began moving as if it had been choreographed. They inched slowly and methodically closer to the scene. The young officer with the gun looked at the older policeman still sitting in the car, then looked around at the gathering mob. The young officer ran to get into the patrol car, and a glass bottle hit the car door just as it closed. The police car slowly drove around the woman and the body on the ground as the mob beat on the car. The crowd followed the car, beating it and shouting, "Fuck the pigs!" until the car sped away, disappearing into the night. There were only a few people left in the street with the woman and the body. Ambrose ushered Lucinda and Dinah back into the house. He asked Dinah if she still had Delray's rifle.

"Yes, why?" she asked.

"Because I'm going to take that woman and her child to the hospital. We all know that nobody is coming out here."

"No, it's too dangerous," Lucinda pleaded.

"How would you feel if that was Jonathan or Tamar lying in the street?" he asked sternly.

Lucinda threw her arms around Ambrose and held onto him. He looked over his shoulder and asked Dinah if she knew how to shoot Delray's rifle. When she nodded in the affirmative, he told her to get the rifle and all the shells she could find. She shook her head up and down, got her house key, and walked quickly out the door. She came back shortly with a rifle, a couple of boxes of shells, and a pearl-handled .22 caliber pistol in the pocket of her dress. Ambrose had managed to detangle himself from Lucinda and had her sitting on the floor when Dinah returned. He went to the linen closet, got a blanket, grabbed his shotgun, and told them he would return as soon as possible. He placed his weapon on the front seat of his car and laid the blanket across the back seat. Ambrose backed out of the driveway and pulled up next to the woman. He got out of the car and kneeled beside her.

"Ma'am...ma'am. I'm going to take you and—."

"Virgil, my boy's name is Virgil," said the woman, looking at him for the first time.

He looked down at the boy, who had to be no older than eleven or twelve. He groaned as he picked up the boy and told the mother to open the car door and get inside. The woman did as he instructed and reached out for her son. She hugged his torso in her arms, rocking his lifeless body back and forth. Ambrose drove to Mission Hospital in Huntington Park, the nearest hospital. The drive was surreal. He had become part of the madness that they watched on TV. Instead of watching the chaos on the screen, he was now in its midst. The metallic scent of the boy's blood clotted his nose as he forced himself not to throw up. He turned off the radio out of respect for the woman and the dead boy in the back seat. The woman hummed to her son as she rocked him and occasionally stroked his cheek with her thumb. The woman's soft humming calmed him as he drove. Her voice traveled through time, crossing the Atlantic Ocean with the thousands of stolen people. It joined the woeful songs sung in cotton, rice, and tobacco fields. It sounded as sweet as the sugar cane that their ancestors harvested. Ambrose listened to the collective stories of their people in her moans as he watched people running down the street with their arms full of stolen items. Most were stealing things they could carry, but some were pulling sofas down the street or pushing TVs in shopping carts. Storefront windows were busted out, and small fires burned in vacant lots. He turned off streets whenever he saw police cars up ahead blocking the intersection. He traveled down dark neighborhoods where porch lights hadn't been turned on. He parked in front of the emergency room door and got out of the car. He opened the back door and tried to pick the boy up, but the woman tightened her grip on her son.

"Ma'am…come on now, we're at the hospital."

She squeezed her son tighter and howled. Exhausted, she looked at Ambrose, wiped her tears, and asked him. "What's the use?"

Ambrose didn't answer her question because there wasn't an answer that would make it easier for her to let go. He lowered his head and exhaled loudly before looking at her again. After a few seconds, the woman kissed the boy's forehead and released her hold. Ambrose pulled Virgil toward him as gently as possible and struggled to pick him up. He carried the boy inside with his mother trailing behind him. The receptionist looked up, assessed the situation correctly, and picked up the phone. Before Ambrose knew what was happening, the young boy was being grabbed from his arms, placed on a gurney, and wheeled into the area closed off from the waiting room. He stood with his arms held out before him as if he were still holding the boy. The adrenaline that he had been operating on poured out of him, and he stumbled backward into Virgil's mother. The woman wobbled, and her legs buckled. Ambrose grabbed her but was too weak to keep her standing upright. He eased her onto the floor and sat beside her, too tired to do anything more. A lady in the waiting room got a cup of water from the receptionist and handed it to Virgil's mom. Ambrose asked the woman if he could call somebody for her. She shook her head and told him that he had done enough. She thanked him repeatedly until it sounded like a soothing mantra instead of the shocked recitation of a grieving mother. With the help of the woman who had given them the water, He helped Virgil's mom up. The good Samaritan told Ambrose she would watch out for the woman, and he left Virgil's mother in her care.

The route back home was circuitous because the streets were full of people. Mayhem was in full swing. Gunshots, screams, and sirens filled the air. He stayed off the main roads to avoid running into the cops with a shotgun lying across the front seat. The dark, empty side streets were eerie in contrast to the pandemonium on Florence and Firestone. He got lost a couple of times, having turned around so many times that he lost his sense of direction. Ambrose finally found a main street where he saw people breaking the windows of stores and running inside. He also saw burning buildings and heard so many gunshots that it seemed that the United States was at war with itself. When he arrived home, he sat in his car for a few minutes before leaving its dark, quiet interior. He wanted to know where a Black man could live without being beaten, burned, hung, and made to struggle until there was no more life left in him worth living. He took a deep breath and got out of the car. He stood beside his car and looked at his yard sprinkled with what he thought was trash. *Damned looters taking stuff they hadn't paid for and discarding empty boxes and shit in his yard,* thought Ambrose. He looked at Dinah's yard and saw the same thing, so he pulled the trash can from the side of the house. He went to pick up the trash in the yard but discovered that the stuff on the lawn was cans of food, bags of sugar, rice, and flour. There were loaves of bread, meat packages, orange juice, and milk. Ambrose picked up the items from both yards and placed them on his porch. On his second trip, Lucinda opened the front door.

"What are you doing?" she asked.

"Getting the food off the lawn,"

"What," said Lucinda, looking down at the food on the porch.

"People have been throwing food in everybody's yard," he said, extending his arm and sweeping it from side to side.

She walked down the steps and stood next to Ambrose. She looked at her neighbors' yards, put her hands up to her mouth, and blinked back tears before helping Ambrose pick up the rest of the food. He grinned as he looked at his neighbors, coming out of their homes and discovering the food on their lawns. He took back what he thought about the looters. *Maybe they hadn't paid for the things with money, but they had paid for them in other ways.*

"Ambrose…Ambrose!" said Lottie.

"Huh," he answered, wondering how Lucinda had turned into Lottie.

"Do you want some more lemonade? You don't look so good."

"Yeah, thanks," he said, wiping the sweat from his forehead. He looked around as Lottie went inside to get more lemonade. He saw his house across the street as panic and confusion's icy fingers crept up his spine. He didn't know where he was, then suddenly the fog that covered his brain cleared, and he knew it wasn't 1965 and that his Lucinda had been dead for a long time. He looked at his house and saw that it was a different color than it had been in 1965, and a wire fence surrounded it. The revelation that he was sitting on Lottie's porch in 2010 came to him with such force that he felt as if he had been physically slapped in the face. The rapid beating of his heart began to slow, but he was still a little frightened by his complete submersion into the past. The security door banged, and Lottie appeared with a pitcher of lemonade. He drank his lemonade in one long gulp and made a loud sucking sound when he finished the last of it. She poured more lemonade into his glass, and he drank that one slower. His hand didn't shake as much as it had with the first glass, and his breathing was almost steady. Lottie sat silently on the porch with him until the sun began its descent.

"Dinner is ready. Don't tell nobody, but I made us some fried pork chops, sweet potatoes, and string beans," she whispered.

"Mmm…that sounds good," he said, blinking several times as he looked across the street at his and Dinah's house.

Chapter 8

"How long has this been going on?" Destiny asked.

"Nothing is going on," Indigo protested.

"This nothing, that's not going on...how long has that been going on?"

"Onyx and I are friends. He stops by to make sure Treyvon is not bothering me."

"Speaking of Treyvon, what's going on with him?"

"We're done; that's what's going on." Indigo got up from the couch they were sitting on and stood by the security door.

"It's hard to believe...you know that he did that," said Destiny quietly, so quietly that Indigo didn't catch the last three words, but she knew what Destiny was thinking.

"I thought I knew him."

"Did you think he would ever do something like that? Did he ever make you feel scared?" Destiny asked, leaning forward to watch Indigo as she answered.

"No, never. We lived together for a year, and never did I think he was capable of..." Indigo didn't say the word because she was tired of saying it and thinking about it. She just wanted to forget that it happened. She looked out the door and watched a Hispanic family walking down the sidewalk like ducks. The mother was in the lead while the three kids trailed behind. The silence between her and Destiny stretched on as she watched Roscoe run to the fence and follow the family that walked on the sidewalk in front of his yard. The last little girl in the line stopped and stooped down to put her hand inside the chain link fence. When the mother reached the corner, she saw the little girl squatting at the fence, petting Roscoe. The woman shouted something in Spanish, and the little girl jumped up and began running toward her mother.

Destiny stood up to leave, cutting the short visit even shorter. Since Indigo and Amani had stopped talking, it seemed like Indigo had nothing to say to her. Destiny thought her friend would lean on her for support. Instead, she had become closed-off and hard to reach. Talking to her was like pulling teeth, a one-sided affair, where she asked questions and Indigo gave perfunctory responses. She hugged Indigo goodbye and walked out the door. Indigo walked out onto the porch with Destiny and watched her drive away. She stood on the porch, surveilling the neighborhood. People were out and about on this sunny Saturday afternoon. The neighborhood was alive with people, sounds, and movement. Some were leaning on their fences, talking to each other. Young kids rode their bikes on the sidewalk while teens huddled in groups, laughing at each other's asinine remarks and stunts. Family members sat on porches, talking, laughing, eating, and drinking. Doors banged as people paraded in and out of houses. One man washed his car while others played cards or dominos in the front yard under shade trees. People were doing all the same things that she remembered them doing when she was a kid, except there were more brown faces than black faces. Spanish words mingled with English words, while mariachi and ranchera music competed with rhythm and blues and rap. Big Momma had once loved this place. Mr. Ambrose and Miss Lottie still did. She had forgotten how much she loved it here as a child before she grew up and left the protective borders of her hood. The friends she made in college were surprised to learn that she grew up in South Central Los

Angeles. They believed the media's portrayal of how people on the East Side lived and behaved. Some of her friends respected her ability to break the stereotype of who she was supposed to be, while others waited for the hood rat to show itself. Indigo cut a lot of so-called friends loose when they complimented her on how different she was from other Black girls. This pronouncement, surprisingly enough, came not just from Whites but also from Hispanics and Blacks. She grew tired of hearing the overused phrase, "You're so well-spoken." The first time someone said it to her, she didn't impart much meaning to it one way or another. She assumed the speaker meant well. But when it became a common phrase that seemingly only described her, the compliment caused her to look at the person in a new light. Sometimes, she would give them the benefit of the doubt and explain that it wasn't the compliment they thought it was. Sometimes, she knew exactly what was meant and what the person was. She felt like an outsider now standing on the porch because the sentiments behind that phrase had tainted how she viewed herself, even though she fought against it. Indigo bought into the lie that she was better than the people who lived in the neighborhood that she had come from. But now, the hood was creeping back into her heart. The sights, sounds, and smells may be a little different, but the spirit of the place was the same. Some houses teemed with flowers surrounded by a manicured carpet of grass, while others looked abandoned. The houses transformed into homes helped keep the despondency that grew like weeds in neighborhoods that politicians remembered only during an election year. The neighborhood could have been a wasteland if it wasn't for people like her grandmother. The rose bushes, pansies, marigolds, and sunflowers that grew in some yards lightened weary hearts. The spearmint that grew outside fences encroaching on the sidewalk released its pleasing scent into the air and caused passersby to slow down and breathe deeper. She was amazed to see such beauty overflowing in a place where security bars and doors were required to enjoy a cool breeze. She looked at Big Momma's yard and noticed its sorry state. The rosebushes needed deadheading, weeds were growing where flowers once grew, and the grass needed to be mowed. She went inside and locked the front doors before leaving out of the back door. In the garage, she saw her grandmother's gardening tools and gloves lying on a workbench. Indigo grabbed the gloves and a small hand trowel. She pulled the trash can from the side of the garage to the front yard and got to work pulling weeds. She pulled out the dead plants and clipped blackened stems off rose bushes.

Lottie watched from across the street as Indigo finally did something about Dinah's yard. She went inside her house, poured two tall glasses of lemonade, and put six homemade oatmeal-raisin cookies in a paper bag. Then, Lottie stood at Dinah's gate, holding the two glasses and the bag of cookies.

"Indigo, open the gate, hon!"

"Huh?" Indigo turned to see Miss Lottie and Rosco. She grunted as she stood to open the gate.

"I saw you working in the yard, so I brought you some refreshments."

"Thank you," huffed Indigo.

Lottie went to the porch while Roscoe sniffed around the yard, inspecting Indigo's work. Indigo tossed her gloves on the porch and told Lottie she needed to wash her hands before quickly ducking around to the back of the house. She returned to the porch by the front door, leaving the wooden door open. She handed Lottie a couple of napkins and took a seat before digging into the bag for a cookie. They were sitting on the porch enjoying the warm weather and the occasional breeze when Roscoe and seemingly all the dogs on the block started barking. Roscoe ran to the gate and looked up and down the street, growling.

"What in the world is wrong with him and the rest of the dogs?" asked Indigo.

"Pete's coming," said Lottie, matter-of-factly.

"Who's Pete?"

"He's the mailman," Lottie said, looking at Indigo and taking another bite of her cookie. "You haven't seen Pete since you been here?"

"No."

"Well, Pete will talk your head off and try to get into your business so he can spread it around town. The only reason he doesn't hang outside my house is because Roscoe won't let him. Look down the street; you'll see everybody going inside. Indigo looked to her left and saw a woman pick up her baby and enter her house. A man working on his car hurriedly gathered his tools, leaving the hood up, and darted inside his home.

"Do we need to go inside?" Indigo asked, rising halfway out of her chair.

"Nah, we're good. Roscoe has got it covered, "Lottie grinned. Just as she finished her declaration, the dog looked back at her and barked twice before turning his attention back to the streets. They stayed on the porch and finished the cookies as Pete got closer and closer. Roscoe barked and growled incessantly as Pete delivered Ambrose's mail.

"I'll take care of this," said Lottie, getting up.

"Morning, Miss Lottie. What are you doing over here? Pete asked.

"Good afternoon, Pete."

"Yeah, you got me," he laughed. "It's afternoon, all right. I guess I've been working so hard, delivering mail and all...that the time just slipped by."

"Um-hum," replied Lottie, sticking her hand out. "I'll take the mail, thank you."

"I can't give you your mail yet because I've got a system. You'll mess it up if I went looking for it now."

"I mean, I'll take Indigo's mail."

"Indigo…Indigo, huh? Is she Miss Dinah's granddaughter? Is she gonna sell it or rent it? Because I know someone who might be interested in renting. If she's planning on renting it."

"Pete, you know darn well you know who Indigo is. You knew who she was two seconds after she moved in. What she plans on doing with her grandmama's house is none of your business. Now give me her mail and go on about your business."

"Miss Lottie, I can't give you the mail for this house; that would be a crime. Now, if you would restrain that beast of yours, I could do my job."

"Pete, you know damn well…. Boy, you gonna make me lose my religion. Give me the mail. Indigo is sitting right there and has given me permission to retrieve her mail." Lottie straightened her back, and Roscoe started a new chorus of barking.

"I don't understand why she can't come and get the mail herself. She's right there," he said, pointing at her. Indigo started to get up, but Lottie gave her a look that said she had better not move.

"Pete, I ain't playing with you…you're gonna give me the mail, and you're gonna give it to me right now. Or…I could call your Postmaster and tell him what you do on your route. I know you place bets at the bookie joint on 92nd Street, and God only knows what you do at that cat house two blocks over." Lottie extended one hand out for the mail and placed the other hand on her hip.

Pete's mouth opened and closed, but no words came out. He wiped the sweat from his brow and let a long gust of air noisily out of his mouth before handing over the mail.

"You don't know what you're talking about," Pete mumbled.

"Say, what now?" asked Lottie.

"What?" he asked, feigning that he hadn't heard her. Lottie stared at him, refusing to repeat herself. Pete cleared his throat before mumbling, "I said, have a nice day."

Lottie angled her head skyward before walking away from him. Pete kicked in Roscoe's direction behind Lottie's back, careful not to touch the fence. Lottie handed Indigo her mail and picked up the empty glasses. Indigo gave the mail, mostly junk mail, a cursory glance before placing it on the table.

"Well, me and Roscoe are going to go so you can finish. Dinah would be glad to see you taking care of her flowers."

Indigo could only smile and shake her head in agreement. As Lottie crossed the street, she yelled her thanks again for the refreshments. After she finished the flower beds, she pulled out the old push mower. She was surprised at how well it cut. The blades were sharp and rotated smoothly. The smell of fresh-cut grass reminded her of Saturday mornings when she and her grandmother worked in the yard. Her grandmother cut the grass while she raked the clippings in piles before dumping them in the trash. On Saturday, the humming of lawnmowers was a familiar white noise for weekend warriors. Someone was always outside doing something they didn't have the time to do during the week. She felt like a kid again working in the yard. She glanced at the front door, half expecting Big Momma to walk out and tell her it was time to take a break. She watered the yard just as the daylight was fading. The neighborhood was quiet now; kids were running home, trying to make it there before the streetlights came on. She sat on the porch, tired, but it was a good tired because she had physically accomplished something. She saw Mr. Ambrose returning from his walk with Roscoe. They waved at each other when he noticed her. He walked inside Miss Lottie's house without bothering to knock. *Huh*, thought Indigo, *that's awfully familiar.* She remained on the porch; the setting sun cast a golden hue on everything, always making this time of day seem sacred. In the growing darkness, she fantasized that her grand-mother was inside making dinner and that she was setting the table. After setting the table, she asked her grandmother if she needed help preparing dinner. But Big Momma, as usual, sent her off to finish her homework or watch TV until it was time to eat. Indigo sat in the dark, thinking what she wouldn't give to be a little girl again. She wished she could walk inside and be magically transported back to those days. Sitting on the porch, watching kids make it home just as the streetlights flickered on, Indigo remembered her childhood evenings here in this house.

Big Momma never taught her how to cook, claiming she didn't have time. All her grandmother wanted to do when she got off work was to get off her aching feet. Her grandmother was a well-oiled machine in her kitchen. She knew where everything was and didn't make any unneces-sary movements as she chopped, sprinkled, pinched, and stirred. Usually, dinner was on the table within an hour. They would say grace and dig in. She would tell her grandmother about the girls who were mean to her and how the classroom laughed at some kid who couldn't do the math problem when the teacher called on them. After dinner, when she was big enough, she washed the dishes, swept the kitchen floor, and took out the trash. The best part of the night was after she had taken her bath. She sat on the couch next to Big Momma and watched TV. She snuggled up on the softest part of her grandmother and inhaled the rose fragrant that was a part of her. She would fall asleep to that sweet scent only to be shaken, awoke, and told to go to bed. Indigo also recalled how much she hated rubbing her grandmother's feet and legs. Now, if she could wash her feet and dry them with her hair like the woman in the bible, she would. If only she had known as a kid that she wouldn't have her grandmother forever, she wouldn't have wanted to grow up so fast. She would have stayed under her more and never left home. The streetlights were on now, and the sky no longer glowed. A few faint stars competed with the city's lights, and Indigo looked upward before going inside.

The doorbell rang as Indigo stepped out of the shower. She tied the belt of her robe tight and dashed to the front door.

"Hey!" she said, smiling at Onyx and unlocking the screen door.

"Hey…hey," he said as his voice modulated, taking on a sultry tone as his eyes slid down her body and landed on her polished red toenails.

"Boy, stop being silly." She stepped back to let him in. Indigo locked the door and excused herself. When she returned, He was seated on the couch.

"You could have turned on the TV," she said.

"I'm good," he said, looking at her in the way that men looked at women whom they wanted to know better.

"Boy, stop!"

"Stop what?"

"Stop looking at me like that."

"I'll try," he said earnestly. "I heard you were doing some yard work today."

"I was, and it felt really good doing something physical. Besides, Big Momma would have had a fit if she saw what her yard looked like."

"I'll have to check it out in the daylight. So, what else is up with you?"

"I'm going back to work Monday."

"That's good…what do you do?"

"I'm a Pharmacy Technician."

"So, you're a drug dealer," he joked.

"Yep, you can take the girl out of the hood, but you can't take the hood out of the girl. So, what do you do?"

"I'm a realtor, investor, and property manager."

"So, you're a hustler."

"I'm a hustla baby. I just want you to know," sang Onyx in his Jay-Z's voice.

"I take it that you like your job."

"Yeah, I do. I get to meet some really interesting people. What about you?"

"I do, but it's a formidable responsibility because there's no room for error."

"Formidable," he teased. "You ain't got to use a two-dollar word; it's just us talking."

"Forget you," said Indigo as she playfully punched his arm. They talked for an hour before he got up to leave. They were on the porch saying goodbye when he moved in to kiss her.

"Sorry," said Indigo, backing up.

"No, I'm sorry…it was just that I kissed you the other night."

"I know, but…I don't know what we're doing."

"I'm just trying to get to know you."

"Boy, you have known me since we were kids."

"Yeah, but I don't know the woman you've become."

She looked at him, struck by the truth of that statement. She thought she knew Treyvon, but she hadn't known him as well as she thought she had.

"Do we really ever know someone?" she asked the question more to herself rhetorically and was slightly surprised when he answered.

"We know bits and pieces of people, but rarely do we get to know the whole person."

"Why is that?" she asked with a child-like wonder.

Onyx looked down at Indigo and saw that she was seriously asking him to reveal a mystery. "Because." he hesitated and stared at her. "Most of us don't really know ourselves. We have an image or idea of who we think we are, but if we look closely, we find that the image is distorted or has changed from what it was the day before."

She looked at him and saw not only his surface beauty but also something deeper. His skin was smooth and silky and glowed despite its darkness. Slanted tight eyes were surrounded by lush black lashes framed by thick arched brows. *Yes,* Indigo thought, *this is an extraordinarily beautiful man, but he is also wise.*

"So, what's up with you? Are you seeing anyone?" she asked.

"Yeah, I see people." Onyx's mouth stretched into a wide grin.

"People?"

He chuckled and replied. "Yeah, people."

"What's so funny?"

"You're funny. You act like you wanna be my woman or something." He stepped closer to her, backing her up against the door. He placed his hands on her hips and stooped to kiss her. The gentle sweetness of the kiss soon turned prurient, and their bodies moved in a slow, sinuous motion. He stopped moving his tongue long enough to confirm she was kissing him back. When her tongue searched for his, he kissed her deeper and squeezed her tighter. Heavy breathing and the quiet rattling of the iron door mixed with the moans that slipped from her mouth. Onyx slid a hand inside the front of her jeans. Indigo jerked her head back and banged it hard against the wrought iron screen door.

"Whoa! You good?" he asked.

"We need to stop!"

"Okay—okay," he said, backing up to give her space. "I'll see you tomorrow, but can you answer the question before I go?"

"What question?"

"Do you wanna be my woman?"

"Do you want me to be your woman?" she teased.

"I asked you first."

"Maybe we'll see after we get to know each other again."

"So, I can't get any nookie no time soon?" he asked, slowly turning his smile into an exaggerated frown.

"No, and you can't get any from those people you used to see either."

"What am I supposed to do about this?" he asked, looking down at the bulge in his pants.

Indigo looked down at his crotch and threw her head back, bumping it again against the door. She cradled her head and laughed before saying, "Looks like a personal problem."

"Funny, real funny," he kissed her forehead before turning to go to his car.

Chapter 9

Indigo was up early the next day, which was the Sunday before she was scheduled to return to work. She watered the flowers and the grass out front before starting to work in the backyard. She was the only one on the block out in her yard. Indigo surveyed her work from the day before and plucked up the offending weeds or grass growing in the flowerbeds. Although she didn't see many people milling around in the street, she could tell they were unfurling from their beds and beginning their day. The smell of sizzling pork wafted in the air, and she almost went back into the house to make breakfast. But this would be the last opportunity to spend the entire day in the yard before she returned to work, so she soldiered on without breakfast. She was in the backyard, weeding the flower bed against the back fence, when Ambrose greeted her.

"Good Morning!" yelled Ambrose from his back porch.

"Good morning!" She stopped weeding to look around at him.

"You got the front yard looking good."

"Thanks."

Ambrose, wanting to keep an eye on her, got the water hose and began to water his yard. He glanced at her while watering and gasped when she stuck the shovel in the rose bed to turn over the dirt. A small amount of saliva went down the wrong pipe. He was choking so badly that Indigo stopped what she was doing and went to the side fence.

"Are you okay," she asked.

"Just choking on my own spit," he answered between fits of coughing.

He dropped the water hose and went to his back door, making a hacking sound as he tried to clear his throat. He was so shaken by what he saw that he barely reached the kitchen table.

Oh, my God, what am I going to do if she... Ambrose couldn't bring himself to finish the thought. After a few minutes, he got up to get a glass of water, but when he reached for the glass in the cupboard, his hand shook so violently that he changed his mind. He sat back down at the kitchen table and placed his head in his hands. He mumbled to himself that he had made a promise to Dinah and would keep it if it were the last thing he did. He sat at the table, trying to figure a way out of this mess. After all these years, the thing that almost made Dinah lose her mind could be found out by the one person she had never wanted to know. He got up and peeked out the kitchen window; what he saw made him grip the edge of the sink to keep from falling. Ambrose held onto the kitchen counter and edged along until he reached the back door. Holding onto the back door, he crept onto the porch.

"Indigo!"

Indigo turned to acknowledge that she had heard him, but she knew something was wrong when she saw him. She dropped the shovel and hurried to the fence.

"What's wrong?"

"I'm not feeling too good. Can you come over for a minute?"

She instantly started moving to the other side of her yard. She walked around to his backyard and entered his kitchen. She saw him sitting at the kitchen table, looking old and feeble. Tears immediately sprung into her eyes, knowing that it would be too much to endure if anything happened to him.

"What's wrong? Are you hurt?" she asked tenderly.

"No, nothing's hurting me. I just got weak and felt like I was going to faint. Maybe I need to eat something. Do you mind fixing me something?"

"Of course not. What would you like?" she asked, relieved.

"Toast and scrambled eggs would be nice."

"What about some coffee or tea?"

"Coffee would be good. Thanks, Indigo, I appreciate you."

She washed her hands at the kitchen sink and got busy making his breakfast.

Within minutes, the smell of freshly brewed coffee filled the room, and a plate of toast and eggs was placed in front of him. She had made herself a plate as well and sat across from him.

"Thanks, baby girl." He gulped his coffee and attacked his toast and eggs. Ambrose breathed a deep sigh of relief when he finished.

"Are you sure you don't want me to take you to urgent care or the emergency room?"

"Nah, baby girl, I'm good. Sometimes, my blood sugar drops too low at night, and I don't always feel like eating anything when I get up. I feel a lot better now."

"Okay, then. I'm going to get back at it."

"Back at what—what are you planning on doing?" His tone was suddenly harsh.

"I was thinking about making the flower bed along the back fence wider and more natural-looking," she answered, slowly aware of the jarring difference in his tone. "I'm going to dig up some of the bushes and plant some groundcover and other plants in the bed."

"You gonna dig up Dinah's rose bushes?"

"Yeah, I'm going to spread them out a little bit. I'm not going to get rid of them!" she explained, thinking he had misunderstood her plan.

"What you wanna do that for?" he asked, beginning to feel sick again.

"The bushes need more room." She looked at him curiously, wondering why he was getting so upset.

"I don't think you should mess with your grandmother's roses. What if you killed them? How you gonna feel then?"

"Mr. Ambrose, I'm not going to kill them. They'll probably look a whole lot better."

"I don't know about that. I think you need to leave your grandmama's roses alone."

Nobody asked you, and why do you care? The questions jumped into her head, but she would never say those words out loud to him. She had been raised to respect her elders. Once again, she told Ambrose to call her if he needed anything and quickly escaped out the back door.

What had started as simply cleaning up the backyard had now morphed into a bigger project. She decided to make the backyard a memorial garden honoring her grandmother. The backyard would be where she could sit and reflect on who she was after everything that had happened. The woman she was a few weeks ago was gone. What Onyx said the other night had resonated with her. She didn't know who she was anymore. Before the rape and death of Big Momma, she would have said she was a happy, confident woman who was secure in her relationship and job. She had made it out of the hood and saw a future where every one of her dreams would come true. Now, her confidence was shaken, and she didn't know if she could trust Onyx not to hurt her. She questioned whether Amani was ever really her friend, examining every disagreement, slight, or misunderstanding until the bonds of their friendship lay limp and threadbare. Her future had been altered, and now she didn't know what it held or what she wanted. The only thing she knew for sure was that she must survive.

She had been digging up the grass where the enlarged flower beds would be. She had been at it for over two hours when the hairs on the back of her neck bristled. She looked over her shoulder, expecting to see Mr. Ambrose watching her from his back porch, but he wasn't there. She finished edging the shape of the new bed with the shovel when the feeling of being watched returned. She looked back at Mr. Ambrose's porch, then at her back door. Indigo gripped the shovel handle tight when she saw a shadow move past her kitchen window. Without thinking of the danger, she rushed toward the back door with the shovel raised to strike. Swinging the door open, she stood on the threshold, afraid to enter.

"Hello!" she shouted, trying to remember if she had gone out the front door and left it unlocked. She went around to the front of the house. The security door was locked, just as she thought it would be. She breathed a little easier and scolded herself for letting her imagination run away. Walking briskly to the back door, she entered the house, still holding the shovel. She got a cold bottle of water out of the fridge, took a few gulps, and breathed in and out a couple of times before searching the house. She half expected to see drawers opened and clothes tossed about, but everything was in place. Her laptop was still on the dining room table, and her watch and jewelry were on the China platter on the nightstand. Indigo walked out of her bedroom feeling better, and then she glimpsed a shadowy shape in her peripheral vision at the end of the hallway. In the seconds that it took her brain to process what she saw and for her to obey her brain's command to turn her head to confirm the impression, it was too late. Whatever she almost saw was gone. She knew that whatever it was wasn't of this world. Just as she acknowledged the thought, she felt a gush of wind behind her. The wind was neither warm nor cold but thick with the scent of roses. The smell clogged her nose and throat; she dropped the shovel and placed a hand on the wall as she rode a wave of nausea and fear. *Something evil is here*, screamed inside her head as she stood at the front of the hallway. She was stuck in another dimension as she stood wet from the sweat that fear produced. Her blouse clung to her, and a bead of sweat dropped from her forehead into her right eye. The moment her eye blinked, her body was freed from paralysis, and she ran to the front door. Her hands shook so violently that it took several attempts to unlock the deadbolt, even with the keys already inserted in the lock. Once outside, she felt foolish, but she was too afraid to go back inside the house. She crossed the street when she spotted Lottie sitting on her porch, hoping to be invited to sit with her until she got the courage to return home.

"Good morning, Miss Lottie. How you doing?" asked Indigo, standing outside Lottie's gate.

"Morning, baby. How you?"

"Good—good. Everything's good."

"You done working in the yard?"

"No, I was working in the back until I had to stop and help Mr. Ambrose. He wasn't feeling well."

"What! Ambrose, not feeling good?" Lottie struggled to her feet.

"He's all right now, Miss Lottie. I made him breakfast, and he felt better after he ate."

She knew Miss Lottie heard her say Mr. Ambrose was fine, but that didn't stop her from dashing across the street as fast as her plump body and short legs could carry her. Picking up on Lottie's anxiety, Roscoe followed behind her without bothering to give Indigo his customary growl.

"Ambrose—Ambrose, are you all right in there?" Lottie shouted as she banged on the front door. Ambrose opened the door and looked accusingly at Indigo before asking Lottie what she was fussing about. After his third reassurance that he was fine, he lost his patience with Lottie and closed the door in her face.

"That old fool don't have the sense that God gave him," Lottie huffed, storming off the porch, leaving Indigo nowhere to go but back home.

She took a few deep breaths on the front porch before opening the front door. Once inside, she locked the door and walked rapidly through the house and out the back door. Shaken by the earlier events, she concluded she was done working in the yard for the day. She collected the garden tools, including the shovel she had left inside the house, and put them back in the garage. Back in the house, she stood still in every room, trying to gauge whether or not a supernatural presence was there. She stood in the doorway and looked in her old bedroom. Everything looked and felt normal. No shadowy figure lurked in the corners, and there was no heaviness in the atmosphere. The room where she and her girlfriends had spent hours perfecting their dance moves like the Running Man, Electric Slide, and the Cabbage Patch was flooded with sunlight. Two twin beds were in the room, separated by a nightstand, and on the wall opposite, a TV sat on top of a dresser. Gone were the toys that littered the floor when she was a child, but the boyband posters she had posted as an adolescent remained on the wall. Indigo went to Big Momma's room, which was now hers; no sinister presence awaited her, but there was an undeniable scent of roses. The fragrance was soft and pleasing; she stood in the doorway, breathing it in. The smell calmed her, and when it drifted away, she went to the living room with her cell phone in hand. Whenever she needed an answer to something she didn't understand, she did what she laughingly referred to as "*Google that shit.*" She was fascinated with the information that she gleaned. An hour later, Indigo was convinced she had two spirits in the house; one was her grandmother's, protecting her from the haint she had seen earlier. She wasn't as afraid as before because she now had the information needed to protect herself. She clicked on the Amazon app and bought a bundle of smudging sage to cleanse the house. The sage would be delivered in two days, so she went into her bedroom to look for Big Momma's bible. The Bible wasn't on top of the nightstand, the usual spot as long as she could remember. She looked inside the drawer of the nightstand and the chifforobe's drawers, but it wasn't in either of the places. She could picture the old Bible held together by duct tape. Scriptures were highlighted in a rainbow of colors depending on whatever highlighters were readily available. The neon colors glowed on the thin, yellowed pages. *It had to be in the house somewhere,* she thought. She searched all over for it, places where it should and shouldn't be, before entering the room she now slept in. The most logical place for it to be because her grandmother read her Bible every morning before getting out of bed and every night before going to sleep was the nightstand. Sitting on the bed, trying to think where it could be, she remembered the boxes in the closet. She pulled down both boxes and looked in the heaviest box first; then she looked in the box that contained the shoebox full of photos and a large manilla envelope. The manilla envelope couldn't possibly contain the Bible, but she remembered that she never looked inside it because the photographs sidetracked her. Then, another thought occurred to her.

"Her purse! It's got to be in her purse!" she shouted. The nurse had given her Big Momma's purse, and she had put it up in the closet. She grabbed the purse from the closet shelf, but she knew it wasn't there before she even looked inside. Although the purse was big enough, it wasn't heavy enough, but she looked inside anyway. She dumped the contents on the bed. A coin purse, wallet, lipstick, cough drops, a hand-embroidered handkerchief, loose change, three pens, one pencil with a broken lead, and a crumpled piece of paper spilled out onto the bed. She un-balled the paper to discover that it was an old grocery store receipt. She looked down at the debris and picked up the lipstick, wanting to see the only shade her grandmother had ever worn. These were her things, the everyday things she touched, just as she was doing now. She touched them wistfully and smelled the handkerchief, which still held the faintest hint of roses. Indigo put everything back inside the purse, crumbling up the store receipt before placing it back inside and putting the purse back on the closet shelf. The box containing the manilla envelope was still sitting on the floor, so Indigo knelt and took out the envelope. The envelope contained a small ream of College Ruled 3-hole Punched Paper covered with her grandmother's beautiful cursive writing.

April 29, 1992

The world has gone crazy and me with it. Black folks are rioting in the street again. Police are still killing us, and we are still killing each other. Lord, what am I gonna do now?

May 5, 1992

Ambrose says the riots are over and that I have to get myself together so I can go back to work and take care of Indigo. I can't sleep. I spend my days and nights looking out the window at what I've done.

May 8, 1992

Ambrose left Indigo alone with me today. For a little while, I had my little girl and Delray back. It scared me for a minute how completely I thought it was true. Ambrose was scared, too, because he didn't bring Indigo to visit me every day like before. Instead, he sits with me after Indigo goes to sleep. Ambrose watches me eat and searches the house for the liquor that I buy when he's at work. After he pours whatever is left down the drain, he threatens to be done with the whole business and leave me be. We both know that if it hadn't been for Indigo, he wouldn't have helped me.

May 10, 1992

I went for a walk with Indigo today. I expected storefronts to be boarded up, vacant lots full of trash, burnt cars, and houses like before, but the neighborhood looked the same. On our walk, Indigo asked me about her mother, and that knocked the wind out of me. She started crying, and before long, I was crying too.

Sept. 15, 1992

Indigo is back in school, and I've been at work for a while. Things are better for both of us. She forgets about her mother for longer periods before she has a crying spell. I can forget for a few hours every day while I clean houses and figure out how to, Rob Peter, to Pay Paul.

December 28, 1992

I can't believe it's been eight months. This was the first Christmas without my baby. Indigo cried most of the day. I did my best to make it a good Christmas for her, but I'm glad it's over.

March 16, 1993

Today is Wanda's birthday. I took Indigo to school and came back home. I didn't go to work today. I'm so tired; if it weren't for my grandbaby, I would ask the good Lord to take me home. I wonder what

I did wrong in raising Wanda. She was a sweet little girl; she was daddy's little girl. When she got older, her nose was wide open for any boy who paid her any attention. How a woman could choose a man over their own child, I'll never know. Anyway, Indigo didn't know it was her momma's birthday today. I surprised her with a special dinner and a cake for dessert. She didn't know it was a secret birthday dinner for her momma.

April 29, 1993

It's been a whole year, and Indigo doesn't ask about her momma nearly as much as she used to. Sometimes, I catch her looking out the window or down the street looking for her. I don't say anything; I just let her have her moment. Sometimes, she climbs in my lap like a little baby, and I cradle her and rock her like she's one. It does us both some good because I feel better when I rock her to sleep. Looking at her asleep in my arms, I know I did the right thing.

Indigo flipped the pages, looking for more entries, but there were none. *Big Momma did something she regretted, which was why her momma never came back. The diary also alludes to her mother choosing a man over her,* Indigo thought. She reread the pages three or four times, becoming more confused with each reading. *Looking out the window at what she had done, Mr. Ambrose had to keep her because Big Momma was too distraught to care for her or herself. Drunken binges, not eating, none of it made sense.* Indigo left the bedroom with the pieces of paper that she read and reread. *What did her grandmother do that made her mother leave and not come back? Why would she do that? Mr. Ambrose knows! Why did Mr.*

Ambrose have to keep her? Indigo felt sick to her stomach, and her head hurt. The questions came so fast that they got jumbled inside her brain and tumbled out into a crazy conspiracy theory between Big Momma and Mr. Ambrose to keep her from her mother. For what rhyme or reason, she couldn't fathom. A feeling deeper than sadness came over her as she sat on the couch, pondering what the words her grandmother wrote meant. Sorrow mixed with anger burned her gut until tears extinguished the pain. Indigo sat in the dark with the wooden front door open, and she watched the brightness of the day soften into nightfall. The sounds that only a city makes at night could be heard. They were sounds that she had not paid attention to in a long time. Sitting in the living room, she heard cars speeding by. After a while, the cars sounded like waves crashing on the shore. The distant sounds of horns and sirens faded. The crickets chirping right outside the door melded into the crashing waves of the cars. The muffled sounds of people talking and laughing and the barking of dogs grew faint. The calliope of noises lulled Indigo into a more serene state as she tried to weave together who she thought her grandmother was. She was so entranced in her thoughts that she didn't see Onyx standing in front of the security door.

"Indigo."

"Onyx?" she asked, unsure if he was standing in front of the door.

"Yeah, let me in."

The loose papers fell from her lap as she stood and inched her way to the door. Onyx's fingers searched the wall for the light switch by the door.

"Why are you sitting in the dark?" he asked, flicking on the light.

"It wasn't dark when I started sitting here,"

"So, why didn't you turn on the light when it got dark?"

"I didn't know it had," she said as if no further explanation was needed.

"Okay, that sounds crazy as fuck. You're sitting in the dark because you didn't know it was dark? Is that what you're saying?" he asked, looking at her with a mixture of concern and amusement.

"I was reading something my grandmother wrote, and I guess I got caught up because I didn't realize I was sitting in the dark. Here, look at this." Indigo bent over to pick up the papers scattered on the floor. She arranged the pages in date order because they were not numbered. He read the pages standing up. When he finished, he sat on the couch next to her.

"So, what do you think this means?" he asked.

"It sounds like Big Momma told my mother not to come back for me, and she did something to make sure she stayed away."

"Are there more pages?" he asked, waving the pages in the air.

"No."

"Are you sure?"

"Yeah, I'm sure. There was a small ream of paper with these pages, but she didn't write anything else after April 29, 1993," she said, taking the papers from his hand.

"What do you think your grandmother did?"

"I don't know, but look here..." She flipped to May 5th and 8th. Your grandfather knows what she did. First, he told her to get herself together so she could go back to work and take care of me; that was on May 5th. Then, on May 8th, he brought me over to visit my grandmother. Your grandfather was keeping me because Big Momma was mentally unable to take care of me. He had to make her eat and he got rid of the liquor in the house. Since when did Big Momma drink, let alone have a drinking problem? Something really messed up happened between my mother and grandmother, and your grandfather knows all about it."

"I don't remember you staying with us. He kept me and Zari on the weekends when our mother worked."

"I remember you guys at your grandfather's house on the weekends, but I don't remember staying with him. I need to talk to him."

"Talk to him about what?"

"About what he knows! Come on, we can ask him now," she said, clutching the papers tighter and leaping from the couch.

"Hold on a minute." Onyx grabbed her arm harder than he meant. Indigo toppled back onto the sofa next to him. The paper fluttered in the air, and time did that thing that it did when Treyvon was raping her. The papers stayed in the air so long that they transformed into bird wings flapping. They became the birds she watched out the window as she lay beside Treyvon after he had finished…when she was afraid to move or breathe.

Onyx immediately saw that he had frightened her and apologized repeatedly, but he was seemingly not getting through to her. He rubbed her arms softly and spoke to her in a cooing fashion.

"It's okay…you're okay…I'm sorry. I would never hurt you…you know that, right?"

The span of time was less than a minute, but for Indigo, it felt like the days and weeks that had separated her from the rape had been compressed into a millisecond, and she was back in that moment. Finally, she heard his voice, and instantly, she was back in his presence.

"You're right. He wasn't feeling well this morning. How is he doing?"

"He wasn't feeling well this morning?" he repeated, careful of the modulation of his voice.

"I was working in the backyard when he called for me to come over. I think his blood sugar dropped, so I made him breakfast. After he ate and had a cup of coffee, he said he felt better."

"Why didn't you call me?" he asked, forgetting to adjust his tone.

"After he ate, he was fine. "I'm sorry, Onyx, I should have called you," she said, not wanting to tell him that she had forgotten about his grandfather because she had a ghost in the house. "How was he doing when you checked on him?"

"He didn't mention that he wasn't feeling well, but he didn't seem like himself. He said he was tired and was going to bed, so I came here. I think I'll check on him again before I go home."

When Onyx mentioned going home, the fear that lay just beneath the surface leaped up, causing her heart to beat faster. She clutched his arms.

"What's wrong with you?" he asked, shrugging his arms free. "What the fuck is wrong with you?"

"Can I tell you something without you thinking I'm crazy?"

"I don't know, I kinda think it's too late for that." He would have found her behavior comical if not for the wild look in her eyes. Her eyes opened wider, and she grabbed his arms again. "Hey—hey, what's going on with you?"

"I'm scared to stay here alone," she confessed, releasing her grip and looking down at the floor.

"Has that motherfucker, been back?"

She shook her head from side to side.

"Then, what? Onyx lifted her chin with his finger. "Then, what? Tell me…what is it?"

Her face was turned upward, but her eyes remained lowered. "There's something in the house."

"Something like what? A mouse?" When she shook her head again from side to side, he asked if she had roaches. "Okay, look, we could do this all night, or you could just tell me what's in the house."

"A ghost."

Onyx almost laughed, but he saw that she was serious. "Indigo, babe, seriously, you think you have a ghost in the house. Come on…"

"I can smell roses in the house. Sometimes, the scent is overwhelming; sometimes, it's barely there. I'm not afraid when I smell roses because that's Big Momma's spirit. But sometimes, I can feel an evil presence, and today, I saw a shadow moving around in the house."

"Whoa, slow down. Roses, evil spirits, and shadows? Tell me about each time you saw or felt something."

Sitting side by side on the couch, she told him about the first time she felt something, including what she saw that morning.

"Do you believe in that stuff?" he asked.

"Yeah, don't you?"

"No, not really."

"What do you think happens when you die?"

"I don't know, man. I don't think about shit like that. I guess you just stop being."

"Don't you believe in God the Father, Son, and Holy Spirit? Don't you believe in heaven and hell?

"I guess."

"What do you mean, you guess?" she asked, standing up.

"I mean, I went to church as a kid, just like you did, but I don't go to church now. I haven't experienced ghosts or spirits floating around."

"I'm telling you that I'm not crazy and that this is really happening."

"So, you think your grandmother is trying to hurt you. You think she's an evil spirit now?"

"No, I think my grandmother is trying to protect me from the evil spirit." Indigo stood looking down at him with her arms across her chest. "Well," she said after a few moments of silence.

"Well, what do you want me to say?" he asked, completely at a loss for words.

"Will you stay with me until I can figure this out?"

"Figure what out?"

"Figure out how to get rid of the evil spirit."

"Indigo, look...I think you're tripping. I'll stay with you tonight, but..."

"But, what?"

"I need to get some clothes. Are you coming with me or staying here?" he asked, his lips twitching as he tried not to smile.

They checked on Ambrose before going to his place. The subject of her grandmother's diary or ghosts was not brought up at his grandfather's house. Neither were the subjects brought up on the drive to Onyx's house. Indigo had almost drifted off to sleep when he pulled into his driveway.

"Nice," she said, getting out of the car and looking at the Spanish-style house. "Love your landscaping; this is nice."

"Thanks." He unlocked the front door and stepped back, allowing her to enter first. Onyx turned on the light after she entered. The light revealed dark-stained hardwood floors, a beige, overstuffed sofa, and a large wooden coffee table. There was a fireplace with a chunky rustic mantle and hand-painted Spanish tiles on the hearth and fireplace surround. He excused himself to go pack, and Indigo sat on the sofa. She sat looking around until she couldn't contain her curiosity and began snooping. The dining area was part of the living room, and the dining table was the same wood as the coffee table. The kitchen had a vintage vibe, but the white cabinetry looked too pristine to be original. On closer inspection, she could see that the cupboards were original and had been stripped and restored by a master carpenter before being professionally repainted. The patina of the old porcelain kitchen sink contrasted with the stark whiteness of the quartz countertops but matched perfectly with the hand-painted Spanish tiles backsplash. The large hexagon terracotta floor tiles and stainless-steel appliances told everyone that vintage was fine up to a point. The kitchen had just enough room for a small wooden table and chairs. She left the kitchen, backtracked through the dining and living area, and walked down a hallway. Instead of peeking into unlit rooms, she followed the light and entered his bedroom. His bedroom was very modern. The curtains were navy blue linen, and the large area rug that covered most of the room was an abstract pattern of cream, navy blue, and rust colors that worked well with the dark wood of the floor and the pewter gray walls. The tufted caramel leather king-sized headboard completed the room's sophisticated masculinity. On each side of the bed were wooden tables instead of nightstands. The tables were not a matching set, but the cream-colored ceramic lamps on top of them were. A book lay open on one table, face down, and on the other table lay a pair of gold hoops. Onyx looked up when she entered the room.

"I'm almost done." He continued to put items into a duffle bag.

"Um, hum." Indigo walked over to the side of the bed with the gold hoops and picked them up. He saw her pick up the earrings but kept quiet. He zipped the bag and pulled the straps onto his shoulder.

"Ready…let's go." He waited for her by the doorway with his hand hovering over the light switch. She returned the gold hoops and turned to leave the room.

On the drive back to her house, she was quiet, trying to control her feelings. She was jealous of the woman who owned the earrings. She wanted to be the only one who meant something to him, the only one who mattered.

"You good?" he asked.

"Yeah, I'm good," she answered defensively.

"Then, why are you so quiet?" he asked cheerfully, smiling at her.

"No reason. Just thinking."

Looking over at him, she wondered if she could trust him. He was a tall, muscular man who could easily overpower her. She was conflicted by her desire to be with him and the fear that he could hurt her like Treyvon had. She knew Onyx as a boy but didn't know him as a man. The fact that he respected and checked on his grandfather proved he was a good person, but Treyvon was good to his mother. He had treated her well until that day. Once, she had felt safe in his arms. Indigo rubbed her temple with both hands, wishing she could stop thinking about everything.

When they arrived at her house, he put his bag in her old room before poking his head into the kitchen, where she was making a chicken salad sandwich. He told her that his grandfather had called and wanted him to come over. She trailed behind him, turning on the dining room and living room lights and locking the door behind him. The show she was watching had ended, and the news had been on for a few minutes when Onyx finally returned. He was not as relaxed as he was when he left, but when she asked if everything was okay, he shrugged it off and said he was going to bed. She checked that the back door was locked before turning off the lights in the house. She got her pajamas, and then she went to the bathroom to take a shower. She compulsively checked the bathroom door, reassuring herself that it was locked before undressing. When she wasn't physically checking the doorknob, she looked at it to see if it was still locked. After showering and dressing in cotton pajamas, she stood in the hallway, afraid to go to her room alone. Indigo tapped on her old bedroom door before she opened it.

"You wanna sleep with me?" she asked, standing in the doorway.

"What?" Onyx's head popped up from his pillow.

"Can you sleep with me in the other room?"

"Yeah, sure!" he answered, throwing back the covers and following her into her bedroom. He removed his T-shirt and dropped his pajama bottoms as Indigo got in bed.

"Whoa—what are you doing?" she shouted.

He stood naked in front of her with his pajama bottom pooled around his ankles. "What do you mean, what I'm doing?" he asked, attempting to cover his erect penis with his hands. She tried to look at his eyes, but once her eyes glided down his chest, rolled over his flat abs, slithered past his pelvis, and landed on the mass of curly hair that surrounded his manhood, her feeble attempts were unsuccessful.

"Oh, my."

"What the fuck!" Onyx swore, realizing he and Indigo had two different things in mind. He ordered her to close her eyes. She placed one hand over her eyes, then splayed her fingers. She saw him as he fumbled to put his pajamas back on.

"I can see your monkey ass, close your eyes," he fumed.

She closed her fingers for a second, then splayed them again. By the time he had his pajamas and t-shirt back on, she had collapsed on her back, laughing uncontrollably. He also laughed as he jerked the covers off her and jumped on the bed. They continued laughing as he unbuttoned her top and pulled her bottoms off. He twirled them around in the air before sailing them across the room. It was not until they stopped laughing and she saw his eyes roam up and down her body that she became fearful. He straddled her, and he leaned down to kiss her when he stopped abruptly. He rose and removed his legs from around her and lay on his side, propped up on one elbow.

"Sorry, I misunderstood," he said so softly that it came out as a whisper.

In that delicate moment, the fear that surfaced dissipated with the last notes of his voice, and all she could see were his eyes looking back at her. She studied his face and traced the frown lines on his forehead with her fingers; she outlined his thick dark eyebrows, circled his cheekbones, and glided her fingers down to his lips. Indigo pulled and plucked his lips with her fingers, and when he parted his lips to speak, she placed a finger inside his mouth. He sucked her finger before she could remove it.

"I'm not that dude. I would never hurt you."

"I know," she responded repeatedly while Onyx inflicted the sweetest pain.

Chapter 10

Indigo couldn't believe she had been back at work three weeks now. She watched Mrs. Milton from behind the counter. Mrs. Milton came into the store two or three days a week and shoplifted. Lennie, the elderly security guard, followed behind her and noted the items she placed in her purse. Mrs. Milton's daughter had an arrangement with the store's owner to pay for the things her mother stole. The elderly woman's husband died a few years ago, and that's when she started taking things from the store. It wasn't from a lack of money because Mr. Milton had a large insurance policy and pension. Mrs. Milton was lonely; most of her friends had died or no longer lived in their homes, and her only child lived in a different state. Her daughter was trying to stave off the inevitable placement in an assisted living home, but Mrs. Milton's time was rapidly running out. Indigo looked around the neighborhood pharmacy and thought how lucky she was to work there. She could have worked in a hospital pharmacy or a large drugstore chain, but she loved working for this independently owned store. The store had a pharmacy, postal service, utility payment center, and greeting card/gift departments. She had heard about this quaint store from one of her classmates who opted to apply for a position at a hospital instead. The day she went to apply for the position, the line at the pharmacy was almost at the front of the store. She waited in line and presented her resume to the clerk behind the counter. Just as she walked out the door, Caleb Eisner, the pharmacist, stopped her. That was seven years ago, and she has never regretted accepting the job even though she could have made more money working elsewhere. Working for Caleb, she got to know the people for whom she filled prescriptions. She felt responsible for them and took extra care that there were no harmful drug interactions. Sometimes, she felt like a country doctor because her elderly customer's consultations usually ended with them showing her pictures of their grandchildren. And as the years passed, she saw the children in the photos grow up. She surprised her customers and herself when she began to remember the children's names in the pictures and even inquired after them. Going back to work gave her life a certain normality, except for the tiny increments of times that she forgot that Big Momma was dead. Those were the times that she spontaneously picked up the phone to call her grandmother because she wanted to tell her something funny that had happened at work. She would stop herself from hitting her grandmother's number, and she remembered. Like a phantom limb, the hole in her heart would ache, and tears would flow unrestrained until grief loosened its grip. And she would be all right until she forgot and remembered again the next time.

Being at work was the best thing for her; it was only on the drive home that she had time to reflect on what she no longer had. But going home to Onyx made that easier because new love was like that. There's an urgency about a new love that demands a personal touch for it to flourish. So, most nights Indigo and Onyx spent together, tangled in soft cotton sheets, learning things about each other that people who had known them longer would never know. On weekends, they would go to a restaurant or a hipster café to listen to a band or the spoken word. Her plans for a backyard tribute to her grandmother weren't forgotten but delayed; she promised herself that she would get back to it soon. She never asked Mr. Ambrose about Big Momma's journal entries because Onyx told her to wait. Onyx soon became an all-consuming distraction that filled up almost all the emptiness that Big Momma had left.

Ambrose was pleased that his grandson was dating Dinah's granddaughter. Indigo was a good girl, much better than the women he occasionally brought around. He didn't know what those women did for a living, but by their looks, he wouldn't be surprised if a pole was involved. One high yellow gal called herself "Butter," and Ambrose believed she could melt in a man's mouth. He had brought that gal Butter around longer than any of the others, and he had been afraid his grandson would run himself ragged chasing behind her. So, his grandson dating Indigo was a good thing in more ways than one. Onyx had taken pictures of what Dinah wrote so Ambrose could read exactly what was written. Onyx had also told Ambrose about Indigo's ghost theory. Ambrose agreed with Indigo but kept that opinion to himself. Wanda was the spirit in the house that Dinah was protecting her granddaughter from. She was protecting her grandbaby in death just as she had done in life. Onyx had also told him that Indigo had ordered some sage to cleanse the house, so he had watched for the package to be delivered. He had stolen that package off her porch, and when he turned around, Lottie was looking directly at him. Lottie waved at him so that he knew that she had seen him. He walked across the street and sat in the rocking chair beside her.

"Why you stealing that package, Ambrose?"

He sang like a canary, explaining why Indigo ordered the sage to cleanse the house of an evil spirit. He told her he stole it because he believed Dinah was already protecting her from the evil spirit, and if Indigo wasn't careful, she might get rid of Dinah instead of the bad one. He concluded his confession by commenting on its absurdity.

"Nah, I don't think it's silly at all. I believe in spirits, and Dinah protecting her granddaughter from the grave sounds about right. But who do you think the evil spirit is?"

"I can't think of anyone wanting to hurt the girl," lied Ambrose, looking across the street at Dinah's house.

To Ambrose and Lottie's surprise, Indigo opened the front door and appeared to be looking for the purloined package. When she spotted them, she walked across the street and stood in front of Lottie's gate. Roscoe no longer barked at Indigo, but he wasn't pleased to see her. He trotted to the gate to block her entrance or nip at her ankles. Either option was acceptable to him.

"Good morning," called out Indigo.

"Morning," replied Ambrose.

"Good morning, hon!" chimed Lottie.

"Did you guys see the delivery truck?" asked Indigo.

"When?" asked Ambrose.

"Just now. I got an e-mail saying my package was delivered," she said, turning around and looking up and down the street.

"Nope, we ain't seen no delivery truck, "he said, answering for himself and Lottie.

"Okay, thanks," she said, turning to go home.

They watched Indigo enter her house, and when she did, Ambrose slipped the small package out from under his shirt.

"What you gonna do now? Become a whatchamacallit, a porch pirate, and steal all her packages?" Lottie asked.

Three weeks ago, when Onyx told Ambrose about Indigo's ghost story, he knew what happened in 1992 wasn't over. That night, when his grandson came over for the second time and told him he was spending the night at Indigo's, he knew there was no way out but to have Onyx do the unthinkable. Ambrose sipped his morning coffee on his back porch and tried to think of another way out...but there wasn't one. He wished he could spare them the gruesome ordeal of digging up the past. He had told Onyx his theory about the two spirits in the house. Ambrose grimaced because he had yet to tell Onyx what he felt needed to be done. Although Onyx would be reluctant, Ambrose knew he would agree to do it. He knew his grandson didn't believe in ghosts and hauntings, but Onyx knew he and Indigo did. Onyx would do anything to appease him and hopefully give Indigo some peace.

While Ambrose was on his back porch pondering how and when to do what needed to be done with his morning coffee, Onyx was sitting at his desk in his office. He was thinking that the last few weeks had gone well. Indigo hadn't brought up the subject of ghosts, and his grandfather wasn't bugging him to do some creepy ass shit. He enjoyed Indigo's company even though she differed from the women he usually dated. She was fine as hell but didn't need to be validated by every man who crossed her path. She didn't trip when they went out if he appreciated a woman built like a brick shithouse. Onyx laughed out loud at his desk, and Jerry paused on the way to the printer room to ask him what was so funny.

"My grandpa would see a fine woman and say she was built like a brick shithouse."

"You mean a brick house," corrected Jerry.

"Nah, man. He always said a brick shithouse."

"I don't get it," said Jerry, looking at Onyx for a second before moving on.

"I don't either," smiled Onyx, shaking his head, before his thoughts returned to Indigo. That little shitty brick house had him watching Jeopardy and playing badminton in the front yard for the whole world to see. There was something different about Indigo; she was cool and everything, but being with one woman every night playing badminton and shit was doing too much.

After his last showing, Onyx met some of his colleagues at "The Itchy Foot," a bar that they frequented to celebrate getting a listing or escrow finally closing. On the way to the bar, he called Indigo and told her he was pitching some investors and didn't know when he would be done. He purposely omitted whether or not he was going to her house after the meeting. He was beginning to feel a little too domesticated, so when he ended the call, he blasted UGK (Underground Kingz) – *Da Game Been Good To Me*, placed his right elbow on the console, leaned to the right, and bopped his head, feeling the beat. The music pumped him up as he sped down the freeway, but it didn't make him okay with lying to her. He was pissed at himself for feeling the need to lie. He was a grown-ass man. He didn't have to get her permission or explain himself to her. When he got out of the car, his shoulder moved up toward his ears twice in rapid succession, trying to shake the feeling that he was quite possibly going to fuck-up his life tonight. The feeling subsided a little when he walked into the bar, and his colleagues greeted him as if he was the prodigal son returning home. Onyx spotted Butter shortly after sitting down at the table with the guys. He nodded when their eyes met and quickly looked away, but he wasn't surprised when she approached the table.

"Hello, fellas," said Butter in a voice that dripped like hot-buttered soul.

"Hey, Butter!" sang all the guys except Onyx. Each one wished he was the one she had walked over for, but they knew for whom the trip was made.

"Wassup, Onyx?" she asked, standing before him.

"Nothing much. Just having drinks with the fellas. Wassup with you?" He took a swig of his drink before satisfying her with a long, slow gaze at her stiletto-clad feet before roaming up to rest for a few moments on her hips. He licked his lips as his eyes continued traveling upward, remembering how good it was. Butter knew exactly what was going to happen next. He knew, she knew, and the guys knew. She felt her power as all women do when strong men quake with desire. She smiled broadly, parted her legs, and leaned back. The stance caused her hips to thrust slightly forward as if daring him to grab what he wanted.

"I don't know what's up because I haven't seen you in a minute. So, you tell me."

The guys at the table snapped out of their trance and started making the same noise they would have made if they were rooting for their favorite sports team.

"You know what it is," said Onyx.

"I know what it used to be," she retorted loudly.

"You wanna do this here?" he asked, smiling. His smile evaporated the anger that had steadily built up from the moment she caught his eye and had risen with each step it took for her to arrive before him.

"No. I would much rather be doing this at your place," she said in a husky voice, bending forward, placing her hands on his thighs, and placing her face inches from his.

The table exploded with whoa, damns, and whoops.

"Damn dog!" shouted Jerry as they walked out of the bar.

While Onyx was out, Indigo lay in bed with the bedroom door locked, the bedside lamps, and the ceiling light on. She wanted to call Onyx and ask him when he was coming over, but his earlier call made it clear he wasn't coming. Unable to sleep and tired of hearing the news loop around, Indigo turned off the TV and reached for her laptop. After hearing the creaks of the old house as it expanded and contracted, she remembered the stolen sage and ordered more. But this time, she changed the delivery address to the drug store instead of the house. The popping and creaking noises that occurred every night were not noticed because of the noise that the two of them made. One of them was either cooking dinner, watching TV, listening to music, talking on the phone, or talking to each other. The house was usually filled with the life they were living, but tonight, it was a quiet, lonely place. She sat in bed, going down innocuous rabbit holes only Twitter could provide. She left the chat rooms when spirited conversations deteriorated into vicious, personal attacks on anyone brave enough to disagree with the majority opinion. Indigo's insecurities and fears lurked behind the bedroom door in the dark rooms of the rest of the house. From time to time, when she lifted her eyes above the computer screen, the room's dark corners frightened her.

Meanwhile, Onyx lay on his back in bed, exhausted from Butter's antics. It was as good as he remembered…but that feeling was back. He felt like he was about to lose the biggest listing of his life. He had just got his rocks off with a woman that most men could only dream about having. Her head was on his chest as her hands began to travel up his legs, trying to get something started again. He grabbed her hand.

"Look, Butter…I need to tell you something. I've been seeing somebody," he said, lifting his head to see her face.

"Onyx, boy, when haven't you been seeing somebody? I know we're not exclusive." Butter lifted her head to look at him.

"Yeah, man, but this someone is different, so we can't do this anymore," he said, sitting up in bed dislodging her.

"Ain't that a bitch. I've been waiting for you to fall in love with me all this time, and now you're telling me some bullshit like this," she screeched.

She got out of bed, yanking the covers with her. One tear rolled down her face before she swiped her eyes so hard that one false eyelash was lost. Onyx had only managed to put on his boxers while she had put on her clothes and was sitting on the bed putting on her shoes. He walked over to her and told her he wasn't sure until tonight what he was feeling. She stopped fussing with the strap of her shoe and sat up to face him.

"So, you slept with me to see how you felt about another bitch?"

"Well…when you put it like that…."

Rolling In The Deep

He never finished what he would say next because she balled up her fist and hit him as hard as she could in his mouth. Onyx flinched and grabbed her by both wrists before flipping her on her back. He penned her down on the bed until she lay spent from kicking, screaming, and crying.

"Are you done?" he whispered in her ear. Butter shook her head. "I never meant to hurt you." He held on to her a little longer to gauge whether she was truly done.

"But you did," she whimpered. He stood up and backed away, waiting to see what she would do next.

Butter lay exhausted on the bed, feeling all used up. She sat up and looked around for her shoes. She walked out of the bedroom with them in her hands, not wanting to spend another second in his bedroom.

"Wait a minute," said Onyx. "You forgot these."

She made a sucking sound with her teeth when she saw the earrings in his hands before she continued down the hall and out the front door. She had opened her car door when he yelled, "What do you want me to do with these?"

"You can stuff them up your ass!" she shouted before sliding into her car.

Chapter 11

The next morning, Indigo and Caleb worked side by side, filling prescriptions.

"Consultation," announced Stella as she rang up a sale.

Indigo looked up and saw Mrs. Milton smiling at her. "I got it." She told Caleb, placing the bottles in the plastic bin for Stella to pick up. After the women greeted each other and Mrs. Milton showed Indigo the latest pictures of her teenage grandsons, she told Indigo what was bothering her. When asked if she had any other symptoms associated with a cold, Mrs. Milton shook her head and said she didn't have a cold, only a persistent cough. Just as Indigo was prepared to ask if the cough was wet or dry, Mrs. Milton coughed. Indigo heard the slight rattle in her chest. The wet cough was concerning, so she asked Mrs. Milton if she took her heart failure medications daily.

"I forget sometimes, but I take them when I remember," she said, smiling.

Indigo asked if she had a pill pack. "That way, you can be sure to take your medication every day," she explained, smiling back at the woman. Indigo stepped from behind the counter and showed Mrs. Milton the pill pack with boxes for morning and evening. The older woman thanked Indigo and showed her the pictures of her grandsons again. Indigo looked back at the pharmacy counter and gently informed Mrs. Milton that she had to get back to work. Lennie, the store's loss prevention officer, thought the old lady was done. She had stolen a tube of toothpaste before talking to the pharmacist, but he followed her anyway. Mrs. Milton walked surreptitiously around the store before slipping a pill pack into her purse.

That afternoon, when things slowed, Indigo looked up Mrs. Milton's daughter's number. She informed the daughter that her mother had a cough that might be due to her mother not taking her heart medication consistently. The daughter thanked Indigo profusely and assured her that she would make a doctor's appointment for her mother and put a plan in place to ensure that she took her medication every day. Indigo hung up the phone, feeling better than she felt all day. The feeling vanished when she saw Bruce Mitchell and his sidekick Bo strutting down the aisle.

"Oh no…oh no," groaned Stella under her breath.

It was too late to take a break, so she closed the small opening, where filled orders were passed as if closing it would make the clear glass partition opaque. Indigo kept her head down and pretended to be busy. Stella slid the opening open and whispered instead of the customary yell. "Consultation with Indigo requested." Caleb turned his back and snickered, trying not to laugh. Indigo shook her head in the affirmative without looking up. After a deep breath, she opened the pharmacy's locked door and stepped down to the counter.

"Look here, Doc…I was wondering if it was okay for me to take my Viagra every day on my vacation?" grinned Bruce, licking his lips and looking for a reaction from her.

"Mr. Mitchell, you should never take more than one dose of Viagra per 24-hour period. It may be safe to take one daily if your doctor feels it is safe for you. Mr. Mitchell, I suggest you consult your physician before you go on vacation," she said in the mechanical voice she used whenever she spoke with him.

"Well, you know I don't need no Viagra when I'm messing with these old freaks at home, but if I'm gonna be messing with those young freaky deakies on vacation, I'm gonna need some help." Bruce turned around and stuck out his hand for Bo to slap his palm.

"Sho, you're right," declared Bo, slapping Bruce's palm before looping his thumps on the top of his belt and moving his feet from side to side like James Brown. He ended his footwork with two stomps of his right foot, threw his head back, and roared with laughter.

The two old men had accomplished what they had set out to do. They loved messing with Indigo. Her lack of inflection when she spoke let them know they had hit a nerve. She concluded the consultation by returning to the locked room where the drugs were kept. Because of the glass partition, the room only slightly muffled Bruce Mitchell's booming voice.

"These young bucks today don't know half of what I know," laughed Bruce, watching Indigo, waiting for her to look up at him. When she didn't look up, he continued to tell Bo and everyone within earshot how crazy the young girls were about him. Indigo knew that Stella was trapped outside, and that Mr. Mitchell wouldn't leave until she looked at him. She held her breath so nothing on her face moved; her head rose slowly until their eyes met. Bruce and Bo were thoroughly satisfied with Indigo's reaction to their shenanigans. Bruce's sexual prowess was pure fantasy. His great-nephew sold his Viagra to supplement his Social Security check, but he took great delight in people thinking that he was a dirty old dog. When the old men left the store, Stella turned, smiling and shaking her head to look at Indigo, but she was looking down, filling an order. Caleb was pulling a bottle from a top shelf near the back of the room. Stella turned back to face the front of the store and watched the two old men walk out of view of the large storefront window.

The workday was over; Onyx hadn't called, and neither had she. Indigo watched Ambrose unbuckle Roscoe's leash and walk into Lottie's house as she drove past. There was something sweet about how he walked in with Roscoe without knocking, as if he was going home instead of visiting a friend. She wondered for a nanosecond if they were doing anything. Her body shuddered in reaction to the image that flashed in her head. Mr. Mitchell and Bo's vulgarity had definitely got inside her head. She pulled into her driveway and went inside long enough to put down her purse. She hurried back outside to water the yard to beat the already setting sun. While watering the roses against the back fence, a heaviness overtook her. She looked back at the house, which seemed to stretch away from her, and wondered how she would ever reach the back door. She started walking toward the house with the water hose, but the weight of the hose increased with each step she took, so she dropped it. When she dropped the hose, she looked down at it, fighting the urge to sit next to it. Her hand trembled, and she barely had the strength to turn off the water spigot. The instant she entered the kitchen, the crushing heaviness lifted, and her body became buoyant. The momentary buoyancy caused her to become lightheaded. She sat in the nearest chair for a few minutes until the dizziness passed. When she felt more like herself, she made a large salad for dinner with plenty of chicken, thinking the drop in her blood sugar was the cause of the strange sensation. She took her dinner to the living room and ate in front of the TV.

She couldn't tell if she was sitting or standing in the blackness because she couldn't feel her body. No light penetrated the darkness; the black was complete, soft, and comforting. She knew things here in the dark. She knew she existed somewhere in the universe beyond the stars in a space where there was no limit to the expansion of one's consciousness. A supreme peace filled her as she floated in the vast emptiness she was becoming a part of. She wondered how long she had been here and wished she could stay. Somehow, she knew that her time here was running out. Suddenly, a jarring flash of light tore into the space, and she became aware of a persistent buzzing sound. Indigo was back in her body on the couch in front of the TV. The empty salad bowl was on the coffee table; the only light came from the TV. She turned on the light before opening the door. Onyx stood on the other side of the security door. They looked at each other, not saying a word. She unlocked the iron door, knowing that love was within reach. He picked her up in a bear hug and told her that he missed her. She closed her eyes when he wrapped his arms around her, wanting to drift weightlessly into the empty place with him.

Chapter 12

Seven-year-old Indigo was asleep when a thump against her bedroom door woke her.

"She's my baby, not yours, Momma, and she's coming home with me!" shouted Wanda.

"You still with that man...huh? That same man who wants to hurt her?" Dinah asked, shoving Wanda away from the door.

"You know Indigo lies. Why would he want a little girl when he's got all this?" Wanda slapped her backside.

"Wanda, get your drunk ass out of here and go on home. You can see Indigo tomorrow. Come on now," she said more persuasively as she nudged Wanda down the hall with her body.

"Naw, momma, I'm taking her home tonight. Ronnie told me to bring her back tonight."

Dinah blocked the hallway entrance, determined that her grand-baby wasn't going anywhere. Wanda bounced off her mother and laughed, but when Dinah wouldn't move, she got angry.

"Move, Momma! Move out the damn way!"

"Wanda, you're not taking that baby back to that house with that sick bastard. That's my grandchild, and if you won't protect her, I will."

Wanda pulled a chair away from the dining table and sat down heavily. She opened her purse, took out a flask, unscrewed the top, and took a long, satisfying pull.

"Are you so desperate for a man that you would let him have your child too?" Dinah asked.

"That's a lie, Momma, and you know it!" Wanda slammed the flask down on the table. "He only wanted Indigo to bring him some water."

"Some water in the shower. Are you for real right now?"

"He wasn't in the shower; he was in the bedroom watching TV."

"Yeah, okay. And what do you think he would've done if she had gone into that bedroom?" Dinah screamed.

"I don't know, Momma, the same thing my daddy did, said Wanda flippantly, walking over to her mother to grin in her face. Dinah slapped her so hard that she staggered backward.

"See, you don't like it when someone accuses your man, do you? " Wanda said in a silly, mocking tone. "Ooh, ooh, you better be glad you're my momma." She said, rubbing her face.

"That's your father, not some man. My God, Wanda, what's wrong with you?"

"Look, Momma, I'm tired of playing games with you. Move out of my way so I can get my daughter and go home."

When Dinah didn't move, Wanda shoved her against the door jamb; soon, the women were striking each other with their fists. They fought all the way down the hall; Wanda had her mother pinned against the back bedroom door.

"Momma, don't make me have to cut your ass. Move out of the way," she hissed, breathing heavily.

When Dinah didn't move, Wanda walked back to the dining room. Dinah ran to the front of the hallway to block the entrance. The dining table where Wanda's purse lay was about two feet from the hallway where Dinah stood guard. She saw her daughter reach into the purse for what she thought was a cigarette because the flask was on the floor. But when Wanda's hands emerged, she was holding a box cutter. For a moment, the women froze, not daring to breathe. They appeared to be playing a game where the person who blinked first would be declared the loser. Wanda held her mother's gaze as she pushed the metal slide of the utility knife forward. Dinah's eyes ricocheted from her daughter to the knife back to her daughter several times as Wanda waved the opened box cutter in the air. Wanda waved the weapon above her head and told her mother to get out of the way over and over again. Dinah pleaded with her to stop and go home as she inched away from the hall toward her bedroom. Wanda walked down the hallway and opened Indigo's door. Indigo was lying in bed with her eyes closed so tightly that they were beginning to hurt. She was hugging her stuffed giraffe with both arms across her chest. Wanda retracted the blade and stuck it in her pocket.

"Hey baby, wake up; it's Mommy!"

Indigo opened her eyes slowly and saw a silhouette of her mother with hair sticking out all over her head.

"Momma," she said, clutching her giraffe tighter.

"Yeah, baby, it's me. Did you forget your Momma?"

"No, Momma, but you look scary in the dark with your hair sticking out."

Wanda turned on the light, raked her fingers through her hair, and patted it down. "See, it's me. Come on, get up. Momma's taking you home."

Indigo jumped out of bed, leaving her giraffe, and hugged her mother. Wanda took her daughter by the hand and started to walk out of the room.

"Wait, Momma. I need to put on my clothes and shoes."

Wanda released her hand and told Indigo to only put on her shoes. Indigo did as she was told and smiled as she took her mother's hand again.

"Momma, if we're going home, does that mean Ronnie is gone."

"No, why do you think that."

"Big Momma said I wasn't going back home until Ronnie leaves."

"Well, Big Momma was mistaken. Your stepdaddy is at home waiting for us."

Indigo stopped moving and pulled her hand free.

"I don't wanna go home; I wanna stay here with Big Momma."

Wanda snatched her daughter's hand and dragged her down the hall. Indigo was crying and trying to pull away from her mother's vice-like grip. Wanda suddenly stopped moving, and so did Indigo.

"Momma, you ain't gonna shoot nobody. Gon' and get out of my way," said Wanda with more bravado than she felt. Wanda didn't move because she wasn't entirely sure that her mother wouldn't shoot her.

"Wanda, let her go. You're either drunk, high, or both, but either way, we're done for tonight. Go home, and we'll talk about you spending some time with Indigo tomorrow."

"Why do I have to spend time with my baby? I'm her mother," Wanda's voice rose with indignation. "You're the one who should be spending time with her, not me."

"Then act like her mother. Stop bringing men around your baby girl."

"Ronnie ain't did nothing to her."

"Not yet, but it's just a matter of time. Why do you think she's afraid of him?"

"She's scared of him because you filled her head with that sick shit." Wanda turned and looked down at her daughter. "Ronnie ever touched you?"

Indigo shook her head from side to side.

"See, Momma, I told you, Ronnie ain't never touched her."

"I guess we got a different definition of touching. Ask her how he makes her sit on his lap and how he bounces her and moves her around on his lap while she watches cartoons when you're at work. I wonder why he doesn't have her sitting on his lap when you're home? Why do you think that is, huh?"

"That's a lie! Indigo would've told me!"

"When you come home, you start drinking, and then pretty soon, you and Ronnie are going at it. When is she supposed to tell you that she's afraid? I've told you not to have men around your baby. That's why you didn't tell me that he was living with you in the first place. If that baby hadn't told me, God only knows what would've happened to her."

"So, that's why you came and got her. You said it was only for a little while…that you were giving me a break."

"I am giving you a break. You need to realize what's more important: a man in your bed or your baby girl."

There was a brief silence where Dinah thought her daughter would make the right choice. Wanda yanked Indigo's hand and started walking toward the front door with the box cutter raised.

"I'm taking my baby home. I'm tired of you lying about me and Ronnie."

"Stop!" screamed Dinah. "I'm not gonna let you take her. Wanda, I swear to God, If you don't stop."

"Momma, you ain't gonna do shit."

"Indigo, close your eyes, close them now, and don't open them again until I say so," ordered Big Momma in a voice that sounded strange even to herself.

Indigo heard something in her grandmother's voice that made her obey. Her world turned black as she scrunched her eyes tight. She kept her eyes closed even when she heard loud booms and screams. Her ears and head hurt from the ringing that wouldn't stop. Her mother's grip loosened and slid free. There was a dull thud as something heavy fell next to her. Indigo put her hands over her ears and squeezed her eyes tighter.

"That's right, keep your eyes closed," whispered Big Momma next to Indigo's ear.

Indigo felt herself being picked up; she was moving around in total darkness, no longer able to feel her body. Her grandmother's soft skin brushed against her skin as she was carried back to her bed. Indigo's cheek rubbed against her grandmother's bare shoulder, and the scent of roses, which her grandmother always gave off, was released. Big Momma had taught her to rub rose petals together to release their fragrances, so that's what Indigo was doing as her grandmother carried her to her room. Dinah pulled the covers over Indigo and told her to stay there and not get up. Indigo opened her eyes when she heard the door close. She found her giraffe and held it against her chest before pulling the covers over her head and squeezing her eyes shut again.

Indigo jerked up in bed, her heart pounding from the sound of the explosion that had awakened her. Onyx was lying beside her, sound asleep. She didn't move as she tried to determine whether she had actually heard an explosion or if it was part of the dream. She remained upright momentarily before easing down next to Onyx, needing to touch him. She needed to know that she was fully awake and not dreaming within a dream. Once she was convinced that she was awake, she wondered if she was dreaming or remembering something that had happened to her.

Indigo woke up a few hours later, feeling out of sorts. She dragged herself to the bathroom to brush her teeth and shower. She hoped to be invigorated by the warm water beating down on her body. She felt better when she entered the kitchen, the smell of coffee promising to reset her day.

Onyx ate grits, bacon, eggs, and toast for breakfast. He stopped eating long enough to tell her that he had left her some bacon on the stove. Indigo tore a hunk of bread from the French loaf, buttered it, and placed it under the boiler. She didn't want the bacon but took the plate with the three pieces anyway. After she poured herself a cup of coffee and retrieved her toast, she sat across from Onyx.

"You good?" he asked, looking across at her.

"I had the weirdest dream…it felt more like a memory, really. A horrible memory. It felt so real, but I can't remember most of the dream, memory whatever it was now. The longer I'm awake, the more of it I'm forgetting. I can't remember most of it now, but I know that it was bad, that something bad happened, that something bad happened to me. But I don't know whether it only happened to me in the dream or if I was dreaming about something that happened in real life."

"That sounds like a riddle wrapped in a mystery inside an enigma," he said before sipping his coffee.

"I know, right? I dreamt I was a little girl in my old bedroom here in this house, and there was a lot of noise. A big bang, like an explosion, woke me up. I actually woke up thinking something had blown up, but you were sound asleep. Anyway, I can't shake this feeling that something is falling into place."

"Do you want to hang out with me today? I have a showing at three, but we can do anything you want until then."

"As good as that sounds, I think I need to go to work and act like a big girl." Indigo picked up her plate and placed it in the sink.

"You don't have to act; you are a big girl." He slapped her plump backside.

"Funny, ha, ha," Indigo said, smiling.

Onyx walked Indigo to her car and continued next door to his grandfather's house. He waved at Miss Lottie, who was already sitting on her porch. He stood in Ambrose's living room, peering through the curtains, waiting for her to go inside.

"You might as well sit down and wait. Lottie ain't going inside until her shows come on," Ambrose said, looking at his watch. "you got twenty minutes."

Onyx sat down, but he couldn't relax. His thoughts kept running to the gruesome thing that awaited him after eighteen years of being buried in the backyard. *What*, he thought, *would be left*? When he arrived, he had thrown the shovel, three rose bushes, and an empty duffel bag over the back fence into Indigo's yard. The plan was for them to casually walk over to Indigo's backyard, dispose of the problem, scatter the bushes around, and fill in the area they dug up. He went back to the window after the twenty minutes were up.

"Okay, she's gone inside. Let's go," said Onyx.

At Ambrose's direction, they waited a few more minutes to give Lottie a chance to fully immerse herself in whatever court show or paternity show she was watching. When Ambrose thought enough time had passed, he and Onyx strolled next door.

"Where?" asked Onyx.

"It should be right about here," said Ambrose, walking over to the flower bed.

Onyx stuck the shovel in the ground and started digging. Ambrose pulled one of the chairs from under the tree and moved closer to the flower bed.

Onyx had been digging for just over an hour and had found nothing. He picked up large rocks he unearthed with the shovel and tossed them aside. His face was smeared with dirt as he frantically wiped sweat from his face.

"Are you sure this is the spot?"

"Yeah, I'm sure," Ambrose said, getting up to look at the coffin-like hole. "Keep digging. You should hit something soon."

After several more shovels full of dirt, he suddenly stopped and called his grandfather over. They looked down at shredded pieces of cloth and a green knob-looking thing. Ambrose's heart slammed into his chest when he saw pieces of the blanket he had wrapped Wanda in. He struggled to get enough air in his lungs. Onyx held on to his grandfather and guided him back to the chair. Ambrose clutched onto his arms, not wanting his grandson to let him go. He fought the rising panic within him as Onyx inhaled and exhaled slowly with him. Seeing the evidence of the thing that he had done all those years ago brought back that horrible night.

Ambrose was tired that Friday night, May 1, 1992, as he was most Fridays. It was the third night of the Rodney King Riots, but most of the unrest happened on the city's west side. His drive home was unaffected by the civil unrest. He went to work because if he hadn't, he might have found himself out in the streets setting fires to the liquor stores that infested his neighborhood or burning the stores of the latest immigrants to invade Black neighborhoods. Korean store owners openly followed Blacks around in their stores before taking Black folk's money for the cheap imported products they peddled. Ambrose hoped the rioters burned the store down to the ground where a Korean store owner killed a 15-year-old girl because she thought the girl was stealing a bottle of orange juice. The crying Korean store owner was convicted of manslaughter and received five years of probation, community service, and a $500 fine. The dead little Black girl was portrayed as a thief, and the store owner was depicted as a hard-working immigrant forced to protect her profit margin from the likes of *those people.*

Ambrose remembered being mentally tired that night. He and Dinah ate dinner and watched the news, shaking their heads at how much things had changed and yet stayed the same. How could a major city like Los Angeles have a Black Mayor, Tom Bradley, and have a police chief like Daryl Gates? He left Dinah's house early, wanting to be alone, unable to stand seeing the implosion of so many deferred dreams on the news. He went home, gave in to the hopeless feeling, and fell asleep to Sam Cooke's melancholic crooning of *A Change is Gonna Come.* He was asleep on the couch when the shrill, persistent ringing of the phone woke him, and BB King's, *How Blue Can You Get,* was playing when he rushed out the front door. After that night, the woman he secretly loved disappeared molecule by molecule before his eyes. She became a flawed human being again instead of the precious thing he had imagined her to be. Killing Wanda hadn't been an accident; Dinah had chosen to stop her daughter for good. In the early morning hours after he had done the unthinkable, he fell to his knees and begged God and his dead wife to forgive him. He asked God to forgive him for his present transgression while he asked Lucinda to forgive him for all the years that his heart had stopped beating for her.

He thought love was a funny thing as he looked down into the hole and held onto his grandson's arm. After that night, he told himself he didn't love Dinah anymore. But if that was true, why was he standing in her backyard looking down at Wanda's skeleton? Onyx dug up the rest of Wanda. The skull, two long bones with knobs on the end, the rib cage, small fragments of the rest of the skeleton and teeth. There were only pieces of fabric that hadn't disintegrated or been carried away by burrowing animals.

"Where's the rest of her?" asked Onyx.

"Gone back to the earth, I guess. Ain't that what it says in the bible? Ashes to Ashes: Dust to Dust." Ambrose looked down and saw what looked like a few strands of hair. "And the animals. I'm pretty sure worms and maggots did their part."

Onyx's body involuntarily shook as he thought about gophers, rats, and maybe a snake taking some part of Wanda away. He threw what was left of the blanket, her clothes, and shoes in the trash can. He placed the bones, two rings, and a necklace in the duffle bag. Looking at the hollowed-out eye socket was the worst because he could still imagine the humanity that was once reflected from those empty eye sockets.

Ambrose's breathing had returned to normal, and he was sitting quietly in the chair, remembering while Onyx filled in the hole. A frightened little Indigo had knocked on his door when he got home from work three nights after he buried Wanda. She pulled on his arm, walked him to Dinah's house, and told him something was wrong with her grandmother. He couldn't believe the change that had occurred in such a short period of time. Dark circles under Dinah's eyes accentuated the gauntness of her face. Indigo told him that she tried to take care of her, but Big Momma wouldn't eat, and she was talking to somebody Indigo couldn't see. He took Indigo home with him that night. He kept her with him until Dinah returned to herself or as close to who she was before that night. For days, he watched Dinah sink into a world where reality didn't exist and feared she would be lost forever. She had stopped going to work, eating, bathing, or combing her hair. After a week, Ambrose called out sick and stayed home with Dinah. He took Indigo to school and returned to Dinah's house. He was desperate to snap her out of the hellish depth of despair she was trapped in.

"You can't keep doing this, Dinah. I can't keep doing this." When there was no response, Ambrose continued. "What did you do it for…if you were going to let the State have her?" Ambrose saw something stir in Dinah's eyes. "What do you think is gonna happen to her in the system?"

Dinah's eyes slowly found him. He saw a glimmer of understanding flicker in her eyes and spread across her face. He left her to process what her mind would have her forget, but necessity could not. He found a can of soup and heated it up. In the kitchen, he saw evidence that she was surviving on peanut butter and jelly sandwiches and whiskey. When Ambrose placed the spoon in front of her lips, Dinah parted them. Halfway through the bowl, her lips refused to open. He smiled, encouraged, and murmured silly words that he said to his kids and grandkids when they were little and wouldn't eat. As he fed her, a muskiness escaped the folds of her housecoat, so he ran her a bath. Ambrose squeezed toothpaste on her toothbrush and began brushing her teeth before she took over. He left her in the bathroom to take her bath, but after thirty minutes, he found her sitting in a tub of cold water, staring into space, her body dry where the water hadn't reached it. He ran more hot water into the tub and took the dry face towel from the edge of the tub, sloshing it around in the water. He washed the crusty corners of Dinah's eyes first, then worked up a good head of lather from the bar of Ivory soap on the towel and washed her face. He was careful not to get soap in her eyes. He went systematically down her body, helping her to stand up so he could wash her private parts. Ambrose helped her out of the tub and patted her body dry. As he dried her body, she caught his hands and pulled them up to touch her breasts. He recoiled, but she held on to his hands.

"Please." Dinah's voice cracked from disused.

It's too late, he thought. He looked into Dinah's eyes and shook his head.

"I know. But do it for me. I need you, old friend."

"This ain't right, Dinah!"

"I know it ain't right. But I can't feel nothing, Ambrose. I need to feel something. Help me to feel something."

"Help you. Damn, ain't I helped enough. What more do you want from me?"

"This one last thing."

With trembling hands, Ambrose walked with Dinah to her bedroom. He sat on the edge of the bed with her and waited for something to happen. Dinah was the first to move; she began to unbutton his shirt. She pulled him up to stand before her so she could unbuckle his belt. When his pants dropped to the floor, she touched him, and he began to do the things that he vowed that he would never do. After the heated rush, touching and tasting, Dinah lay in his arms and wept. She cried because he wasn't Delray, and he stared up at the ceiling. He listened to her pain as silent tears ran down the side of his face into his ears.

That day was a turning point for both of them. There were times that she seemed lost, and there were nights when she needed a couple of drinks to sleep. She stepped back into her life with his help, but never in that way again. A life that faded into a routine with more good days than bad ones. Ambrose couldn't forgive Dinah for what she had done or for getting him mixed up in it, but when he saw how close she had come to losing her grip on reality, he felt compelled to be there for her. He kept her secrets, and they became more connected than ever because of that horrendous thing that happened on May 1, 1992. Anyone looking in from the outside, like Miss Lottie, would have thought they were lovers. But Ambrose's desire for Dinah lay dead and buried in the backyard with her daughter. They never spoke of the day they made love; that afternoon was another secret they kept even from themselves.

Chapter 13

Indigo thought the feeling would have gone by the time she arrived at work. Instead, the feeling had morphed into a premonition. The feeling that something bad was going to happen wouldn't go away. She was behind the glass partition filling a prescription when Stella knocked on the glass. When she looked up, she saw her waving an Amazon box. Indigo nodded and finished the order before going to the counter and opening the package.

"Do you know what to do with that?" Stella asked.

"I guess. I'm just going to burn it and wave it around every room of the house."

"My grandmother can cleanse your house if you want," Stella said, looking at Indigo.

"I think I can do it."

"Well, if it doesn't work, let me know. My Granny Grand is from Louisiana and does all that Voodoo stuff."

It was late morning, almost noon, and Indigo was still having trouble concentrating. She told Caleb that perhaps it would be better if she went home. Caleb took a short lunch break before she left to go home.

Indigo waved at Miss Lottie before pulling into her driveway. She was glad to see Onyx's car still parked in his grandfather's driveway. *A lazy afternoon stretched out in bed with Onyx's fingers massaging her neck and shoulders before they moved slowly down her back*—Indigo jumped when Miss Lottie interrupted her daydream. Miss Lottie was tapping on her car's window.

"Are you supposed to be home now?" asked Lottie

Indigo opened the car door, "What?"

"You're early. I don't think they're expecting you this early." Roscoe barked at Indigo and Lottie stomped her foot at him. The dog continued barking, but his attention was no longer on Indigo. The furry terrorist ran toward the backyard with Lottie in pursuit. Indigo looked at them before trailing behind them.

"What are you doing?" asked Indigo, seeing Onyx standing with a shovel and rose bushes dug up and scattered along the back fence.

"We—I was trying to surprise you," he said. "I wanted to have this done before you got home."

"What exactly are you trying to do?" she asked, walking toward him. "And why are the holes so deep?"

"I was getting rid of the tree roots and rocks and everything. I guess I got carried away." He began shoveling dirt into a hole.

Indigo gave him a curious look before her face erupted into a big grin. "Aww, thank you, baby." She stood on her tiptoes and kissed his cheek. "Let me change my clothes so I can help. Besides, I want to place the roses. You need to fill in those holes and let me figure out where I want to move the rest of the roses before you put in any new ones."

"Okay," said Onyx, not knowing what else to say.

"Well, since the surprise is ruined. I'm going home." Ambrose picked up the duffel bag that Roscoe had been clawing at. He flung the straps of the bag over his shoulder, and Roscoe repeatedly jumped up, nipping at the bag.

"Stop it!" shouted Ambrose, startling the dog and women.

"Come here, Roscoe," commanded Lottie, but the dog continued to jump and nip at the bag. Lottie picked him up, and Ambrose walked out of the yard as fast as he could, leaving Lottie dumbfounded.

"I guess we'll go back home too," said Lottie quietly, already walking down the driveway.

"What are you doing home so early?" asked Onyx.

"I couldn't concentrate, so I decided to come home before I messed up a prescription and killed somebody," Indigo chuckled.

Onyx stopped abruptly and looked at her.

"I'm kidding," she said, giving him a side-eye. "I'm going to change; I'll be right back."

While Indigo changed clothes, Onyx began filling the holes and looked around the yard, praying no loose teeth or small bones were mixed in with the dirt. They spent an hour in the yard placing the rose bushes that Onyx had bought, digging new holes, and replanting old rose bushes.

"Babe, it's getting late. I thought you had a showing at three?"

"I do, thanks." He handed Indigo the shovel, kissed her on the lips, and ran inside the house.

She stayed in the backyard working on her tribute to Big Momma. When she had all the bushes planted, she sat in a chair and admired their handiwork. She had forgotten about the rose garden when she found the diary pages. Sitting there, thinking about her grandmother, she remembered that she had never asked Mr. Ambrose about what her grandmother had written. Indigo put the tools away in the garage and watered the roses before going into the house to reread those pages. She sat on the couch, trying to tap down the anger that had flared up again. Mr. Ambrose had the answers that she needed, and this time, Onyx wasn't there to stop her.

Mr. Ambrose didn't answer the repeated knocks on the door. She looked across the street at Miss Lottie's house and figured he must be there, so she went back home. She dug in her purse, got the bundle of sage out, and went to the kitchen. She turned the burner on high and stuck the sage in the fire, wondering if the dry clump of weed would ignite into a fiery torch. The sage quickly caught on fire and just as quickly went out. Indigo continued lighting and relighting the sage until it occurred to her that the bundle was burning as incense did. She stopped lighting the bundle and watched the plume of smoke float upward. When the smoke continued to drift up, she turned off the burner. Since she was already in the kitchen, she started there. She went from one corner of the room to the next, moving horizontally as she blessed the house and asked God to rid the house of anything that was not of him. She moved on to every room, even opening up closets. As she fanned the plume of smoke and watched it dance around the room before it vanished, she became more confident and spoke boldly to God. After cleansing the house, she spoke to her grandmother as the sage continued to burn.

"I know you're here still watching over me. I've cleansed the house, so whatever was here is gone now. You've been taking care of me all my life, but I'm grown now. I can take care of myself. You can rest now. Mr. Ambrose and Onyx are looking after me, even Miss Lottie. You know nothing is going to happen to me on her watch." She swallowed twice before she was able to continue. "Big Momma, you have taken care of me long enough. I'm good… you can rest in peace like people say when someone dies. Rest now…you deserve it. Be with Jesus. I'll tell you all about my life when I see you again."

She waved the sage around while tears rolled freely down her face. A hint of roses replaced the earthy scent of sage. She felt a rush of wind at her back, but before she could turn to see the cause of the wind, it was gone, and only a piney, peppery fragrance remained. Indigo sat down on the couch, knowing that her grandmother was gone. She also believed that whatever evil had been in the house was gone because her grandmother wouldn't have left if it was still there. The house felt lighter as if all its secrets had been released. Indigo was relieved; she was falling in love with Onyx, and yet she wasn't losing herself as she had done with Treyvon. She could be herself with Onyx; she didn't feel the need to be what she thought he wanted her to be.

When Lottie pounded on the front door, Indigo had bathed and was lounging around in sweats and a t-shirt.

"What's wrong?" she asked, seeing the expression on Miss Lottie's face.

"Ambrose didn't come for Roscoe, and he's not answering his door," said Lottie.

Indigo called Onyx; she and Lottie hurried next door to get the spare key hidden under a flowerpot on the back porch. Onyx remained on the line, repeatedly asking her if she had found the key, if she was inside, if his grandfather was there, and if he was okay. Indigo put the phone in her pants pocket as she lifted pots, searching for the key. Her hand shook as she inserted the key into the lock. The kitchen was dark as she fumbled for the light switch. She and Lottie called out his name as they advanced into the house. She found him lying in bed. She turned on the light and screamed, forgetting that Onyx was still on the phone. Ambrose's face was contorted, his mouth stretched open as if frozen in mid-scream. His eyes bulged, and dried spit left a dry, ashy riverbed that traveled from the corner of his lips down the side of his chin. The dried saliva streaked down the side of his neck and pooled in the conclave of his clavicle. Lottie bumped into her and began screaming as her own scream died down. Indigo remembered the phone in her pocket and told Onyx what she saw.

"Is he alive?" he shouted.

"I don't know," yelled Indigo over Miss Lottie's wailing.

"Check for a pulse. Damn it, check his pulse!"

She placed her index and middle finger just under his jawline along the side of his neck. There was a weak pulse. She put her finger under his nose and thought she felt a slight breeze. She told him that his grandfather was breathing and there was a pulse. Onyx ordered her to call for an ambulance and told her he would meet them at the hospital. Indigo hung up and left the room to hear and be heard. She called 911.

The paramedics worked on Ambrose in his bedroom while Lottie and Indigo watched from the hallway. Lottie's loud weeping was reduced to sniffles accompanied by the occasional *Lordy, lordy,* as she held Roscoe in her arms. Indigo waited in the car while Lottie put Roscoe inside the house and locked her front door. Indigo took the same route she had taken when Big Momma was in the hospital. Neither woman spoke, each knowing their faith was being tested yet again and praying that healing would be here on earth. They were sitting in the waiting room when Onyx ran in and asked what was going on. He went to the front desk even though Indigo told him they were running tests and would let them know when they were done. He returned to them and repeated the same information as if it were new. He sat next to Indigo and called his mother and sister. When he finished his calls, he rested both elbows on his thighs and looked down at the floor. Indigo leaned against him and reached for his hand.

Onyx's mother and sister were present when the doctor spoke with the family.

"Your father is resting now. His breathing is normal; there is no evidence that he suffered a stroke or heart attack. It appears…" The doctor lowered his head to consult his notes and looked up before speaking again. "It appears some woman named Wanda frightened your father, but we couldn't get him to tell us anything about her or what she did. Every time her name was mentioned, he became upset. Your father has been given a mild sedative and is sleeping soundly. Adult Protective Services has been notified due to possible elder abuse."

"What!" shouted Tamar. "Who's Wanda?" she asked, looking at her son and then at Lottie and Indigo.

"Wanda is my mother, but she has been gone for at least twenty years!"

"Wanda," muttered Lottie.

Onyx eyes widened; he hunched his shoulders up and down and looked at his mother.

"My father must be delusional; there is no Wanda. What exactly did he say?"

"I can't discuss what your father has told us. He will be admitted soon so that we can monitor him tonight. Barring any unforeseen complications, he will be released tomorrow. I suggest everyone go home, get some rest, and come back tomorrow," the doctor concluded, turning to go.

"Is there any medical reason why I can't see my father?" asked Tamar sharply, barely containing her rage.

Indigo took Lottie home: Onyx and his family stayed at the hospital, taking turns sitting in Ambrose's room, complying with the two visitors' rule. His mother and sister had left to get coffee and something to eat, so he was alone in the room with his grandfather. He sat beside the bed and held Ambrose's hand, grateful that his grandfather was still with him. Onyx's heart thumped in his chest, and his lips spread wide across his face as his grandfather's hand twitched and his eyes opened. Onyx's smile faded as he saw Ambrose's eyes roam wildly around the room.

"Grandpa, you're okay. You're in the hospital. I'm here with you." Onyx squeezed his hand tighter. The bewildered look on Ambrose's face faded as he focused on his grandson. "Relax, breathe…I'm with you," chanted Onyx as he squeezed with one hand and rubbed his grandfather's arm with the other hand. A few seconds later, Onyx asked what happened.

"Wanda was in the house. Get them bones out of the house."

"What!" exploded Onyx, unconsciously releasing Ambrose's hand and sitting back in his chair.

"I know it sounds crazy, but she's not at peace."

"Yeah, it sounds crazy. The doctor thinks Wanda did something to you," he whispered, looking around the room.

"She did. She scared the shit out of me. You need to get rid of her bones, but be careful, grandson!"

"What do you mean, get rid of? I can't just throw them in the trash!" hissed Onyx.

"No! Don't do that, but you need to get them out of the house—wait, no—yeah, get them out of the house, but don't take them to your house. Put them in the garage for now."

The door opened, and Tamar and Zari walked in with coffee and a bag with a sandwich inside.

"Hey, Daddy, you're awake! How are you feeling?" asked Tamar, walking over to kiss her father.

Onyx got up from the chair and offered the seat to his mother. Zari handed her brother his coffee and sandwich before moving closer to her grandfather's bed.

"I'm going outside to eat. I'll be back," he said, furtively glancing at his grandfather.

He walked out of the hospital and found a round cement table and bench set which was close to a light pole so he wouldn't be in the dark. He sat on the cement table with one foot swinging between the semi-circular benches while the other foot rested on one of the benches. He was far enough away from the emergency room not to be interrupted but still close enough to see the terrified expressions of the people as they rushed into the building. His body was weak from the fear of what might have been. He bit savagely into the foot-long sandwich. His forehead was wrinkled with worry, and his jawline twitched. First, Indigo with witches and ghosts. Now, his grandfather said he saw a dead woman. When he finished his sandwich and coffee, he sat outside for a while, wondering what to do with the duffel bag full of bones. Reluctantly, he headed back to his grandfather's hospital room.

"I think we should leave and let your grandpa get some rest," said Tamar, looking at her son.

I don't know. I think someone should be with him when he wakes up."

"Your grandfather is sedated; he's going to be out for a while. Why don't you go home and get some sleep? I'm coming right back; I just need to get some things." His mother placed her hand on his arm. "I'll call you the minute he wakes up. Zari went home already, so I'll let you both know what's happening with your grandpa in the morning."

They walked out of the hospital together, parting at the parking structure. He went straight to Indigo's house. Indigo and Lottie were sitting on the porch. Indigo had a mug of tea, and Lottie had something much stronger in her mug. The bottle of Royal Crown was on the small table with the purple cloth pouch next to it. Indigo stood up for Onyx to sit in the chair and then sat on his lap.

"How is he doing?" asked Lottie.

"He's good. He woke up, and I talked to him for a little bit. He was sedated, so he went right back to sleep. My mother is staying with him tonight, and I'm going back first thing in the morning."

"Whew! He scared the shit out of me. Sorry, hun." Lottie reached over and picked up the bottle, tilting it toward him. "You want some of this?"

"Naw, I'm good."

"We've been trying to figure out what Wanda has to do with this," said Lottie, pouring two fingers of whisky into her mug before placing the bottle into its pouch.

"Do you think my mother went to see your grandfather, and they argued or something?" asked Indigo, looking hopefully at him.

"What? That's crazy; my grandfather was delirious."

"Yeah, but why would he even say my mother's name…unless she came to visit him?"

"You're tripping. Why would your mother go see my grandfather?" He looked at Indigo, then at Lottie.

Lottie shrugged her shoulders as if to ask, "*How would I know?*" but instead said, "That's what we've been trying to figure out."

"I don't know. Maybe she wanted to know if I was receptive to her coming to see me. After all, he knows why my grandmother wouldn't let my mother take me home."

"I think the doctor got it wrong," said Onyx.

"The doctor specifically said that Wanda scared your grandfather," said Indigo.

"I know, but it doesn't make sense," Onyx said. He wrapped his arms around her tightly. Roscoe lifted his head, looking up at them before plopping his head back on the porch. The three remained on the porch, testing different scenarios until Lottie announced she was sleepy.

"We'll just have to wait until Ambrose comes home," announced Lottie, getting up stiffly. She rebuffed Onyx's offer to walk her across the street to her house.

Indigo and Onyx stood on the porch and watched Lottie and Roscoe enter her house before they went inside. Lottie wasn't buying the story about Wanda scaring Ambrose or Ambrose being delusional. Something was going on, and Onyx knew all about it. Rosebushes and the duffel bag, Roscoe kept sniffing around. *Nope,* thought Lottie, *Something fishy is going on.* She fed her faithful companion and locked herself in the house after he had done his business in the front yard. She sat in the dark living room with the curtains slightly parted. Roscoe had given up standing watch with her and was asleep at her feet. It was around 4 am when she saw Onyx slip out of the house. At first, he looked like part of the night, a shadow that opened the gate and slowly crept up to Ambrose's house, but she saw him clearly when the streetlight flicked on. Lottie slipped out of her front door without waking up her dog. She walked across the street and inside Ambrose's yard as quickly as her short legs could carry her. She gingerly crossed the porch's wooden planks, not wanting to be heard. The front door was unlocked, so she opened it slowly and slipped inside. She heard Onyx moving around in Ambrose's bedroom. She looked around in the darkness for a place where she could hide and still be able to see what he took out of the house. She hid inside the coat closet next to the front door, leaving the door cracked.

"What the fuck!" shouted Onyx before there was a loud crash.

Lottie opened the closet door, and Onyx slammed into it. When she stepped out of the closet, Onyx let out a scream that rivaled any female soprano and lasted longer than she thought was necessary.

She waited a beat for the scream to end before saying, "It's me, Lottie. What's going on, Onyx?"

He rubbed his forehead, turned around in a complete circle before asking Miss Lottie what the fuck she was doing in his grandfather's closet.

"You better watch your mouth, boy; who do you think you're talking to?"

"Sorry, Miss Lottie, but you scared the …."

"What you doing over here, huh? What you running from?"

Onyx looked back at the hall before reaching past her to turn on the living room light. The light helped Onyx regain his composure, and he ventured toward the hallway and turned on the hall light as well. He crept down the hallway with Lottie shuffling behind him.

"I thought I saw something in his room," he said, reaching into the room to turn on the light.

"I don't see nothin," Lottie said, peeping around Onyx's back.

"Yeah, well, there was something in this room."

"Well, there ain't nobody in here now."

"I said there was something, not someone."

"What are you talking about something? Is that why you came running out of there, like a bat out of hell?"

"Just what I said. There was something in this room."

"If there was something in here, it's not here now!" quipped Lottie.

Onyx took a breath and exhaled slowly. "Shit—, sorry, Miss Lottie."

"It's all right," she said, looking at the overturned chair and TV. "What were you looking for?"

"Uh, nothing. I was just coming to get my grandfather some clothes for tomorrow."

"At 4 a.m., boy, what kinda fool do you take me for?" Onyx knew better than to answer that, and Lottie didn't expect him to. She asked the next question without waiting for a response. "What's in the bag?" she asked, staring pointily at the bag in the corner.

"Nothing."

"Look, boy, I ain't got all night. What's in the bag?"

"Nothing is in the bag, Miss Lottie. Come on, let's get out of here."

"Okay, we can leave after you get whatever it is that you came here for."

"Come on, let's go." He picked up the duffel bag.

They made it to the living room before she threatened to wake Indigo and tell her about his little visit to his grandfather's house and the duffel bag. Onyx stopped and turned to look at Miss Lottie.

"Tell me, maybe I can help."

He looked nervously at the hallway. "This is going to sound crazy, but can I tell you at your house?"

"Sure, she said softly, looking up at him.

He locked the front door and told Lottie to wait for him by the gate while he took the bag to the garage. Onyx was sweaty and jittery as he and Lottie walked across the street to her house. Roscoe woke up when they entered the living room; Lottie let him out the front door. She and Onyx sat in the semi-dark living room while Onyx told her his campfire ghost tale and what he and his grandfather were doing in Indigo's yard yesterday.

"Oh my God!" Lottie exclaimed before summarizing the story she had just heard. "Dinah killed her own child…but why? Ambrose buried Wanda in the backyard, and now she's haunting Indigo; she came after Ambrose earlier and you tonight after her bones were dug up."

"I know. I didn't believe it until I saw what I saw tonight," said Onyx.

"What exactly did you see?"

"I guess I felt it more than I saw it, but it was there. It felt like something was in the room with me hovering in the corner. It felt like it was trying to suck me into a void. An emptiness so complete that if I got sucked in, I would die." Onyx shivered when he finished. "No wonder my grandfather was almost scared to death. I never want to feel like that again."

"So, Wanda is back."

"I guess we brought her back when I dug her up."

"Or maybe she never left. Dinah was keeping her at bay when she was alive and most likely after she died. Give me a couple of days to figure out what we can do; until then…." She got up and went down the hall. Lottie came back with four white candles. She placed a candle on the coffee table and lit it. "Here." She handed Onyx the remaining candles. "Burn these and leave those bones in the garage until we figure out what to do with them." She patted his shoulder. "Don't worry, we're gonna figure this out."

Roscoe slipped back into the house as Onyx walked out. Onyx waited until he heard the lock click before walking back to Indigo's house. Lottie sat in the candle-lit room, the soft light of a new day filtering into the room. She watched Onyx cross the street and disappear into Dinah's house.

Chapter 14

Ambrose came home later that day. Lottie was exhausted from keeping watch and thinking about what Onyx had told her. She waited until Tamar and Zari left before she and Roscoe went for a visit. Roscoe ran ahead, jetting across the street. Lottie thanked God that no cars were zipping by, or he might have been run over. The dog stood by the gate, barking, impatiently waiting for her.

"Hold on. I'm coming as fast as I can."

Onyx opened the door for them and looked at Lottie with a look, warning her to be quiet.

"Roscoe, get down!" she commanded.

"It's all right, Lottie," said Ambrose, patting the dog's head.

"Roscoe!" Lottie barked again, slapping her hands against her thighs to no avail. Her dog wasn't interested in her now that he was in the presence of his other favorite person. The dog jumped into the old man's lap and made numerous attempts to slather his face with doggie kisses. Roscoe had done what no medicine could do. Ambrose's head turned up, and he released a belly-bursting laugh that soon had everyone laughing. The tension in his shoulders relaxed, and for the first time today, he thought maybe things would work out. Ambrose gave up trying to put the dog on the floor only to have him leap back into his lap and let him remain.

"I'm fine, everybody," Ambrose said, moving his head slowly to look into each of their eyes as he absentmindedly petted his furry friend. "According to the doctor, I should rest for another day or so, and then I can go about my business as usual."

"Roscoe, you hear that. You can't go for a walk for a couple of days," said Lottie. The canine lifted his head at the mention of his name and looked at Lottie, then at Ambrose.

"Not today, buddy, but tomorrow. I promise we'll go for our walk tomorrow," said Ambrose.

"Well, I just came over to check on you and see if you were up to having dinner with Roscoe and me."

"I think my grandfather needs to stay home tonight," answered Onyx, looking sternly at Lottie.

"That's fine, we can have dinner here," Lottie replied unperturbed.

Ambrose caught the look that passed between Onyx and Lottie. He stood up, dropping Roscoe from his lap. "I'm going over to Lottie's for dinner." Roscoe began barking and running around in circles.

"Oh, for goodness' sake! Stop all this foolishness, Roscoe!" Lottie opened the door for the dog to twirl himself out. Onyx locked his grandfather's front door and watched Ambrose, Lottie, and Roscoe cross the street and enter Miss Lottie's house.

"Let's go somewhere to sit down and have a nice dinner. My treat!" said Indigo, smiling up at Onyx.

Lottie waited until they had finished dinner before telling Ambrose she knew about Wanda. They were still seated at the dining table. Ambrose patted his stomach and sighed appreciatively.

"Which one of you killed Wanda?" Lottie asked, her face as flat as her voice.

"Whoa—What?" The drowsiness of a second ago was replaced by a jolt of confusion, rapidly cycling into discombobulation, and finally understanding what the look between Onyx and Lottie was about. "What did Onyx tell you?"

"I ain't worried about what Onyx said. I'm asking you." Lottie slammed her hands hard on the dining room table. Roscoe growled to remind the humans to play nice.

"It's a long story, Lottie. Trust me. I didn't kill nobody, and you know Onyx didn't either."

"I know Onyx didn't kill Wanda; he would have been a boy when Wanda went missing. You wouldn't have killed Wanda unless Dinah asked you to, so again, which one of you killed Wanda and why?"

"What the hell is wrong with you, woman? I wouldn't have killed anybody, let alone Wanda, because Dinah asked me. Are you out of your ever-loving mind?"

"Okay—okay. Why did Dinah kill her baby?"

"What you got to drink?"

"I got some wine or some Royal Crown."

"This here's a brown liquor story. Put a little ice in the glass."

Ambrose had moved to the living room and was seated on the couch. She handed him his whiskey and sat beside him with her glass.

"You remember the riots, right?" he asked.

"Which one? The Watts Riots or Rodney King?"

"The last one in 1992."

"Well, that wasn't a good riot, not like the riots in 1965."

"What do you mean by a good riot? There ain't no such thing as a good riot."

"The King riot didn't even get this far down. The Watts Riot, now that was a riot. It was like a war zone, the national guards, shooting, fires, looting—"

"Lottie!" shouted Ambrose. "You want me to tell you about Wanda, or do you want to debate which riot was better?"

"I'm sorry…go ahead. I'll be quiet." She took a sip of the amber liquid in her glass and leaned forward.

"It was the second or third night of the riot. Wanda had gone to her mother's house to take Indigo home with her. Apparently, they got into a fight, and one thing led to another, and Dinah ended up shooting and killing Wanda."

"Oh…" gasped Lottie.

"Dinah was beside herself when she called me over to help her. When I got there…I couldn't believe what I saw. Wanda was lying on the floor in the living room, her blood creating a man-made lake around her. Dinah was standing in the middle of the room, her clothes bloodied and torn, hair all over her head. I thought she had been shot or stabbed because there was a box cutter and a pistol on the floor, but it was only Wanda's blood on her. She was hysterical, and she didn't want me to call for help."

"She's dead, Ambrose. Look at my baby. She's dead," cried Dinah.

"How do you know she's dead? We need to call for an ambulance."

"She ain't breathing—look at her!"

He looked at Wanda, trying to see if her chest was moving. After a moment, he walked over to her, stepping cautiously into the slick pool of blood. He placed his index and middle finger on Wanda's throat; when he didn't feel a pulse, he shook her shoulder as a final test.

"I can't go to jail," wailed Dinah. "What's going to happen to Indigo?"

"What happened?" he asked, stepping away from the body. Dinah began to pace back and forth as she told him that Wanda wanted to take Indigo home. Suddenly, Ambrose noticed the bloody shoe tracks on the floor and told Dinah to stop moving. They removed their shoes and moved further away from the blood. Ambrose drew the living room curtains and locked the front door. He stood in front of the drawn curtains, gripping Dinah's shoulders, wishing he could shake her like an "Etch a Sketch" until the macabre scene vanished.

"Why would you shoot her for wanting to take her child home?" he asked to restart Dinah's telling of the story.

"That nasty-ass man Ronnie wanted Indigo to go back home. Ronnie was gonna hurt my grandbaby. He was already sitting her on his lap. He was getting her ready. It was only a matter of time before he hurt her so badly that she wouldn't ever be able to forget. I know about that kinda hurt; it never leaves."

"What are you saying?" Ambrose's fingers splayed in the air away from Dinah as if she had suddenly become too hot to touch. He knew what she meant but asked the question anyway, not knowing what else to say.

Dinah shook her head from side to side at first slowly, and then her head moved faster and faster until he thought she would break her neck. He hugged her and cradled her head against his chest until the river of tears stopped. Exhausted from everything that had already happened that night, along with old wounds that had been ripped open, Dinah's body went limp. He eased her onto the floor where she sat, rocking back and forth with her arms, wrapping herself in a hug. He stood frozen, not knowing what to do next. Dinah sitting on the floor with her sanity seeping out of her like the blood that was leaving her child's body. The silence in the room was smothering him until her voice brought him from the depths of hell and spurred him into action.

"What's going to happen to Indigo?"

"Nothing's going to happen to her. You're going to take care of her like you always have."

"How?" she asked, looking up at him.

"I don't know, I don't know...give me a minute. I need a minute to think."

She looked across the room at the daughter that she had loved from the moment that she knew of her existence, nestled in her womb, now lying dead by her hands. How many times had she told her rebellious teenage daughter, I brought you into this world, and I can take you out. The saying had been one that her mother had also spoken to her. Looking into the vacant eyes of God's gift, she realized that the idle threat uttered by so many frustrated mothers was actually a curse.

"Get me a blanket," Ambrose demanded. "I need a blanket to wrap her in."

Dinah took a blanket out of the hall closet. After she handed it to him, she went into the bathroom and got the bottle of Old Foster whiskey from the medicine cabinet. She carried the bottle into the kitchen and got a teaspoon. She was heading toward the hallway with the bottle and teaspoon when Ambrose saw her.

"What are you doing?" he asked, rolling Wanda onto the blanket.

"I'm going to give Indigo some of this to knock her out," she said, holding up the whiskey bottle with the sludgy brown liquid that fizzed when she shook the bottle. The bottle had whiskey and other things a root worker had put in it. Her mother gave it to her when she had Wanda and told her to give only a little to her colicky baby instead of the medication the doctor had prescribed.

"Are you sure about that?" he asked.

"It's for colicky babies to make them sleep."

"Ain't that too old...maybe it's gone bad or something?" asked Ambrose, concerned that she might also kill her granddaughter.

"It doesn't go bad. I'm just going to give her a little."

Dinah slowly opened Indigo's bedroom door. "Keep your eyes closed, baby. It's me, Big Momma. I got something to help you sleep."

She sat on the side of the bed. Her grandbaby's eyes were shut so tight that her little face was crunched up.

"That's good, baby. Keep your eyes closed. Now, open your mouth for Big Momma."

Indigo opened her mouth slightly.

"Open wide, That's a good girl." Dinah lifted Indigo's head so she could swallow without choking. "I know it doesn't taste good, but you'll be able to sleep now. Grandma loves you so much. I'm not gonna let anybody hurt grandma's baby." Dinah sat on the edge of the bed until Indigo's face was relaxed, and her breathing slowed down. She wanted to hug her granddaughter, but she didn't want to smear blood on her. She wished she could sit there and watch her forever instead of stepping back into the evil she had unleashed.

When she went back into the living room, Ambrose and Wanda were not there. Panic rose in her, causing her to buckle to the floor. She threw up twice before Ambrose came back into the house.

"Damnit, Dinah. You have to clean that up. Matter of fact, you need to clean all of this up. I'll be in the backyard."

"No, no, no, no, no...you can't bury my baby in the backyard like she's a dog!" She scrambled up from the floor to run to the backyard, but Ambrose stopped her.

"Look, we have to do this thing quick. It's going to take me hours to dig a grave deep enough so nothing can dig her back up."

She stopped fighting him when he made that statement. Instead of struggling to be released, her body went limp. Ambrose groaned under the sudden dead weight of her as he tried to keep her standing upright. He dropped her pendulous body on the couch, annoyed that he was dragged into this and the constant battle to keep Dinah from falling apart.

"You got any liquor?" When she didn't answer, he told her he would be right back. He returned with a bottle and two ice-filled glasses. He poured two large glasses of whiskey and handed one to Dinah.

"Okay, let's do this. I'll be in the backyard; you clean this up and place everything with blood on it in a plastic bag. You got bleach?"

"Yes."

"When you clean everything, mop it again with a lot of bleach." He left her in the front room.

Ambrose knew he was running out of time as he looked up and saw only a few remaining stars in the night sky. Soon, a new day would dawn, and what had been done under the cover of darkness would be discovered if they had not been careful. He looked up at the sky and knew that heaven bore witness to this night. He wondered for a moment how God would judge him. Surely, he thought God would see that he only took part in this to save a child. He rolled Wanda into her grave, wincing because he should have lowered her gently into the hole. He went into the house half expecting to see blood and vomit on the floor, and Dinah collapsed on the couch. Instead, she stood with a mop in her hand, looking to see if anything had been overlooked. She watched him come into the room. His nose involuntarily wrinkled from the pungent scent of bleach.

"I wanted to know if you want to say anything before I finish."

She walked past him without speaking. Dinah stood, looking down at her daughter wrapped in an old blanket. He waited by the back door, giving her space to say goodbye.

"You're my baby. I carried you for nine long months. I gave birth to you, fed you, and took care of you when you were sick. I would climb into that hole and lay down with you if I didn't have Indigo to see after. Everything in me wants to. I wish you could have seen what I saw in Ronnie because I refuse to believe you saw it and turned a blind eye to it like so many others do. Could you have lived with yourself knowing you had a part in that? I don't believe you could, and I know I couldn't. I did what I did because I love you both, and sometimes love requires you to roll in the deep to prove how real it is. Tonight, I'm rolling in the deep." She looked back at Ambrose and knew that he was rolling in the deep with her in the treacherous waters of love that this night had brought. *"Lord, have mercy on our souls,"* she prayed before walking toward the house.

Ambrose went to the edge of the yard where Dinah's garden was and what would be Wanda's final resting place. Dinah stood by the back door and watched him pick up the shovel. Her breath caught in her throat when dirt landed on the shrouded thing that once was her child, and she retreated into the house. She was sitting on the couch staring into space when he came in from the backyard for the last time that night, locking the door behind him.

"It's done," he declared, sitting beside her. He poured himself a drink and tilted the bottle in her direction. She nodded in the affirmative. After he poured her enough whiskey to knock her on her ass, he poured the rest into his glass. *"Put all your clothes, including your underwear, in a plastic bag; I'll pick it up later and burn everything."* She nodded, and he left to go home.

Lottie was quiet for so long that Ambrose looked at her to make sure he was really sitting in her house and that he had just confessed to burying Wanda.

"You carried that around for all these years?"

"Yeah," nodded Ambrose, looking down at his hands, letting the tears fall unchecked.

"You loved her, didn't you?'

"Yeah, I did."

"So, you guys were more than friends?"

"I loved Lucinda and Delray more. I couldn't dishonor them like that, and after that night, everything changed. Dinah chose to kill her daughter. She could have fired the gun in the air to scare her off or shoot her in the foot. She didn't have to kill her. Dinah knew that, and she knew I knew that."

"Then why? Why did she kill her?"

"I think she knew that Wanda would keep making the same bad choices when it came to men." He looked at Lottie and wiped his eyes, and she did the same.

"It's all right now, Ambrose. I can help you carry the load. Y'all done dug up Wanda, and now her spirit is floating around, kicking up dust and scaring people."

"I think she's been scaring Indigo before we dug her up."

"Then, why is she in your house?"

"We let her in when we put the bones in the house. I'm telling you, she's real. I felt her presence, and her emptiness almost ate my soul."

"That's what Onyx said that she was empty."

"I've got to do something with her bones, but what?"

"She needs to be put to rest. Maybe she doesn't know that she's dead."

Ambrose looked at Lottie with a tentative smile. "We sound like crazy old country people, believing in haints, spirits, voodoo, and God knows what else."

"We are old country people, and there is a spirit world just as sure as we're sitting here."

"Well, Lottie, thank you kindly for listening to me. If I had known how good it would feel to talk to you about that night, I would have done it a long time ago."

"You and Dinah never talked about it?"

"Not really. We talked around it but never about it."

"What about the boyfriend? He didn't come around asking where she was?"

"He did, but Dinah flipped the script on him. She told him that Wanda never came over that night, and she was going to the police and would let them know that he used to beat her daughter, and now she's missing. When she got through screaming, yelling, and accusing him of killing Wanda, he took off. Me and Dinah went to the apartment and moved her out, so nobody was looking for her. I kept Wanda's car in my garage until I found someone to buy it. That money is what I used to pay Dinah's bills until she got herself together enough to go back to work. Later, if anybody asked about Wanda, she was off with some man again. Pretty soon, nobody asked about her anymore."

They sat quietly in the living room, contemplating the situation as they consumed another two fingers of whiskey. When Ambrose rose to go home, he realized that he had had one drink too many. Lottie watched him high step to the door as if he were taking a field sobriety test that required one to march instead of walking. He was at the front door when she collapsed into giggles.

"You're stepping in high cotton now," she laughed. "Why don't you stay here until we get rid of them bones?"

"Onyx took them out of the house; they're locked up in the garage."

"She's a ghost; you don't think she can walk through walls?" Lottie roared with laughter.

Ambrose high-stepped like a toddler with outstretched arms back to the couch. He fell onto the couch and held on to Lottie. Soon, his laughter turned into silent crying as relief washed over him.

Chapter 15

Lottie and Roscoe were in Ambrose's kitchen. Lottie lit the sage on the stove burner and blew the flame out with the soft wind of her breath. She began at the back door and walked around the room, casting out evil spirits. When she finished ridding the house of any manner of wickedness, she ran water over the bundle and left it in the kitchen sink. They were in the living room, watching her court shows, when Onyx let himself in the front door.

"Hey, Grandpa. Uhh, good morning, Miss Lottie."

"Hey, Grandson," said Ambrose.

Lottie emitted a loud, ear-piercing scream. She jumped from the couch and pointed at the duffle bag strapped across Onyx's shoulder. He stood glued in place, wondering what was wrong with her.

"That's not the same bag!" said Ambrose, standing up to grab her. Lottie hadn't heard what he said because she was still screaming.

"Get it out of here!" she shouted when she stopped screaming.

"It's not the bag," Ambrose said, gripping her shoulders.

"You told her?" shouted Onyx, clasping his fingers behind his head.

"Yeah, after you told her," answered Ambrose.

Lottie wasn't convinced that it wasn't the same bag. She had stopped screaming but was shooing Onyx with her hands and telling him to take the bag outside.

"Miss Lottie, calm down. This is my gym bag with my clothes in it."

He unzipped the bag and tilted it so Lottie could see inside. "So, why did you tell my grandfather that I told you about the bones?

"Because you both told me…duh!" retorted Lottie, extending her neck forward and slightly to her left.

"Sit down!" Ambrose shouted. "It's good everybody knows. Now, all of us can try and figure out what to do with them."

A couple of weeks later, the group still hadn't figured out what to do with Wanda's bones, although they met daily at Ambrose's house to discuss it. Their meetings were short and usually ended with Lottie getting into it with Ambrose or Onyx. The bones were hidden in plain sight in the farthest corner of the garage as tiny dust particles collected on the duffel bag. Every morning, the sun seemed to shine brighter when Ambrose opened his eyes because the preceding day and night had been incident-free. Some nights, he stayed over Lottie's house. He liked going to sleep with her beside him, and he knew she did as well, despite their complaining about the other. He complained about her breaking wind in her sleep, and she complained about his snoring. But just before they fell asleep, they would extend their legs until their feet touched.

Ambrose was in his kitchen making a pot of coffee for their customary morning meeting. He had buttoned the last button on his favorite plaid shirt when the doorbell rang. He ran a hand down the front of his shirt, which was paper-thin and faded from years of washing and ironing. He told himself to remember to ask Onyx to buy him another shirt just like this one. Ambrose smiled as he opened the door, expecting to see Lottie and Roscoe.

"Yes," he said, but it sounded more like a question. He was taken aback by the White woman standing at his door, and his smile quickly vanished.

"Hello, my name is Summer Collins. I'm with Adult Protective Services. I'm here to investigate the incident that led to your hospitalization. May I come in?"

"Investigate?"

"Yes. You are Mr. Ambrose Linton, correct?"

"Yes, I'm Mr. Linton."

"I'm here to determine if elder abuse has occurred. I'm here to interview you and see if there are any services or programs that may be able to help you. So, if you don't mind, can I come inside?"

He looked at the solid-looking woman who wore her authority with the same self-assurance as she wore her privilege. The woman moved forward to enter the house while Ambrose moved forward to block her.

"No, you can't."

The woman was baffled for a second until she assumed the reason for the refusal. "Is she in the house?" she whispered, leaning in to complete the conspiracy.

"She?"

"Wanda. Is Wanda inside?" she asked as her eyes darted crazily around, trying to see inside the house.

"Nobody is here but me, and there is no Wanda." Ambrose stepped back from the woman, mainly because he was close enough to smell a pungent mixture of coffee and garlic on her breath. Summer Collins took his retreat as an invitation to enter and squeezed past him. She was seated on the couch with her clipboard and pen when she asked.

"Is Wanda a friend, or does she work for you?"

"Look, Miss Summer, there is no Wanda. I don't know what the doctor told you, but there is no Wanda. I had a nightmare. I must have fallen asleep in front of the TV. Maybe a horror movie was on, and I got frightened or confused."

"Mr. Linton, are you telling me that a trained medical profession-al…a doctor filled out a report, indicating a woman named Wanda fright-ened you to the point that you were hospitalized, but he was mistaken because there is no woman named Wanda?"

"How many times do I have to tell you there is no Wanda? Miss Summer, I ain't got time for this mess. So, go on and let yourself out." Ambrose held the door open for her.

Summer Collins clutched the clipboard to her chest and sighed noisily.

"Mr. Linton, are you refusing to proceed with the investigation?" she asked before standing up.

"There's nothing to investigate."

She pulled out a business card and offered it to him. "Please take my card and let me know if you change your mind. I'd be happy to re-open the investigation." Her lips attempted to smile but couldn't quite pull it off. "If you get frightened again, you can call. There are people who can help."

He felt sorry for her until he heard air quotes around the word frightened. He didn't reach for the card. Summer Collins walked out the door, got into her car, and drove away. Lottie and Roscoe were crossing the street when she pulled away from the curb, and Onyx was closing Dinah's gate. Ambrose waited at the front door for the group.

"Who was that?" asked Lottie.

"Somebody from Adult Protective Services," he answered. Then, he quickly explained that there would be no investigation without his consent and continued into the kitchen. Once they were seated at the kitchen table with coffee mugs in hand, Ambrose started the discussion.

"The way I figure it is—A, we need to get rid of the bones."

"Duh," murmured Lottie, crossing her arms over her chest and rolling her eyes.

Ambrose looked at her and cleared his throat before continuing. "And—B, we need to do it as soon as possible."

"Tell us something we don't know. What we need to know is how do we dispose of the skeletal remains," complained Lottie.

"I see someone has been watching CSI. Dispose of the skeletal remains," mocked Ambrose.

"All right, all right, everybody calm down. Did anyone come up with a plan?" Onyx asked, looking at his grandfather and then at Lottie. "Okay, since no one has, I suggest we take the bones and bury them in the mountains."

"What if they're found, and they trace them back to us?" asked Lottie.

"Who's going to identify a skeleton that has been buried for 18 years with a woman who has never been reported missing?" Onyx asked.

"What if someone sees us drive up to the mountains and follows us into the woods, writes down the license plate number, waits until we leave, digs up the bones, and calls the police?" said Lottie, finally stopping to breathe.

"Lawd have mercy. This woman has lost her mind. Look, Lottie, you're done. Why don't you go back home and forget about all of this? Me and Onyx will take care of this." Ambrose rose from his chair. "Just let Onyx and me handle this."

Ambrose tried to pull Lottie's chair back from the table, but Lottie swatted at him and grabbed the table's edge.

"Ambrose! Leave me alone. You put me in this mess, so I'm in it. I'm not going anywhere. I'm just trying to make sure your monkey ass don't get caught!"

"Get up, Lottie!" ordered Ambrose, struggling to pull back her chair.

"Are you two done?" asked Onyx, his voice hard and cold even to his ears. Alarmed by Onyx's tone, Ambrose and Lottie stopped and looked at him. "Miss Lottie is right. She's in this mess, and we ALL need to get it together. Tomorrow morning, we're going to go fishing. You two will be on the side of the road fishing while I hike into the woods and bury the bones. That's it, end of the story."

Lottie and Ambrose felt like little kids who had been scolded. They were solemn for a few seconds. Ambrose went back to his seat and drank some of his coffee. Lottie looked sheepishly across the table at Ambrose before drinking some of her coffee.

"What time should we be ready to go, grandson?"

"After Indigo leaves for work, say 9 o'clock."

"That's late to be going fishing," said Lottie.

"Even better. Hopefully, no one will be around," stated Onyx.

"Okay, I'll go get my fishing gear out of the garage." Ambrose's voice dropped to a whisper when he said garage.

"Shit," spilled out of Onyx's mouth and echoed in the room.

"But that's where the bones are," Lottie stated the obvious.

"I'll get your gear," said Onyx, trying not to look as apprehensive as he felt.

"Nah, wait a minute." Ambrose looked at his grandson. "We both felt that thing, and it's evil, so I don't think riding around with it in the car for two hours is smart."

Onyx and Lottie agreed and concluded that they were back at square one. The coffee was bitter because Ambrose had forgotten to remove the grinds, but he poured himself another cup anyway. They were just about to disband when Lottie jumped out of her seat.

"I got it. Y'all need to hear me out before saying no."

After Lottie explained her plan, Ambrose and Onyx agreed it might work.

"But where can we get something like that?" asked Ambrose.

Looking like the cat that swallowed the canary, Lottie provided the answer.

Chapter 16

The week it took for the item to be delivered seemed endless. The trio met every morning at Ambrose's house to discuss whether or not it would work and check whether the order had been shipped. Onyx would leave to go to work, and Lottie and Roscoe would go back home to watch her shows while Ambrose relaxed in his recliner and enjoyed the quiet of his home without Lottie's constant yammering.

Indigo had no idea about the secret morning meeting after she had gone to work. Her days were consumed by work and her nights by Onyx. There were times when she almost called Big Momma to tell her about Onyx and how happy she was. After the fresh wave of grief passed, she would almost call Amani until she remembered that she, too, was lost to her. This was the longest time that she and Amani had gone without speaking to each other. Destiny called a few times, but the calls were always short and superficial. She felt guilty about the way she had been treating Destiny. She was angry with Amani, but she treated Destiny poorly because she wouldn't engage in bashing Amani. Whenever she complained about Amani, Destiny would either change the subject or mitigate Amani's reaction by explaining Amani's point of view. It infuriated her, and she knew it was immature of her to want Destiny to be angry with Amani, but it didn't stop her from wanting it. She didn't want to understand how Amani felt. She just wanted Destiny to agree with her. She ended the call with Destiny and tried to stifle her annoyance when Onyx walked into the bedroom. He was still wet from his shower and was drying himself off. She would never understand why he walked out of the bathroom and down the hallway into the bedroom without drying himself. It was an annoying idiosyncrasy that drove her crazy. A healthy dose of lust replaced her irritation as she watched him dry himself and get dressed. Her relationship with Onyx was easy, and it scared her that something could be so good. He made her feel strong and confident. She laughed at the looks that other women gave him when they went out. He was so used to women vying for his attention that he was almost oblivious to it. Sometimes, she caught him looking at other women, but it was only a cursory glance that one gave a beautiful object. She understood it because she still noticed other men and was attracted to their swagger, and as exciting as they might be, she didn't want anyone but Onyx. He was not only physically attractive, but he was also mentally stimulating. They discussed environmental, social, and political issues as well as theology. He was buttoning his shirt when he asked what she had planned for the day.

"I just got off the phone with Destiny. I thought maybe we could do something, but she's tripping."

"Tripping, how?"

"She's always trying to get me to understand how Amani is feeling. She wants me to sit down and talk to her."

"What's wrong with that?"

"What's wrong with that is I was the one who was raped!"

"So, Amani can't feel what she feels?"

"What are you talking about? Amani's feelings, what about my feelings?"

He stopped fastening his pants when he saw how upset Indigo was. He reached out to embrace her, but she jerked backward.

He pulled himself upright, disturbed by her reaction. "Are you okay?"

"Yeah, I didn't know what you were gonna do."

"Did that nigga use to hit you?"

"No."

"Some other nigga?"

"No."

"You think I might hit you?"

"No...just that...."

"Just what?" asked Onyx, lowering himself on the bed beside her.

"Since the rape...I'm very aware of how vulnerable I am as a woman. How any man is capable of hurting me."

"Indigo, I'm not any man, and I've never been that dude. I don't have to hit a woman, and I damn sure don't have to force myself on one." He held his hands up. "You see these hands? All they will ever do is give you pleasure and work so I can buy you whatever your heart desires."

"I know." She placed her hands in his. "I didn't mean to make you feel bad. I'm just being honest."

"So are Amani and Destiny," he said, standing up.

She remained sitting on the edge of the bed as Onyx finished dressing. He kissed her on the forehead and told her he would be back after his showings. She heard the front doors open and close; the car engine rev then purred as it drove away. Indigo sat on the bed, stung by the simple truth of his words. She knew she needed to forgive or at least understand Amani. She should have given Amani time to process what Treyvon had done. Yes, Treyvon had victimized her, but she was not a victim, and she needed to stop carrying his shame. She needed to appreciate Destiny's loyalty to Amani and herself. She needed to forgive Big Momma for running off her mother and to forgive her mother for staying away. Forgiveness didn't mean that she would forget; understanding didn't mean that she would agree, but forgiveness would allow her to move away from the pain. Indigo picked up her phone off the nightstand and called Destiny back.

Sunday morning promised to sizzle into another hot day. There wasn't a wisp of clouds in the sky when Indigo arrived at IHOP. As planned, she was the last to arrive. Destiny was laughing when she saw Indigo walking toward their table. She continued laughing and gave Indigo a slight nod. Amani noticed the gesture and automatically looked in that direction. Amani's laughter died immediately.

"I'm not feeling this," said Amani, standing up.

Indigo blocked her path. "Please, Amani, don't leave," she said quickly.

"Why shouldn't I?"

"Because I need to apologize to you. Please stay so we can talk."

"Please," implored Destiny.

Amani sat and scooted over in the booth, making room for Indigo.

"Thank you," said Indigo, taking a seat.

The group sat in silence for a minute. Destiny sat nervously, tearing up a paper napkin, and Amani tucked her lips, trying to quell her anger.

"Destiny, Amani, I owe you both an apology, so let me start with you, Destiny." Indigo focused only on Destiny. "I'm sorry for trying to make you turn against Amani."

"What the what?" Amani blustered, scooting toward Destiny to get out of the booth.

"Wait, let me finish," said Indigo, turning her attention to Amani. "Every time Destiny called to check on me, I would bring you up and try to make her take my side in our disagreement. That wasn't cool, and I'm sorry, Destiny, I shouldn't have done that. Please forgive me." Indigo turned her gaze back to Destiny.

Destiny looked at Indigo with an expression that Indigo couldn't read. When Indigo spoke, Destiny's forehead had a crease etched across it, and her fingers were in constant motion. They were either balling up the paper napkins or tearing them into tiny pieces. Now, Destiny's hands lay flat on the table perfectly still, and her face stared blankly at her.

"Is that all that you're sorry about?" asked Destiny.

"No, of course not." Indigo looked at Amani to speak but was interrupted.

"Is that all that you're sorry about with me? Destiny asked again, slower and louder.

It was Indigo's turn to look perplexed. She shook her head slightly from side to side before asking what else she should be sorry for.

"Oh, I don't know…maybe for pushing me out and treating me like I wasn't a part of your life anymore."

"What?"

"You made me feel like our friendship couldn't stand on its own. No, that's not quite right either…it felt like there was never a friendship. I felt like I was a friend of a friend but not your friend. You didn't want to do anything with me, and we barely talked."

"That isn't true; we talked."

"You answered questions. If I didn't ask questions, you didn't have anything to say other than bashing Amani and getting pissed when I disagreed. I thought you might need me because friends are supposed to be there for each other during bad times. I wanted to be there for you, but you pushed me away instead of leaning on me."

Indigo opened her mouth to deny the truth of it but closed it instead. Bitter tears stung her eyes, but she wouldn't let them fall. Everything Destiny said was true, and because it was the truth, it was painful to hear. Looking across the table at Destiny, she saw someone new. The old Destiny had always been the timid, weak one in the trio. She was often overlooked or an afterthought when they made plans, which was partly her fault. She never had an opinion and always acquiesced to whatever she and Amani wanted to do. She looked at Destiny and saw that she was trying really hard to stand up to her. Although Indigo was offended by what Destiny said, she knew Destiny couldn't take the clap back, so she remained silent. Destiny had just told her she was a self-centered bitch who discarded people when they no longer served a purpose, and she couldn't do anything about it but lump it if she wanted Destiny as a friend. Indigo blew out a long breath through her mouth before responding.

"You're right. I've been selfishly caught up with what was going on with me, and I never considered your feelings," croaked Indigo. "I'm sorry. Your friendship means everything to me; please forgive me."

Destiny couldn't respond because the server came to the table to take their orders, which gave the group time to settle their emotions. When the waitress left, Indigo continued.

"I'm sorry I made you feel like I didn't value you." Indigo touched one of Destiny's hands.

"I wanted to bring it up, but you already had a lot on your plate. This, what we're doing now, is what grown women do. If we're unable to talk to each other about how something makes us feel, then I don't know if we could have called this a friendship in the first place. Of course, I accept your apology," said Destiny, smiling at Indigo.

"What about you, Amani?" Indigo turned in her direction. "Can you forgive me for not letting you have a moment to process what I told you about someone who means so much to you?" asked Indigo.

Amani cleared her throat before answering. "I can forgive you, but what you said about my brother hurt me to my core. That same loyalty you demanded of me is the same loyalty that Treyvon deserved from me.

Treyvon and I grew up together, and we've been through a lot, so when you said what you said, I couldn't believe it just because you said it."

Indigo scooted out of the booth and stood to leave in one fluid motion.

"Hold up. Let her finish," urged Destiny, grabbing at Indigo's hand.

"Yeah, let me finish. If I believed what you said about him, it would have changed who he is to me." Amani wiped her eyes before she continued. "What you're asking of me is too much...if it was anyone else...." She shook her head from side to side before she murmured, "But not him."

The silence between them was deafening; a majestic tree miles away fell somewhere deep in a forest. Everything that they had once been to each other died in that moment. It shook the earth and rippled the air. Startled birds flew from the tree's canopy, and small animals that had once made their home in its hollowed-out tree trunk fled. But no one at the restaurant except Indigo and Amani heard or felt its demise. Indigo collapsed into the booth, suddenly too tired to stand. Amani bowed her head, wanting to lay it on the table and wail because she couldn't have one friend without betraying the other. Their food arrived at that moment, and Indigo remained. They ate and somehow managed to talk about things that didn't matter one way or the other. Every once in a while, Indigo caught Amani's eyes and saw only a parting of the ways in them. When the bill came, Indigo insisted on paying it. They walked out of the diner like so many times before, except there were no promises to get together soon. They hugged in the parking lot and separated to go to their cars. Indigo turned back to watch Amani walking to her car.

"Amani!" yelled Indigo as she hurried toward her.

Amani turned to see what Indigo wanted and saw her barreling in her direction. Indigo nearly knocked Amani down when she wrapped her in her arms. Amani's body shook as she wept in Indigo's embrace. The women stood in the IHOP parking lot, sobbing because they were letting go of a precious, irreplaceable thing. Destiny sat in her car, feeling excluded yet again.

When Indigo got home, she sat in Big Momma's rocking chair, looking out the window. She and Amani would now play the game that civility required. They would say hello and ask how the other was getting on when they met in public spaces or at mutual friends' events. But there would be no more sharing of the things that made life worth living. They were no longer friends now. They were only tenuously connected by people they both knew.

"Hey, girl," Destiny answered on the first ring.

"Hey, I was calling to say thank you for getting her there. We can't say we didn't try," said Indigo.

"So, you guys didn't make up in the parking lot?"

"No, but getting together was a good thing for us. We all got to be heard. Oh, and just so you know, Miss Thing—I heard you; I'm thinking about having a barbecue next weekend. Nothing big, just a couple of people. You wanna come through?"

"Sounds like fun. Can I bring someone?'

"Someone? What's his name? Is he fine? Where did you meet—no, wait a minute, when did you meet?" laughed Indigo.

They stayed on the phone for almost two hours, with Destiny doing most of the talking. After they hung up, she went to her bedroom and took the book that she had never had a chance to read off the nightstand. She poured herself a glass of iced tea and retreated to the backyard. Indigo sat in one chair and put her legs in another. She managed to read a few pages before scooching so far down in the chair that her butt was barely on it, and she fell asleep. The book she was reading fell from her hands, and her head fell back on the top of the chair, her neck perfectly positioned for the guillotine. She was emerging from unconsciousness, becoming painfully aware that her neck was in an awkward position. She was about to move when what she heard kept her frozen.

"I don't want you in the backyard as long as Wanda is in the garage," hissed Lottie.

"Be quiet, woman. I told you not to say her name. What if Indigo hears you?" said Ambrose.

When Indigo's name was mentioned, they looked in the direction of Dinah's house and saw her sprawled out on chairs in her backyard.

"Oh my God, do you think she heard us?" whispered Lottie.

"I don't think so. She must be asleep or dead from the looks of her. Come on, let's get inside."

Indigo stayed frozen in that painful position, afraid to move. Sweat rolled down her face, back, and other places. She didn't move because she knew Ambrose and Lottie were most likely looking at her from the kitchen window. She heard them talking about her mother being in the garage. She asked herself how two old people could have tied up her mother and kept her held hostage in the garage and concluded that they couldn't have, not without help. Her heart began to pound with that revelation, and she forgot about the pain in her neck. The sweat, running down her back, chilled her spine. Onyx must have tied up her mother. When she thought she had stayed in the position long enough to fool them, she counted to fifty just in case. After fifty, she waited a couple more seconds, and just as she decided to move, the brightness of the sun was blocked, and someone touched her shoulder. Indigo screamed loud and long, causing Ambrose and Lottie to shuffle out the back door and to the fence. She lunged forward and screamed again, not because she was frightened like before, but from the pain that shot down the nape of her neck.

"Sorry, I didn't mean to scare you. You looked uncomfortable like your neck would hurt if you stayed that way," said Onyx.

"You scared the shit out of me," she said, rubbing her neck. "I must have fallen asleep," she said loud enough for Ambrose and Lottie, trying to sell the lie.

"Uh-huh." Onyx picked up the book and handed it to her. He waved to his grandfather and Lottie.

She stood up and stretched, gingerly moving her head from side to side before walking into the house while Ambrose and Lottie looked on. As she walked toward the house, she tried to think of a way to check out Mr. Ambrose's garage.

"You want a neck massage," Onyx asked, wriggling his eyebrows up and down.

"I'm not feeling too hot. I think I'm going to go lie down."

"Okay, but what about dinner later? Do you wanna go out or want me to pick up something?"

"Probably, just pick up something. Like I said, I'm not feeling too good."

"I'll check with you before I go."

"Okay."

She closed the door to the bedroom and lay on top of the covers. She went over in her head what she heard Lottie and Ambrose say. *Could her mother really be in the garage? No! That's crazy...but what other explanation was there? If it's true, then why? Why would Onyx help them? He definitely would've been the one to tie her up. How long has she been there? What are they planning to do with her? What would they do to her if they thought she knew? I gotta look in that garage and get her out of there tonight.* These thoughts raced through her mind and tormented her, making her body twitchy. She forced herself to wait until Onyx was out of the house instead of running half-cocked into the garage while he was there. She would go when he went on a food run. The simple plan let her calm down a bit because it was simple and doable. She closed her eyes, attempting to meditate. As she concentrated on her breathing, the sounds of the neighborhood drifted in. She could tell it was early evening because there weren't many children outside. She thought she heard a lone basketball bouncing outside her window; she listened to its rhythm until the sound became too faint. Her heart raced when she heard Onyx walk past the door. She released her breath when he continued to the bathroom. On his way back to the living room, he stopped at the bedroom door and stood there as if deciding whether to come in before continuing. Muffled noises came from the TV. She heard him walking again, but this time, his footsteps were walking away from her. He must have gone into the kitchen. She could hear them again, and they were getting louder. Indigo's eyes flew open from the sheer panic of knowing that, this time, he was coming into the room. Her breathing was erratic, coming in short, shallow spurts. She drew in a large, deep breath, counting to five, and then exhaled. Indigo was only able to do it twice before he opened the door. She pretended to wake up and yawned, hoping it would mask her panicked breathing.

"How are you feeling?" asked Onyx, standing on the door's threshold.

"A little better."

"What do you want to eat?

"Uh, um…whatever you're having."

"You know what? I think I'll make you one of my grilled cheese sandwiches on sourdough and heat up some soup."

"But what about you? That's not gonna be enough for you. You should go get you something."

"It will be enough. I've been munching on some nachos Miss Lottie made. I went next door while you were sleeping. You didn't hear me go?"

"No," she muttered, not believing she had fallen asleep. She wondered if he knew that she knew and was gaslighting her.

She followed him into the kitchen and watched him heat two cans of chicken gumbo soup and make giant grilled cheese sandwiches from sourdough bread. They watched two action movies and the news before finally going to bed.

It was 3:00 am, the witching hour, and Indigo woke up with the same panicky feeling she had ever since the rape. She lay on her back, looking up at the ceiling, telling herself that she was safe, that she was with Onyx, not Treyvon. *But was she safe? If her mother was in Mr. Ambrose's garage,* she thought. Indigo slowly turned her head sideways to look at him. She watched him and listened to his breathing for a few minutes before she attempted to get out of bed. She slid an inch toward the bed's edge, held her breath, and waited to see if he stirred. When nothing happened, she moved again, stopped, moved, stopped, repeating the movement until she was out of bed. She gripped the bedroom doorknob and turned it slowly like a safecracker. Indigo tiptoed on the old wooden floors that squeaked in too many places to remember. She felt like a hippopotamus dancing demi pointe across the living and dining room, making so much noise that she knew Onyx had to be awake by now. She began to breathe again when she reached the kitchen, where she had conveniently left her purse with her car keys inside. Before she left the house through the back door, she got a large knife and a pair of scissors and placed them in her purse, which she slung across her body. Once outside, she switched on the flashlight, scurried to the side fence, and climbed over it.

"Damn," said Onyx when he heard Indigo open and close the kitchen door. He knew something was going on with her, and his suspicions were confirmed when his grandfather told him that Miss Lottie had mentioned Wanda when they were in the backyard earlier. He had hoped Indigo was asleep when Miss Lottie slipped up, but now it appears she wasn't. Her reaction when he allegedly woke her was overly dramatic; the sudden illness and now sneaking out of the house confirmed what he suspected. He hadn't told his grandfather because he was hoping that he was wrong. He got out of bed and pulled on his clothes and shoes in the dark. He cussed again before locking the front door. Onyx saw the beam of light bouncing around in the dark cavity of the garage. He slipped into the garage and waited for the light to shine on him. Indigo's scream pierced the stillness of the night, and the beam of light jumped around like a wild animal.

"What are you looking for?" he asked when her scream ended.

"You know who I'm looking for."

"I don't know what you're talking about."

"Where is she? What did you guys do with her?"

"You guys? What guys?"

"Your grandfather, Miss Lottie, and you. You know who I'm talking about. Where is she?"

"Indigo, you're not feeling well. Maybe you have a fever. Come on back home and let me take care of you." He stepped forward.

"Stop! Don't you dare come near me!" She stepped backward, put the flashlight in her left hand, and unzipped her purse. Indigo fumbled around in her purse and retrieved the kitchen knife. "I heard them say she was in the garage."

Onyx raised his hands when he saw the knife, wanting to reassure her that he wasn't going to try anything.

"Indigo, relax. I don't know what you thought you heard, but your mother isn't here."

"What's going on, Onyx? Is she in the house?" She jutted the knife at him and began a sort of crab walk out of the garage toward Ambrose's back door. He let her get halfway up the driveway before he lowered his hands and slowly followed her. She was pounding on the back door when he rammed her into the door, pinning her against it. While she was pressed against the door, he grabbed her wrists, squeezing them so hard that she dropped the knife and flashlight. A second later, he placed her in a bear hug to drag her home. Just as she began kicking, Ambrose opened the back door and received a kick to his shinbone. Ambrose yelped, stumbled back, and began rubbing his leg. Onyx released Indigo to go to his grandfather, and she sprinted into the house, yelling for her mother. When she returned to the kitchen, she was no longer shouting. Her shoulders were slumped, and her chest rose and fell as she caught her breath.

"I heard you and Miss Lottie in the backyard. Miss Lottie said she was in the garage, but she wasn't there now. So, where is she? What did you guys do with her?"

Onyx was kneeling in front of his grandfather with a glass of water. "Are you okay?"

"I'm fine," he said, taking the glass.

"Mr. Ambrose, please tell me where my mother is…please," she begged.

Ambrose turned to look at her, and the glass slipped from his hand. Shards of glass bounced off the floor and scattered across it. All three stood in a trance-like state and watched the water flow downward, pooling at a low point in the floor. Each tried to make sense of how they had come to this moment. Miss Lottie's banging on the front door brought them back to Ambrose's kitchen.

"Let her in before she kicks the door in," said Ambrose.

Onyx walked past Indigo and vanished into the next room. Lottie burst into the kitchen and rushed to Ambrose's side. It wasn't until Lottie pulled his head onto her chest that he began to cry. Lottie stroked his head until he struggled to his feet and clasped her hand.

"It's time you knew the truth," he said, looking at Indigo. "Let's go into the living room. Watch your step, Lottie. Mind you, don't cut yourself with those slippers on."

"I see all the glass on the floor. Who broke the glass, and what am I supposed to be wearing at this hour of the morning?"

Ambrose ignored Lottie's unceasing chatter and gripped her hand tighter as he guided her out of the kitchen. He and Lottie sat on the couch, still holding hands, while Onyx perched on the arm of Indigo's chair.

"Your grandmother loved your grandfather and your mother more than anything. They had a good life together. They struggled like everybody else but had each other, so they were happy. We were all happy living next door to each other. Me and Lucinda and your grandparents, well, we did everything together! Friday nights, we would get together with other friends at either my house or your grandfather's and have a weenie roast or fish fry." Ambrose paused, smiling as he remembered those days. "The men would be gambling, drinking, or playing cards. The kids would be ripping and running between the streetlights, playing that game that the kids played while the women cooked or sat around and gossiped." The smile on Ambrose's face vanished suddenly. "But nothing stays the same. One day, Delray just up and died. We were at work; at first, I thought somebody had cut off their finger or something. When I saw him on the floor, his eyes staring at nothing, I knew he was gone." His body shuddered as he recalled the horror of that day. "The life your grandmother had with Delray died with him. She lost interest in everything and everybody. Me and Lucinda saw that Dinah was struggling, so we included Wanda in our family's outings. That didn't last long because my wife got it in her head that something was going on between me and Dinah." The pain that traveled through his body stabbed his chest. He had again denied his feelings for Dinah, but this time, he wanted to tell the truth. "Nothing was going on between us, but I did love her. I don't know if she ever knew that, but my wife did. I don't know how Lucinda knew that I cared about Dinah, but she did. My wife turned her back on Dinah when she needed her. I'll always feel responsible for that."

When Ambrose stopped to collect his thoughts, the room was silent. Indigo sat on the edge of her seat, leaning forward as she digested every word. He began to speak, shifting the heaviness that was pressing in on them as he recounted to them how a mother had come to kill her child.

"Who can tell a person how long or how to grieve? So, we just let her be. I did what I could for her around the house and took care of the yard. I had to be careful when Lucinda started acting funny. I think it added to Dinah's grief when Lucinda pulled away from her, but after a few years, Dinah seemed to be coming back to herself. She worked real hard to keep food on the table and a roof over their heads but she didn't give Wanda what she needed. I don't think Dinah could see how hard it was for Wanda without her father. By the time your mom was a teenager, she and your grandmother weren't getting along at all. Wanda got pregnant right out of high school, and your grandmother was hard on her. You were a little baby when Wanda left your grandmother's house and got her own place. Things seemed to get better between them when your mother moved out. You were about two or three when Wanda started leaving you with your grandmother off and on. Sometimes, Dinah would have to take you to work with her cleaning houses because your mom hadn't picked you up or she wasn't at home. Dinah would complain and threaten not to keep you again, but I could see that she was living again. You gave her something to live for." Ambrose looked at Indigo, and she saw every line that was etched in his face. His eyes were watery and red. A dull film covered his pupils, giving the eyes a murky appearance. "I need to lay down for a little bit."

"But—where's my mother?" demanded Indigo.

"She ain't here, and she never was…well, it's not what you think. I'm gonna tell you everything, but I'm too tired to go on right now, baby girl. Grandson, help me up."

Onyx pulled his grandfather from the couch. Lottie and Onyx followed Ambrose down the hall into his bedroom. When Onyx returned to the living room, he looked at Indigo.

"Can I go home with you?" he asked.

"Why? Your grandfather doesn't need you to watch me anymore."

"Me and you have nothing to do with this."

"Are you going to tell me that your grandfather didn't tell you to keep an eye on me?"

"He wanted to know if you were going to sell the house. He didn't tell me to be with you. I wanted to be with you. I still do."

"I don't know that I can trust you." Indigo stood and walked toward the door; Onyx reached out to hold her hand, but she jerked it away. "Call me when he's ready."

Indigo sat in Big Momma's rocking chair with a cup of tea. She looked out the window and stared at the neighborhood. Once again that feeling of being alone in the world overtook her. The houses across the street were cloaked in darkness, concealing deferred maintenance. Most stood in total darkness, while a few were softened by the warm glow of porch lights or filtered lighting behind sheer curtains. She had a bad feeling about the rest of the story. She wondered if her mother was drug-addicted, sick, or dying, but nothing she could think made sense out of what she heard about her mother being in the garage. Why she left and never returned didn't matter now; all she wanted and needed was her mother. Maybe the hurt feelings and childhood disappointments could be resolved once she had an opportunity to hear her mother's side of the story. Sleep covered her like a blanket still warm from the dryer, and she barely put her cup on the table before giving in to it. Her head fell forward, and she slept off and on in the chair until sunlight danced around in her closed eyes, nudging her closer to wakefulness. The knock on the door woke her completely from her fitful sleep. The confusion she felt upon finding herself in a chair in the front room only lasted a second before she remembered last night. She knew before she answered it who would be on the other side.

Ambrose, Lottie, and Onyx walked in. They walked in silently. Ambrose and Lottie sat next to each other on the couch while Onyx remained standing. Indigo turned the rocking chair to face the room and sat in it. Ambrose resumed telling the story as if he had only taken a bathroom break or gone to get something to drink.

"Your momma dropped you off like that for years. Dinah didn't mind; even though she fussed and carried on, she really didn't mind. If your mom didn't bring you over, your grandmother would go get you. If Wanda had a man living with her, Dinah would have a fit; they would fall out with each other and stop talking for a while. Even if they weren't getting along, Dinah would check on you. Anyway, Wanda had been living with this one man longer than she lived with anyone else. Dinah couldn't stand him; I can't remember his name, but there was something about him she didn't like. She didn't like the way he looked at you, and she didn't like the control he had over your mother. She tried to get Wanda to see that he was no good, but Wanda didn't believe anything Dinah said about him."

"Like, what?" she asked.

"She said that you were afraid of him."

"Why was I afraid of him?"

"She said you told her he made you sit on his lap when your mom wasn't home." Lottie gasped and covered her mouth with her hands before Ambrose continued.

"Dinah told your mother, but she didn't believe her. Dinah said she was worried sick about you being in that apartment with him. She went by the apartment one day, and you came running out of the bushes. You were crying and hanging on to her for dear life, begging to go home with her. In the car, you told her Ronnie was in the shower and wanted you to bring him a towel. When you brought him the towel, he tried to get you to come in the shower with him. When your mother called that night, Dinah didn't tell her about it; she told Wanda she was gonna keep you for a few weeks. That she was giving her a break."

"Did he hurt me?" asked Indigo, sounding like a frightened little girl.

"I don't think so. Dinah had Delray's shotgun and a little pistol in the house. If he had hurt you, I'm sure she would have gone over there and shot him then and there. It took your momma a long time to come and get you. I'll never forget that night. There was so much going on in the world, so much chaos. Lord have mercy; I'll never forget that night. It was the second or third night of the Rodney King riots, and everybody was wondering if it was gonna be another Watts Riot. Wanda came over to take you home, but Dinah wouldn't let her. Dinah said Wanda was drunk, and they got into a fight. She said your mother pulled a box cutter on her and threatened to cut her if she didn't let her take you home." He looked up from the floor and pleaded with Indigo with his eyes to let him stop.

Indigo whispered, "Then, what?"

"Your momma got you out of bed and was trying to leave the house when Dinah shot her."

"No, no, no, not Big Momma." Indigo bent over in the chair, her elbows on her knees and her hands cradled her head. Her hands squeezed her aching head. Ambrose continued reciting what happened that night as she moaned and rocked. Now, he was unable to stop because he wanted to finish this retelling so that he would never have to speak of it again. Bits and pieces of her dreams that were actually memories were being fitted into place with the help of Ambrose's words. She remembered the loud voices, the sound of bodies being shoved against the walls, the boom of the gun, and the dull thud of her mother's body hitting the floor. She was muttering to herself that she remembered that night, that she remembered it all. Onyx knelt in front of her and whispered in her ear. Standing up, he told his grandfather it was enough for today.

She leaned on Onyx as he walked her into the bedroom and helped her into bed. She motioned for him to lie with her, and he held her as she cried herself to sleep.

Chapter 17

The next day, Ambrose got through the retelling of the night that Wanda was murdered. Three days would pass before they would gather again in the living room where Dinah had murdered her child. Indigo, Ambrose, Lottie, and Onyx were sitting in her living room theorizing about the mysterious events that had happened after Dinah's death. Ambrose, Lottie, and Indigo believed that Big Momma's spirit had lingered on to protect Indigo from Wanda. Everyone, except Indigo, believed that Wanda was a malevolent spirit. Even though Indigo had been frightened by Wanda's presence, she didn't believe her mother wanted to hurt her. She was trying to explain this to them.

"I felt it, too—the emptiness and despair that you felt, but I don't believe she was trying to hurt us," she explained.

"What then?" asked Onyx.

"I think we felt her essence. Mr. Ambrose said it…when my grandfather died, it changed her. Instead of being the happy little girl she was before, she was sad, lonely, and grief-stricken. Everybody's focus was on my grandmother, not Wanda. My mother not only lost her father, but she also lost her mother. People back then never thought about a child being depressed. Nobody worried about her mental health. My mother had to figure it out all by herself. No wonder she self-medicated and went looking for her daddy in all the wrong places. I can't imagine living my life without knowing that someone loved me." She looked at Onyx.

"Are you saying Wanda didn't mean to scare anyone? It's just who she was?" asked Lottie.

"Yes! I'm saying that maybe we can release her from the void that she has been trapped in all these years by letting her know that we know how sad and alone she was when her dad died, and her mother stopped showing her how much she was loved. Maybe she doesn't know that she's dead because of how suddenly it happened." She looked at them, hoping to see that they understood.

"So, if you're right. She's just wandering around, trying to take you home?" asked Ambrose.

"Yeah," said Indigo, shaking her head.

"You're gonna try and release her?" he asked.

"Yes."

"How?" asked Ambrose doubtfully.

"I'll show you," she said. She nodded at Onyx. He ushered his grandfather and Lottie to the backyard, where he had set up the potter's kiln. In the backyard, there were four chairs near the back fence just in front of the expanded flowerbed. A carpet of white and purple alyssums covered the nubby base of the rosebushes. Red, orange, pink, and white blooms glowed against a waxy deep-green leaf background. A small table held Big Momma's old, worn bible and a vase of roses. Indigo asked them to take a seat while she stood facing them. Her hand brushed the top of the bible and lingered there as she began.

"Father, God, we are here today asking to be forgiven and freed from the evil committed here almost twenty years ago. Father, please forgive my grandmother for doing the unthinkable by destroying the gift you gave her. That night, with that one act, so much was lost. I lost my mother, Big

Momma lost her daughter, and my mother lost her life. My mother was rotting in this backyard alone all those years in a place where there was only darkness and despair until she embodied that darkness. But today, Father, I ask that you release her from this lonely place and allow her soul to be reunited with you. You are a just God and do not condemn unfairly, so I'm hopeful that my mother will be with you in paradise today and that my grandmother is already there with you. I know that Big Momma had a relationship with you and that she loved you. I'm confident that she asked for your forgiveness years ago. Your capacity to love is beyond anything I can conceive or hope to understand. I am assured that my mother and grandmother will be together again, loving each other. Thank you, Father, for letting the wickedness of that night finally come to an end. Thank you for breaking that curse today, in Jesus' mighty name, Amen."

After the others uttered *Amen,* silence fell over the group. Each felt a peacefulness spread through their bodies. Each experienced something that they would never be able to put into words. No one moved, not wanting to interrupt what was happening. When a pair of monarch butterflies fluttered around the group and then lingered close to Indigo, she knew it had worked.

"Ready," she said when the butterflies had flown away.

Onyx had battered the duffle bag with a sledgehammer earlier that day and left it near the kiln. He had not opened the bag, unsure of what might be released. They walked to the driveway near the garage where the kiln was set up. They held their breath as he unzipped the bag and collectively released their breath when nothing happened. He opened the lid of the kiln and poured the contents of the duffle into it. When he closed the lid, they hoped it was finally over. The group stayed together for the rest of the day and half of the night, finding comfort in each other's presence. At midnight, Onyx stole into the backyard and turned the kiln off. For the first time, he could sleep without the burden his grandfather had placed on him. He hadn't known how heavy it had been until it was lifted off. Indigo slept in his arms, knowing she was loved and had someone she could love without fear. That night, Ambrose lay in bed, feeling that he was finally forgiven for what he had done. He felt it when Indigo began her prayer. It was a surreal feeling he got whenever he was in the presence of The Divine. That evening, instead of saying her prayers in bed, Lottie knelt and thanked God for the people he had placed in her life. Roscoe watched her, struggling to pull herself up from the floor. After her third attempt, he began barking, urging her to get up. He took a piece of her housecoat in his mouth and pulled on it, which made Lottie angry enough to get up off the floor.

On Saturday, Indigo, Onyx, Ambrose, and Lottie went to the cemetery where Dinah and Delray were buried. Ambrose and Lottie sat in the fold-up chairs that Onyx set up for them while he and Indigo sat on the grass close to the grave markers. Onyx dug a hole between the two graves with a garden trowel. When the hole was deep enough, Indigo poured her mother's ashes into it. Onyx replaced the plug of grass on top of the hole and spread the mound of dirt into the lawn. Indigo was satisfied now; her mother was resting between her parents. *It's over*, she thought. *Now, life can go back to normal.*

Indigo and Onyx continued to see each other, but Onyx didn't spend every night with her. She was no longer afraid to be alone in the house. Big Momma's bible was back where it belonged on the nightstand next to her bed. Indigo flipped through its pages when she needed to feel close to her grandmother. There were times that she found herself crying for both her mother and grandmother. Images of that night still came to her in her dreams, and no matter how hard she tried to change the outcome, she couldn't. The boom of the gun and the sound of her mother falling to the floor always ended her dreams and caused her to wake up crying. Thoughts of Treyvon surfaced at unexpected times. She remembered the good times, how they met and fell in love. Then she would remember the monster he had turned into, and fear would make breathing difficult. Indigo's friendship with Amani had ended, but she and Destiny had grown closer. Ambrose and Lottie continued as they had since Big Momma's death. Lottie resumed her post on the porch, only leaving it to watch her shows, dodge the mailman, and cook dinner. Life had returned to the mundane rituals for which they could all be grateful.

The chill in the morning air heralded the end of summer. Indigo told herself it was time to put a blanket on the bed. *September was almost over, and soon, the holidays would be here,* she thought as she hugged herself and got out of bed. *This will be my first Christmas without her.* She felt a heaviness that, if she didn't fight, would take her to a sunken place where it would take days to climb out of. So, she made herself happy. Indigo clicked on Pandora, and B.o.B.'s "Nothin' On You" leaped from her phone into her body. She c-walked down the hall to the beat of the music, genuinely feeling better. She could barely brush her teeth from smiling. She had to contain herself in the shower until 2 Pac's "Dear Mama" came on. Her tears mingled with the water, and she howled.

Indigo was sitting in the kitchen, shaken by the wild swing of emotions—up, down, up, down. It was exhausting cycling through those feelings. She was wondering why she had never cried for her father. Maybe it was because she had never met the man. No one talked about him. He was not even a footnote in her life because no one knew who he was. Her mother couldn't or wouldn't say who he was, and now she would never know. She realized now that she had never missed not having a father. It hit her then that Mr. Ambrose had made that possible. He had been in her life for as long as she could remember. He was a father to the fatherless. She wiped a tear away and reminded herself she needed to thank him for that. The phone rang, and her mood changed yet again.

"Hey, can you meet me at this house I want you to see?" Onyx asked, forgetting to say hello in his excitement. "It's a new listing I got."

"Yeah, sure."

"Cool, cool. I'll text you the address."

Indigo pulled up to a cute one-story Ranch-style house with native planting in lieu of grass. She took the meandering flagstone pathway to the front door. Onyx opened the door smiling.

"Nice, huh?" he asked.

"It's really cute," said Indigo, looking around the living room.

"Let me show you around."

He took her on a tour of the house, pointing out updates and vintage features. After they concluded their tour, Onyx led her out of the family room onto the backyard deck.

"You wouldn't expect a wooden deck here. Most of the time, you would have a cement patio, but I like it. It's different," he said. "It's a decent size deck, and you still have a good-sized yard. So, what do you think?"

"I think it's a beautiful home. A nice house in a nice neighborhood."

"Exactly; that way, I won't have to worry about you when I'm out late or out of town."

"Wait—what. What are you talking about?"

"I'm talking about us. I can sell my house in a heartbeat and buy this one, where we can have a fresh start. You can decorate it any way you want, and we can get married and start having babies."

"Babies! You want to marry me?"

His body jerked slightly. He was surprised that he had said what he said out loud. His eyes blinked a few times before he quietly answered. "Yes."

"And babies, as in more than one?"

"Yes, babies," he answered louder and more confidently than before.

"Are you proposing?"

"Yeah…I guess I am."

Indigo began to laugh. She laughed even harder when she looked at the hangdog expression on his face. "Negro, please." She said when she was finally able to stop laughing. "You looked scared to death when I asked if you wanted to marry me."

"That's not true," he said stiffly.

"Okay, all right then. Where's the ring?" She held her hand up and wiggled her fingers. When he didn't respond, she continued. "That's what I thought. So, why did you have me come here?"

Onyx smiled before confessing. "I thought maybe we could move in together. I guess I got caught up in the moment."

"So, you don't want to marry me," she teased, poking him with a finger.

"I got this new listing and thought about how we would probably get married and have babies one day. I thought this house would be perfect for us now and in the future."

"I'm sorry for laughing at you, but I didn't know you were thinking about settling down, let alone with me."

He grabbed her arm and pulled her to him. "Why not you?" he asked before he kissed her.

Indigo left the house, not knowing if she was engaged or if he was going to buy the house. The only thing she knew for sure was that he wanted to be with her every day, and she wanted to be with him.

That night, Onyx asked if she would move into the house with him.

"You bought the house?" she asked.

"I put in an offer, but because I'm the listing agent, it gets a little tricky. I'll hold an open house and see if any other offers come in. I made a best and final offer, so if someone outbids me, I won't get it."

"Onyx, I don't want to move, at least not yet."

"I thought you liked the house?"

"I do. I think a house like that would be perfect for us in the future, but right now, I want to stay here."

"Why would you want to live in a neighborhood everyone is trying to get out of?"

"I love this neighborhood. I love this house. This neighborhood and this house keep me connected to my mother and grandmother. A lot of love lived here once; besides, I love living next door to your grandfather and across the street from Miss Lottie if you can believe that. It's hilarious how the whole block hides from the mailman. Onyx, this is home, so why don't you move in with me?"

"Come on, man. You know this neighborhood is dangerous."

"I know, and a year ago, moving back to this place would have been the last thing I would've wanted to do. But, right now, it feels right. I want to be here for as long as your grandfather and Miss Lottie are…you know."

"All right. I know my grandfather would love having me living next door, and I wouldn't have to worry about you being here alone at night."

That weekend, Onyx moved his clothes into Indigo's old bedroom closet and laid the clothes that wouldn't fit into the small closet on the twin beds.

"Well, we'll just have to buy a closet system, and to sweeten the deal, you can make this into your office," Indigo said, smiling up at him. Onyx walked over to her and showed her how she could sweeten the deal.

Chapter 18

Ambrose and Lottie were elated that Onyx had moved in with Indigo. Indigo and Lottie were giving Ambrose's house a makeover. The worn sheets and towels were thrown out and replaced with Onyx's money, his contribution to the makeover. Ambrose fussed, but in reality, he was pleased with the changes. Indigo was in his backyard spray painting his wooden kitchen table set. It had taken some convincing to get Ambrose to let her paint the set. The tabletop was nicked up from years of abuse by his kids and grandkids. Homework and art projects were made on that table, as well as the list of bills or groceries Lucinda made on the table. She had to be creative as she thought of a way to preserve those precious markings and refresh the tired old set. She sanded the maple stain off the top of the table, careful not to remove the imperfections. The top of the table was stained dark brown and sealed with a matte varnish, while the legs of the table and chairs were spray-painted a sage green. She had finished spraying a chair when Ambrose poked his head out the back door.

"Going to take Roscoe for a walk."

"Okay," she said, standing straight to look at him. "I'm almost done."

Ambrose turned to leave, then turned around again. "Hey, you're doing a great job. It looks good!"

"I told you it would."

They smiled at each other for a moment, seemingly unable to look away. When Indigo stooped down again, she broke the spell, and Ambrose turned and closed the door. For a crazy second, Indigo wanted to run after him and tell him how much she appreciated him being there for her when she was little. *Hell,* she thought, *I appreciate you being here for me now because I still need you.*

Ambrose closed the back door, thinking his grandson was a lucky man. He had thought the worst part of growing old was feeling like an old watch that was winding down. But seeing young love reminded him that his body couldn't move the way it used to. He still wanted to satisfy a woman like he did in his youth. He still wanted to be satisfied. He remembered how it felt to caress and be left breathless by a beautiful woman. He thought about Lottie and how grateful he was that there was still someone content with the touch of his feeble hands. He walked across the street to fetch Roscoe. She was sitting on the porch, and the little dog ran to the gate, wagging his tail. Lottie walked to the gate with Roscoe's leash. She bent and hooked the leash on his collar.

"Ready!" she said.

"Ready," he said, reaching for the leash.

She handed him the leash and stepped out onto the sidewalk with them.

"Where you going?" he asked.

"I'm going with you. I told you I was going to walk with you one of these days…and today is the day." She closed his mouth with her thumb and index finger before she bumped him with her hip. "C'mon."

Ambrose threw his cane into the yard and took her hand. He stood looking at her before he squeezed her hand hard and began their walk. He took his usual route and a trip down memory lane. He and Lottie remembered the families that once lived or still lived in the houses they passed.

The Smith family had lived in the house on the corner. The Cole family with all those kids, ten or eleven of them. He and Lottie pointed out the houses that no longer contained the families that once lived there. Lottie knew more than Ambrose could have ever imagined about the families that had moved out of the neighborhood. She knew who had died or moved out of their own volition or was forced out by their kids. She also knew if they lived in assisted living facilities or with their kids or grandkids. While she knew about the people who once lived in the houses they passed, Ambrose knew who currently occupied the homes. He nodded to the stern-faced old men wearing cowboy hats and waved to the smiling faces of the Mamitas or children who came out onto the porches to call the old men to dinner. They stopped in front of the gates of the remaining black neighbors if anyone happened to be outside and chatted. They greeted each other with, "Long time, no see," and ended the conversations with promises to return soon with the caveat, "God willing, and the creek don't rise." They turned left at the neighborhood market. A group of young bloods stood leaning against the liquor store wall in the parking lot. They were smoking blunts and drinking from brown paper bags. One of the guys saw Ambrose holding Lottie's hand and yelled.

"Go head, Mr. Ambrose." The group of young men exploded in laughter.

Lottie, feeling like a woman who is desired, straightened her back, swooshed her hips, and laughed out loud. Ambrose laughed with her before he pulled her to him and kissed her like he was her man. He was surprised he remembered how to kiss anymore, considering he hadn't kissed anyone in decades. Everything he remembered about it came rushing back to him. Heat ignited and traveled throughout his body. He released Lottie, who was for once speechless and thought, *This nosey, meddlesome old woman is mine. I hope I'm Her's.* The boys' cheering caused him to look in their direction, and he saw them salute him. Lottie slipped her arm into the crook of his arm, and they walked arm in arm for the rest of their walk.

Ambrose went home that evening after he had eaten dinner at Lottie's. He was tired and wanted to sleep in his own bed. He looked at the worn sofa and recliner and thought maybe it was time to let go of the past. He remembered how the recliner had come to be in the house. *Lucinda had picked out a sofa set with a matching chair, but instead of getting the matching chair, she surprised him with the recliner. Ambrose sat in the recliner in the furniture store and pushed back until his feet were elevated. He closed his eyes and told Lucinda she could pick out any sofa she wanted as long as he could have the chair. Lucinda left the store in tears, complaining that the recliner didn't go with the living room set she picked out. They had argued that night and stubbornly agreed to forget about getting new furniture if they couldn't get what they wanted. A week later, Ambrose had the living room set with the matching chair Lucinda wanted delivered to the house. When he got home that evening, the recliner was there instead of the matching chair.*

He looked at the duct-taped chair where the vinyl had ripped, saw the areas where the brown coloring had faded to no color at all, and knew he could never throw the chair away. Tomorrow, he would tell Indigo and Lottie that they could get started in the living room, but the recliner would have to remain somewhere in the house. Ambrose climbed into bed, chuckling as the image of Lottie sashaying crossed his mind. A big smile spread across his face as he remembered the kiss.

The next morning, the sun rose like every other morning. Onyx and Indigo walked out to their cars together. Onyx was running late so he didn't stop next door before going to work like usual. Seeing Lottie on the porch made him feel better about leaving before checking on his grand-father. Lottie waved at them as they drove in two different directions to work. She wanted to cook her and Ambrose a special dinner, so she was busy most of the afternoon. She didn't notice that Ambrose hadn't come out to water his yard or that he hadn't gotten his mail. She was cooking cornbread for her dressing and snapping string beans as she sat in front of the TV. She put on a nice dress and a little lipstick before she sat the table with her mother's fine china. She went to the porch and waited for him. Roscoe sat by the gate. When he didn't come, she walked to the gate and stomped her feet to shoo the dog away as she slipped out. She looked across at the house and knew something was wrong. She didn't bother to knock. Instead, she let herself into the house with the key Ambrose had given her and called out his name. The house already had the feeling that no one lived there. She walked down the hall, knowing what she would find on the other side. A portion of the Lord's prayer popped into her head. *Yea, though I walk through the valley of the shadow of death, I will fear no evil....* She was unafraid as she walked down the hallway. This was a prayer that she had heard at almost every funeral she had attended. So, as she walked down the hallway, she was preparing herself for whatever was on the other side. She repeated the verse to herself once more before calling out.

"Ambrose, you decent?" She turned the doorknob.

Lottie saw him lying in bed with the most ridiculous grin on his face. "You old fool," she gasped and hiccupped before she broke down and wept. After a while, she pulled a chair close to the bed and sat. She touched his cool, stiff hand and began singing her favorite gospel songs until no more words came from her lips—the room filled with moans.

By the time Indigo walked through the front door, Onyx had bought Chinese food for dinner and had changed into sweats and a t-shirt.

"Hey, babe," he said, leaning down to kiss her.

"Hey," she said, moving past him to go into the bedroom to change her clothes.

"I bought Chinese," he said, continuing into the kitchen.

When she entered the living room, the cartons of Chinese takeout were lined up on the dining table. Chopsticks for Indigo and a fork for Onyx lay beside their plates. She made a pit stop in the bathroom before loading her plate and joining him on the couch. She insisted on eating Chinese or Japanese food with chopsticks (claiming it tasted better that way). Onyx only ate with chopsticks when dining with clients. He claimed a Black man using chopsticks fascinated his clients and made him appear more worldly.

It wasn't until after he and Indigo watched the reality show "Basketball Wives" that he realized he hadn't heard from or seen his grandfather all day. He didn't expect his grandfather to answer the phone, but he called him anyway. Onyx had hoped to save himself a trip, but since there was no answer, he got off the couch. He told Indigo that, as usual, his grandfather wasn't answering his phone and that he just needed to check on him before going to bed. Onyx walked up to the dark house, thinking that his grandpa had forgotten to turn on the porch light. He didn't bother to knock. Instead, he inserted the key into the lock and was a little surprised that the door was unlocked.

"It's just me!" he yelled, stepping into the black front room. "You forgot to lock the front door, and you didn't turn on the porch light, Grandpa!"

He turned on the living room light and announced his presence again. The house was eerily quiet, and the only light was the one he had just turned on. He walked toward the bedroom and turned on the hall light. The bedroom door was slightly ajar, and when he opened it fully, he saw Miss Lottie sitting next to the bed. He jerked to a stop and excused himself, thinking he had walked in on a private moment. He backed out of the room but stopped just outside of it. There was something wrong with what he had seen. Miss Lottie had turned to look at him, but his grandfather hadn't moved. He walked back into the room and turned on the light.

"Miss Lottie, how long have you been sitting here with him?"

"Since this afternoon, when he didn't get Roscoe for their walk."

"Why didn't you call me?"

"Because I wanted to be with him for as long as I could. He'll be taken away from me soon enough."

He looked at his grandfather and saw how happy he looked. "I've never seen anything like this," he whispered.

"Me either. He looks like he saw Jesus himself standing at the pearly gates," declared Lottie. "Or, maybe he saw Lucinda, Delray, and Dinah waiting for him," she said, wiping her tears.

"Come on, Miss Lottie. I need to call somebody…the police, I guess," he said, reaching down to help her.

"I ain't leaving him alone. I'm gonna sit here until they take him away," she said, swatting at his hands.

He made all the necessary calls, standing in his grandfather's doorway. He called his mother, Indigo, and then the police in that order as he stood watch with Miss Lottie. Soon, Indigo was at his side, holding on to him. His mother and sister made it to the house before the police and paramedics did. They stood watch in the small room, answering the questions of the police until the paramedics arrived with the gurney. Ambrose was zipped into a black body bag and rolled out of the house he brought for his wife Lucinda, who made it into a home for their family. Ambrose was leaving his home the only way he ever wanted to leave it, "feet first."

Onyx turned on the porch light and locked the front door after the others had gone next door. He leaned against a porch post to compose himself before going where his mother, sister, Miss Lottie, and his woman waited for him. His grandpa had taught him what it was to be a man; he had been taught that *A real man doesn't cry.* He stayed on the porch until he had swallowed the pain enough to show the women that he was a man who didn't cry like they did. When he set his face into a granite mask, he walked next door. When he walked through the front door, the women looked up at him. They saw the hardness of his face and eyes, but they were not fooled. They, too, wore the mask that was necessary to move within the inhospitable country that they lived in. They knew how close he was to his grandfather and that it was impossible for him not to feel that loss. So, they watched him surreptitiously from the corners of their eyes. They unconsciously held their breaths as they waited for his mask to slip and the dam to break. Onyx walked Lottie to her house to change into her pajamas and get Roscoe. He waited outside while she fed the dog and then changed. When she was ready, they walked back to Indigo's house, where everyone, including his mother and sister, was spending the night. Roscoe was excited to go on a night walk, so he pulled Lottie forward. When they crossed the street, he veered to the right to go to Ambrose's house. Lottie yanked him to the left, almost dragging him into Indigo's yard. He scampered up the steps and into the house. He wagged his tail violently as he inspected Onyx's mother and sister. The dog eyed Indigo warily and began roaming the house looking for Ambrose. Lottie called for him to come back, but he continued his quest. Finally, after every room had been searched, he returned to the front room and went to the door. He scratched at the door and whimpered, wanting to be let out.

"Do you want me to let him out?" asked Onyx.

"He doesn't need to go out. He's looking for Ambrose," Lottie stated.

They looked at the dog as he continued to whimper and paw at the door. After Lottie yelled at him to "*Stop it!*" he gave up and lay in front of the door, staring back at the group.

Tamar called her brother Jonathan and told him that their father died in his sleep last night. Jonathan, who was pissed that it took her a whole day and half the night to tell him that his father was dead, began speaking before she could explain. She listened to him, knowing that he was angry with himself for not being a better son. She also knew that this was just the beginning of the bitter fighting between siblings whenever the last parent died. Jonathan hadn't been in his father's life, nor hers, for years, but he would want whatever money their father had and most certainly would want the house sold as soon as possible. The wound he inflicted when he married his color-struck wife with bourgeoisie aspirations had scabbed over and hardened years ago. She already knew he wouldn't help her bury their father but would insist on selling the house. Cash, for him, would be the temporary legacy that would allow him and his family to indulge in their narcissistic fantasies. So, when he finished his caustic rant, she informed him that she just found out that their father was dead. Her brother, true to form, explained that it was a bad time for him at work and that he couldn't get away. He told her she should take care of everything since she was there.

Indigo changed the sheets on her bed for Tamar and Zari. The twin beds in her old room, where she and Miss Lottie would sleep, already had clean sheets. She was thankful that Onyx had purchased a closet for his clothes. The room was crowded with beds, the free-standing closet, and his desk and chair. The surface of the large desk was covered with contracts, folders, a stapler, a glass jar containing pens, pencils, markers, and a wireless all-in-one printer. Indigo gathered the papers and folders and stacked them neatly in one pile on the desk. She put stray pens into the jar and put his dress shoes into the closet. Onyx lay on the sofa she made up for him while his mother and sister slept in their bed. Indigo was in her childhood bed, and Lottie was in the bed across from her. Roscoe slept on the floor between them.

"You know, at my age, you don't expect to find love...but I did," Lottie said out of the blue.

Indigo didn't say anything right away. She didn't think Lottie needed her to respond, but she asked a question that stopped her from letting herself go in her relationship with Onyx. "Weren't you afraid you wouldn't have much time with him?"

"Nope, you don't have to be old to lose someone. Love is for everyone; it don't belong just to the young. I'm not going to lie. I knew we didn't have a lot of time left, but I wasn't gonna let that stop me. The time we had was good because we had each other."

"I'm scared, Miss Lottie."

"Scared of what?" asked Lottie, lifting herself on her elbows.

"Loving too much, too hard. Not having enough time together."

Lottie smiled at that. "Chile, ain't no other way to love but to love hard. If it's love you talkin' about, then there ain't no controlling it. You better love that man with everything you got, do you hear me? Everything, and I mean everything." She lowered herself back down. "When you get to be my age, people think you don't have desires, but you do. Desire takes on a different form, though. A peck on the lips, a caress of the face, or simply holding hands becomes a thing to be cherished. When Ambrose touched me, I remembered how powerful being a woman is. He gave me back my power every time he touched me. So don't waste time being afraid of something you can't control."

They lay silently, thinking about the men they loved. Lottie knew her life would be lonelier without Ambrose. Indigo knew she was no longer in control when it came to loving Onyx and how long she would have him to love. She also knew she didn't know the day or hour that he might stop loving her.

Zari fell asleep crying in her mother's arms. She cried because she envied the relationship that Onyx and her grandfather had. She also cried because she knew she had not tried to get closer to her grandfather. She had put herself first, always putting off visiting him until the next time, and now that time would never come. She cried herself to sleep, knowing she would never have what Onyx and her grandpa had. Tamar tried not to cry in front of Zari, but it was impossible. Tears streamed down her face, and she held her daughter tight. Her father had been her rock; he had been the strongest man she had ever known. She would never forget how afraid she was to tell her parents that she was pregnant with Onyx. *She was in her first year at Los Angeles City College when she got pregnant. Her mother was horrified that she was going to be an unwed mother. Tamar shook off her mother's shame with a bravado that was only partly manufactured, but she couldn't shake off her father's disappointment. Her dad never told her he was disappointed, but she saw it every time he looked at her. She refused to become the stereotype that people assumed she was. She gave up going to college and worked two jobs so that she wouldn't have to get on welfare. Although her mother was embarrassed that she was a single parent, it didn't stop her from taking her grandbaby to church, daring anybody to say something negative about her daughter or grandson. Tamar cried harder when she recalled how the disappointment in her father's eyes was replaced with unadulterated love the first time he held his grandson.*

Onyx lay on the couch in the dark, staring up at the ceiling. He knew that he would have to face this moment one day, so he was surprised at the depth of his pain. He thought he had prepared himself, but he wasn't ready for this. He was his grandfather's favorite; he knew it; they all knew it. His grandpa had taught him what it was to be a man because he had never known his father. He was very young when his father stopped coming around. What little he knew of his father was from the stories that his mother and grandfather told him. Even though his grandfather reminded him that he had a father, Onyx thought of him as his father until he was older enough to know the difference. His grandfather taught him how to catch and throw a football, dribble a basketball, and mow the lawn. He took him camping and fishing. His grandfather was the one who told him what to do when the inevitable police contact occurred. He had taught him everything that he knew in order for him to survive the injustice of this world, and now he was gone. The pain that hit Onyx at that moment was a physical one that tore at his gut until it moved up to his heart. The pressure on his chest made it hurt to breathe. Onyx clutched his t-shirt until the pressure eased and tears rolled down his cheeks. Indigo heard him crying and sat up in bed.

"Let him be," barked Lottie.

"No," said Indigo, springing from the bed.

"He's kept that pain bottled up all evening; let him get some of it out before he loses his mind. He'll need you to be with him later, but not now. Now, he needs to be able to cry without shame."

Indigo's hand was on the doorknob when Lottie continued. "His grief will either kill him or drive him mad if you don't give him the space he needs to cry. You know that his manhood is all he has left in this place where we find ourselves. He'll stop crying if you go in there, and crying is the best thing he can do right now."

Indigo lowered her hand but remained standing in front of the door. She knew Lottie was right but hearing him weep tore at her. She wanted to draw him close to her, hold and comfort him. She went back to bed and cried as she listened to the guttural sounds coming from the living room.

Tamar heard her son, and she hurt for him, but she knew better than to go to him. She knew his tears would help him to face the heart-wrenching days ahead. She looked at her daughter and was grateful that at least one of her children could sleep tonight.

The next morning, Lottie and Indigo were in the kitchen preparing breakfast. Indigo was taking the biscuits out of the oven when Tamar walked into the kitchen.

"Indigo, you made homemade biscuits?" asked Tamar, impressed.

"I wish. Miss Lottie made these," she answered, placing the pan on top of the stove.

"If you want me to, I'll show you how to make them next time," said Lottie.

"Good, because Big Momma never had time to show me how to cook, and she didn't write anything down. I guess it was hard to measure if you were cooking by touch."

"I don't measure much either, but if you watch me do it, you'll see what a pinch or a dash is," said Lottie.

"Mmm, it smells good in here," Zari said as she entered the kitchen.

"Right," agreed Indigo. "There's coffee on the counter and orange juice in the fridge."

Indigo left the women in the kitchen and went to the living room to see if Onyx was awake. He was just sitting up when she came into the room.

"Good morning."

"Morning," murmured Onyx.

She walked over to sit next to him but instead decided to sit on his lap and hugged him. He squeezed her tightly, and Indigo began to cry. The two of them sat huddled on the couch, holding each other. Lottie yelled from the kitchen for them to come and get something to eat. Indigo wiped at her tears and kissed Onyx's face before she got up. Then, she tugged him to follow her into the kitchen.

Late that afternoon, Onyx crossed the street to Lottie's house. She was on the porch as usual, rocking and watching the comings and goings in the neighborhood. She saw him approaching her house and wondered why. She was surprised when he said he had come to take Roscoe for his walk. Lottie went inside to get the leash. She locked her front door and snapped on Roscoe's leash.

"I guess I better show you the route," she said.

She handed him the leash and slipped her arm under and over his. They walked down the street, amazed that the neighbors already knew about Ambrose. A heavy-set Hispanic woman rushed to her gate, flagging them down with a dish rag. When they stopped in front of the gate, she gestured with her hands for them to wait and shouted something in Spanish over her shoulder. A girl about eight years old ran out of the house and stopped next to the woman. The woman spoke to the child in Spanish and then turned to look at them.

"My grandmother said she's sorry that Mr. Ambrose is gone and to please let her know when his funeral is," the little girl interpreted solemnly.

"Mis condolencias. Que descanse en paz," said the woman, looking at Onyx and Lottie. The little girl didn't interpret, but the meaning was not lost.

"Muchas gracias," replied Onyx directly to the woman before looking at the child. "Tell your grandmother that we will let her know."

Lottie and the woman smiled and bobbed their heads up and down as Onyx spoke, and the child interpreted. Throughout their walk, neighbors stopped them to acknowledge their loss, offer their condolences, and wish to be apprised of his funeral. When they approached the liquor store parking lot, three of the regulars walked up to them.

"Hey man, sorry for your loss. Mr. Ambrose was a good dude, man. Every day, he and his dog came by. Sometimes, he would get on us for being too loud, you know," said one of the guys.

"But he was looking out for us too. He told us when the County was hiring or when there was a job fair going on," said another of the guys.

The first guy interrupted, "Hey, would it be okay if we came to his funeral? We wanna pay our respects to a real G."

"Yeah, man. That's cool. I'll make sure you guys know when and where." Onyx shook each of their hands in that universal way that Black men did and ended the shake with a shoulder bump.

When he and Lottie got to the park, they sat at the bench she and Ambrose had sat at just two days ago. They sat quietly for several minutes. Roscoe had walked passively, not marking his territory or pulling to go faster. Ambrose was gone, and everyone around the dog was sad. He sat attentively at Lottie's foot, expecting to see Ambrose coming to walk with them.

"Ambrose loved you more than anything or anybody," declared Lottie, bumping his shoulder.

"I know. The feeling was mutual."

"You meant the world to him that you were living next door. He talked about you every day. He was so proud of you."

"Thanks." Onyx didn't look at Lottie. He stared stoically ahead, wishing she would stop talking.

"I'm not gonna tell you that it's gonna get better. It might and might not. It's all going to depend on you. A loss this deep is gonna hurt probably for the rest of your life, but its grip on your heart will ease up."

Onyx made a strange sound when she mentioned the pain in his heart.

"When you get to be my age, you lose a lot of people that you loved. It doesn't get easier. I always say that getting old ain't for the faint of heart. You got to be strong to be as old as me because life gets real hard. There's a piece of scripture that helps me when I get to feeling bad. I can't tell where it is in the bible, but it's here." Lottie thumped her chest twice and continued. "It's here...*Count it all joy*. Even though we don't have him with us now, wasn't it a blessing to have him at all? *Count it all joy*, the good times, and the bad times. The joy in this moment is that Ambrose is with his wife

214

Lucinda and his friends Dinah and Delray. We'll get through this because we know he would want us to keep on living. One day, you'll be able to talk about him and be surprised that you're laughing instead of crying. Then you'll be able to *Count it all joy*."

When she finally stopped speaking, he didn't respond because there was nothing he could say. He tried to make sense of what she was saying, but grief wouldn't allow him to find joy in his grandfather's passing. When they made it back to Lottie's house, he tried to get her to spend the night with them again. She declined, saying that she was okay and that she would sleep better in her own bed. He crossed the street and noticed that his grandpa's house already looked abandoned. He went to the house, unlocked the front door, and turned on the porch light. He walked around the house, ending up in the kitchen. Onyx opened the refrigerator, thinking he needed to clean it out soon. He opened the back door and brought in the kitchen table and chairs that Indigo had painted. He locked up the house and leaned against the porch post. Suddenly, he was too weak to stand, so he sat on the steps and sobbed. He didn't bother to wipe his tears away. Instead, he let them fall. A gust of wind stirred behind him, and he knew his grandfather was there with him.

"It hurts too much," he said.

A clump of leaves danced beside his shoes, making a dry scratching sound against the cement walkway. He heard his grandfather say, "I know it does."

His grandfather was sitting beside him, but he knew if he turned his head, the physical body that once housed him wouldn't be there. The supernatural experience he was having with his grandfather was as real as the people across the street walking out of their house and getting into their car. Onyx watched the people across the street drive away, and the world around him hushed. The feeling that this moment would be his last one with his grandfather was not lost on him. He sat on the step and listened to the last things his grandfather needed him to know. Most of the things he already knew because his grandfather had already told him, but he listened intensely, vowing never to forget. A barking dog brought him back to the steps on the porch, and he knew he was alone again. Onyx waited a few more minutes before he stood up to leave. Indigo had made dinner and was surprised to see he was alone. They had dinner in the dining room, and the TV was turned off. She announced they were starting a new tradition where they would sit at the table without distractions and tell each other about their day. He told her about his walk with Lottie and Roscoe.

"Everybody knew my grandfather. I mean everybody, young, old, Black, Mexican, they all knew him and cared about him."

"I'm not surprised. Mr. Ambrose loved this neighborhood and the people in it. In the evenings, when he took Roscoe for a walk, it was like he was tucking everybody in for the night."

"You know, my grandfather told me once that a man's greatest legacy is his children. I know you didn't believe me the first time I asked you because I didn't have something on me. I don't have it on me now, but… will you marry me?"

"Negro! I can't believe you did this again. I look like hell. I have food in my mouth, and you ask me to marry you, again without a ring!" she sighed.

"Is that a problem?"

"Yes, it's a problem," she swallowed. "But my answer is yes!"

Onyx hadn't told her about what happened on his grandfather's porch. He would never share that with anyone. He would, however, reveal in bits and drabs what his grandfather had said to him, prefacing the revelation with, "My grandfather told me once."

Chapter 19

Ambrose's homegoing celebration was a patchwork of people with brown and black faces varying from young to old. One of his contemporaries hobbled up to the pulpit and remembered his friend. He told sanitized versions of their first few years in Los Angeles carousing Central Avenue. He stopped and looked at the pastor before he mentioned Club Alabam and the Dunbar Hotel but told his story anyway. When the old man finished eulogizing his friend, he limped back to his chair with dripping rheumy eyes. More than an hour passed before all the people who wanted to say something about Ambrose had their chance. Onyx was the last to speak, and he started his eulogy with the words, *My grandfather told me once.*

Onyx and five young men from the liquor store parking lot carried the casket out of the church. He had refused to be just an honorary pallbearer. He wanted to personally carry the casket of the man who had carried him and his mother until his stepfather came along. Even when his mother married his stepfather, Herman, his grandfather helped him accept this new man in his life. His grandfather had shown him more love when his sister Zari was born. He knew that, if not for his grandpa, he could have easily felt like an outsider in his mother's new family. Onyx, along with the other pallbearers, lowered the casket onto the metal trolley when directed by the funeral director. He stood at the rear of the hearse until the casket had been placed inside. Once inside the limousine, Onyx closed his eyes, becoming less aware of the suppressed sniffling of the women surrounding him. The pressure of Indigo's shoulder on his side lessened as he slipped into the past. He remembered overhearing a woman whispering to another woman that the little dark boy wasn't Herman's child. Herman had never made him feel like he wasn't his son; it was the whispering woman who made him feel different. It wasn't until that incident that he noticed that his sister Zari was high yellow like Herman and that he wasn't, not even a little bit.

One day, his mother was sitting on the couch with his baby sister Zari, and she patted the cushion, inviting him to sit next to her. His mother held out his sister to him. He positioned his arm the way his mother told him. He sat stiff and upright, all while holding his breath. When she saw how uncomfortable he was, she laughed and took Zari back into her arms. He relaxed and leaned against his mother. He reached to rub his sister's tiny hand, but she grabbed his finger and wouldn't let go. Onyx jiggled his finger, pretending to tug his finger loose, and asked his mom why Zari was so light.

"All Black babies are born lighter than they will be when they grow up," she answered.

"Will she get dark like me?"

"See the color around the edges of her fingers, shaped like crescent moons, just above her fingernails."

"Uh-huh."

"That's the color that she'll grow into."

"It's just a little bit darker, so she isn't going to be dark at all."

"No," said Tamar, pulling her lips into a frown. "She isn't going to be black and beautiful like us."

Onyx studied his baby sister for a minute. "She might be okay, not beautiful like us, but she's my sister, and we're gonna love her anyway, huh momma?"

"That's right," said Tamar, cheerfully. "Because it doesn't matter what color you are. What matters is that you're a good person, right!"

"Right!" agreed Onyx, smiling down at Zari.

He wanted to ask his mother if he was dark like his father, but he didn't because whenever he asked about his father, his mother looked sad. He knew he would ask his grandpa the next time he went to his house.

Onyx was helping his grandfather in the backyard. Ambrose was trimming bushes while he raked the clippings into a pile before throwing them into the trash.

"Grandpa, why come…"

Ambrose stopped clipping, looked over at Onyx, and mocked him. "Why come?"

"Grandpa, why don't I have a dad?"

"You do have a dad. Who told you that you didn't have one?" he asked, lowering his clippers. Ambrose went over to him and bumped him on his shoulder. "Why come…." Ambrose smiled down at him. "You asking about your daddy?"

Onyx looked up at his grandfather, smiling because he caught the joke, but his smile vanished quickly. "I don't know."

"Come on, grandson, let's take a break for a minute." Ambrose went over to the chairs in the shaded part of the yard and sat down. Onyx followed.

"Grandson, you know why you asked, so go ahead and spill it. You know you can ask me anything in the world." He waited patiently for him to ask his question. "You got a right to know about your daddy, so go ahead."

"Zari's daddy sees her every day, so how come my dad don't see me?" he asked, looking down at the ground.

"Your dad used to see you all the time when you were a baby. I think the reason he stopped coming to see you was because no one taught him how

to become a man. I know he loved you, and I'm sure he still does. Sometimes, boys never grow up to be men."

"Will I grow up to be a man?" he asked, looking at his grandfather.

"Yep, because I'm going to teach you how. Now, go on back to picking up them branches. A real man always finishes what he starts."

"Okay, Grandpa, but how long will it take me to be a man?"

"Huh...let's see. You go to school and do your homework and chores at home. You help me. Oh! I almost forgot you're a big brother now." He stroked his chin and looked up at the sky, pretending to be deep in thought. Onyx looked at him intensely, waiting for his answer. "I would have to say that if you keep up the good work, you'll be a man in no time." Ambrose grinned at his grandson. "Now, let's get back to work."

The pastor was speaking at the grave site, but Onyx was too tired to concentrate. He stood behind the few seats reserved for the family, wanting it to end. When the mourners had thrown a handful of dirt or a lone rose into the grave, he couldn't leave. His mother whispered in his ear that it was time to leave, but he told her that he couldn't. The grave digger sat on the mini excavator, unable to backfill the grave because they were there. When his mother, sister, or stepfather couldn't convince him to leave, Lottie came and stood beside him and didn't say a word. Lottie's daughter rode back in the limousine with Onyx's family and left Indigo the keys to her car. Indigo sat on a chair a few feet away from Onyx and Lottie and waited for them to say goodbye. A man from the office walked up to him and explained that they couldn't fill the grave as long as they were there. Onyx didn't move or acknowledge his presence, and neither did Miss Lottie. The man spoke with Indigo and asked for her help.

"He's not going to leave, so can you make an exception, please?"

Exasperated, the man asked, "Can you get him to step back maybe four or five feet?"

Indigo thanked the man and told Onyx they would fill the grave if he stood back a few feet. He stepped backward, and Lottie and Indigo left him to sit down. The man in the dark suit gestured for the man in the excavator to begin. The machine roared and lurched forward. Onyx fell to his knees when the first scoop of dirt was dropped in the hole. Lottie grabbed onto Indigo's arm. He remained seated on the ground until the excavator drove away. When he stood up, Indigo rushed to his side. Onyx hugged her, walked over to Lottie, and helped her up, holding on to her until they reached the car.

The repast was at Tamar's house in Inglewood. Onyx had wanted it at Ambrose's house, but his mother refused to consider it. There was still a fair number of people there when Onyx, Indigo, and Lottie arrived. Most of the people from his grandfather's neighborhood had already left. The remaining people were relatives, Tamar's friends, co-workers, church, and club members. There were also friends and co-workers of Zari and Onyx. Onyx mingled with the guest, walked them out to their cars, and thanked them for coming. He ate when Indigo brought him a plate and reassured her and anyone else who asked how he was doing. He kept moving, not wanting to remain still, not wanting to recall what had happened at the grave site. When he had stood at his grandfather's grave and looked down into the abyss, he had almost lost all hope. He didn't want to be touched, not by Indigo or anyone. He wanted to be left alone to cuss, scream, and hit something. The funeral man came dangerously close to getting the shit beat out of him. The man must have sensed it because his demeanor changed abruptly, and he backed away. The dirt splashing on the casket snapped him out of his madness, and the only thing he felt was sadness. His knees buckled from the heavy sorrow that washed over him. He wanted to howl like a wounded animal until someone put him down, but he had just enough awareness to know that if he started to howl, he wouldn't be able to stop. The silence that came after the excavator drove away stopped the screams inside his head, and he heard his grandfather say *I'm proud of you, grandson.*

Onyx, Indigo, and Lottie left the repast after the ladies from Tamar's church washed the dishes and packed up the food. Onyx and a couple of his cousins collapsed the rental tables and chairs and leaned them on the fence in the backyard.

On the drive home, Indigo looked out the window. All day, the sun had been blocked by gray clouds, reminding her of the stormy day Big Momma had been buried. That day, the heavens cried intermittently. That night, the sky wept and pelted the earth. Today, the sky had only looked like it would rain, but there was never the scent of rain in the air. The only storms had been the private ones that tormented the bereaved. Jonathan and Tamar's relationship, which was already tattered, was coming apart at the seams, aided by grief, regrets, and recrimination. It came as no surprise to either of them. Indigo had felt their tension and was glad for once that she didn't have any siblings. Onyx's laughter brought her back to the present.

"That was nice of your mother to let the young men be pallbearers," said Lottie.

A genuine laugh erupted before he spoke. "Believe me, my mother had no idea who those guys were, but my grandpa would have been pleased."

"He sure would have been. You know he used to have a drink with them from time to time. Everybody knew not to mess with him because of those guys," said Lottie. "That's why I didn't worry about him and Roscoe going on their walks. I knew they were safe."

"One of the guys…I think it was Smitty who said my grandpa would give them gas money to get to work or money for food."

"You know they paid him back. They didn't take advantage of him. They always paid him back!" Lottie declared. "Ambrose loved them boys, and he prayed for them; we prayed for them," she said quietly. "A couple of the boys are doing all right now. I think one of them even bought a house."

The rest of the ride home was silent. They were too tired to try to lift each other's spirits. The liquor store parking lot was empty when they drove past, and so were the streets. The neighborhood looked deserted. Onyx stopped in front of Lottie's house and waited for her to go inside. When she unlocked her front door, Roscoe shot out to relieve himself, and she turned on the porch light and went inside. Onyx pulled away from the curve and U-turned into Indigo's driveway. He looked over at his grandfather's house, and the feeling which threatened to sink him earlier crept closer to him. He was too tired to turn on his grandfather's porch light, which he did every evening, so the house remained shrouded in darkness.

Chapter 20

A few weeks later, Onyx was out in the front yard mowing the grass. He was pushing the mower next door when he saw Pete speed-walking down the sidewalk in his direction. He could tell by his expression that Pete was pleased to catch him outside. Onyx continued to roll the lawnmower into his grandfather's yard, hoping to start it before Pete got closer.

"Hey! Onyx, man, I'm glad I caught you. I just wanted to express my deepest condolences. Ambrose was a good man, one of the old guards of the neighborhood," proclaimed Pete.

"Thanks, man," said Onyx, bending to pull the cord when Pete spoke again.

"Yeah, Ambrose was an old guard, all right, but he wasn't the last one. Now, with Miss Lottie moving out, there's only about three left."

"What!"

"Yeah, what…you didn't know?" Pete smirked, thoroughly pleased with himself. He was about to elaborate, but Onyx was already hurrying past him. "I thought you guys were close," yelled Pete at Onyx's back.

Lottie was watching one of her shows when Onyx pounded on her door.

"What's wrong with you? Pounding on my door like you're the POPO?" Lottie demanded over Roscoe's barking.

"Why didn't you tell us you were moving?"

"Come on in, Onyx...you're letting the heat out."

"Miss Lottie, why didn't you tell us?"

"I was gonna tell you, but I never could find the right time. What with y'all still grieving and everything. I just didn't wanna contribute to any more sadness."

"But you are if you leave," said Onyx, collapsing into a chair.

"I know, but I won't be gone, gone. I'll be around. You and Indigo can come and visit me in Pomona."

"Miss Lottie, why are you leaving the neighborhood you claim you love so much?"

"I do love it, but I can't stand looking across the street at Ambrose's house. Every night, when you turn on his porch light, it's like he's at home watching TV, too tired to come over and take Roscoe and me for a walk. I keep waiting for him to come over, and it's hard waiting for someone who's never coming."

Onyx didn't say anything for a long while. He looked at the old woman that had come to mean so much to him. She was a living connection to his grandfather; now, he was losing that.

"You understand, don't you, baby?" she asked sweetly.

He looked at her and smiled because he had never heard her speak so tenderly. He wondered if she had used that voice with his grandfather. "I understand. Are you moving to a senior living facility?"

"Hell to da naw! I'm gonna live in my daughter's back house. She got a big house with a...whatchamacallit...yeah, a granny flat. Me and Roscoe gonna have our own little house in back of her big house."

"So, what's going to happen to this house?"

"Oh, honey child!" laughed Lottie. "Y'all gonna have my grand-daughter and her three badass little boys for neighbors." Lottie's chuckle rumbled on for so long that Onyx couldn't help but smile.

He blew out a gust of air before he asked, "When are you leaving, Miss Lottie?"

"I'll be here for another week or so. My daughter is painting and fixin' the place up a little before we move in."

"Well, let me know if you need any help moving," he said, standing up to leave.

Lottie got up and reached up to hug him. Onyx held his body taut, not wanting to fall apart. She thought he was angry with her, so she hung on to him and patted his back.

"You understand why, don't you?" she whispered. Lottie released after he nodded in the affirmative.

Onyx walked out of Lottie's yard, passing Pete as he pretended to sort the mail. He crossed the street and went back to mowing his grandfather's yard. He rode this wave of grief like he did the others. Hearing that Miss Lottie was leaving was almost too much to bear. She was a living memento who brought his grandfather back to him every day. She and her damn dog. He sucked up his pain and finished mowing the yard.

When Indigo got home that evening, he told her the news. Although she was shocked, she understood it was for the best. Miss Lottie would have her family around. While Onyx pretended that it didn't bother him, she knew better. He thought that she didn't see his grief, but she did. She had taken Miss Lottie's advice and let him be strong when he needed to be strong, and she gave him the space he needed when he needed to cry. The day before Lottie moved, she and Onyx took her out to dinner. They went to a barbeque joint in Inglewood, on Market Street, where she wanted to go.

"I haven't been to the west side in decades!" declared Lottie. "It sure has changed. This area used to be so nice."

"It's going to come back up. I got some investors looking in this area," Onyx said.

"Oh, so you're back at work?" asked Lottie.

"I'm not grinding like I should, but I've started to get back at it," he replied.

Indigo was sucking on a rib bone when Onyx and Lottie looked at her.

"What?" she asked. "Can't a girl suck on a bone in peace?" she grinned before wiping sauce off her face.

"Dang, girl. You must be hungry," he said, smiling at her.

"I am, but I don't understand it because I've been eating all day."

"When is the baby due?" Lottie asked, then took a bite of her tri-tip sandwich.

"Wait—what? What makes you think I'm pregnant? Indigo asked, putting down the bone.

"I dreamt about fishes last week. I thought my granddaughter was foolish enough to get pregnant again. But looking at you tonight, I can tell it's you," said Lottie matter-of-factly.

"What do you mean? You can tell by looking at me."

"Your breasts are huge: your hips and ass have spread…oh, honey, you're pregnant, all right." Lottie took another bite of her sandwich. "Think about it for a minute," she mumbled with a mouth full of food.

Indigo dropped the bone onto her plate and wiped her hands on her napkin. Onyx looked at her with a sheepish look on his face. He leaned over and whispered in her ear. Indigo's eyes popped. Lottie watched them do the calculations as she chewed and swallowed.

"Y'all let me know when the wedding and baby shower is." Lottie smiled at their confused faces.

"We're not getting married for another year," said Indigo.

"You don't have a year if you wanna be married before that baby gets here." Lottie laughed so loud that the people from other tables looked in their direction.

They ate quietly for a while as Onyx and Indigo processed the possibility that Lottie was right. Lottie couldn't be happier for them. A baby would give them beauty for ashes and bring back some joy into their lives. When they were able to speak again, they spoke of Lottie's new home and made promises to keep in touch. They spoke in code so that the people at the next table wouldn't hear about the strange events of the last few months. Onyx ordered glasses of wine for Miss Lottie and himself. Indigo drank iced tea as they toasted to the future.

That evening, Onyx and Indigo lay in bed. Her head was on his chest as his fingers glided up and down her naked body.

"We said we wanted to have kids," said Onyx.

"Yes, but not this quick. I wasn't supposed to get pregnant this quick after getting off the pill."

"I guess you didn't know how strong my boys were," he said, smiling broadly.

"Whatever, but seriously, what are we going to do?"

"We're going to get married, then we're going to have a baby."

"You act like that's easy."

"It is easy. All we need is you, me, and a preacher."

"Are you crazy? We need a license, a place to get married, a reception hall, invitations, a photographer, a caterer…I can't think. I know we need something else."

"Relax, baby. My mom, Zari, and your homegirl, Destiny, can help."

At the mention of Destiny, Indigo calmed a little. She wanted to pick up the phone to tell her that she was pretty sure she was pregnant. Amani popped into her thoughts. She desperately wanted to share this news with her, but she knew she wouldn't. She was planning the wedding in her head when she heard Onyx's voice.

"I'll have to pay the tenant to break the lease, and then we can move back into the house."

"Or…we could stay here until the lease is up. I would love to bring the baby here from the hospital."

He wasn't thrilled about the idea, but he didn't say anything. He thought there would be plenty of time to change her mind. Instead, they spent the rest of the night making love and asking each other if they wanted a boy or a girl.

The next morning, Onyx helped Lottie's grandsons load furniture and boxes into the U-Haul truck. He and Indigo hugged Lottie good-bye before she got into her daughter's car with Roscoe on her lap. Lottie glanced across at Ambrose's house and quickly looked back at her old home as her daughter pulled away from the curve. She watched the neighborhood that she had been a part of for decades glide past her from the passenger window. Lottie had her daughter turn left on 87th Street and then right on Beach so she would pass the liquor store when her daughter made a right on Firestone Boulevard. The boys were in the parking lot, standing around a trash can that they had made into a firepit. They were laughing riotously as she sailed past.

Chapter 21

Six months later, on a cold Saturday, beneath a milky gray sky that threatened rain, Indigo and Onyx got married. They had endured the forced gaiety of the holidays. The baby that grew inside Indigo's womb kept Onyx from slipping away from the people who loved him. The baby and planning for the wedding helped Indigo to temporarily forget what she had lost. She was sitting in Ambrose's living room on rented party furniture. All of Ambrose's furniture had been thrown away except for the kitchen table and chairs that Indigo had painted. A crisp white tablecloth covered the table and was serving as a bar in the living room. The chairs were hidden in one of the bedrooms. The hardwood floors were refinished, and the walls were painted white. The house had been transformed into an elegant lounge. Enlarged black and white photos of Ambrose, Lucinda, Delray, and Dinah hung on the walls. The pictures depicted couples dressed to the nines. The women looked glamorous in their evening dresses with shiny brooches, gloves, and jaunty pillbox hats. Ambrose and Delray wore dark suits that hung loose on them and fedora hats, leaning to the side. There was only one large picture of Onyx and Indigo near the front door on an easel. The easel stood next to a small table with a large floral arrangement and guest book. The women in the wedding party used the living room as a dressing room because it was the only room with furniture. Zari held out Indigo's dress and told her to stand up. Indigo stood, slipped the dress over her head, and looked at herself in the ornate floor-to-ceiling mirror. The dress didn't camouflage her bulging stomach, which she constantly rubbed in a circular motion. Zari zipped up the dress, and Indigo automatically began rubbing her stomach.

"You look beautiful," said Lottie.

The apricot dress had a bateau neckline with scalloped sleeves. Small fabric cream-colored roses outlined the neckline and the sleeves. The back of the dress draped low, but not too low, and the scalloped hemline ended just above her knees.

"Where in the world did you get this hat? It's perfect!" Tamar asked, placing it on top of Indigo's afro.

"I found it in Big Momma's closet. I had the dress made to go with the hat."

"Is that why you're wearing an apricot-colored dress?" asked Tamar.

"Yep. I sure couldn't wear a white one," she laughed.

Lottie laughed loudly and finished her mimosa. Destiny and Zari laughed politely, but Tamar was not amused.

"You could have worn white if you had gotten married before you started showing. You wouldn't have been the first pregnant bride walking down the aisle in white," retorted Tamar.

"I know, but I'm not trying to hide the fact that I got pregnant before I got married." Indigo pushed the little hat to the side and more to the front of her head.

"Mission accomplished," murmured Tamar.

"I'm not trying to make a statement one way or another. We were going to get married and start a family right away anyway. I just got pregnant first," concluded Indigo.

"Timing is everything," giggled Lottie, picking up a bottle of champagne from the coffee table.

Tamar took the bottle out of Lottie's hand. "Okay, you've had enough," she said, looking sternly at Lottie.

"Party pooper. Come on, lighten up. You look like you need another glass." Lottie smiled at Tamar. "Come on, let's celebrate love and the fact that your son and this girl here found it."

"You're right." Tamar agreed and poured a little champagne into Lottie's glass. She poured some into each of their glasses except for Indigo's. Destiny followed behind Tamar, pouring orange juice into everyone's glasses, including Indigo's.

Caleb cracked the kitchen door and asked if it was okay for him to come in. He told the women that they were ready to get the show on the road.

"Born ready!" announced Lottie, rising from the couch. She swayed slightly. No one noticed but Tamar.

Tamar kissed her soon-to-be daughter-in-law on the cheek and went into the kitchen. Herman was in the kitchen with the broom that Indigo and Onyx would jump over. He presented his arm for his wife to take, and they walked out into the backyard. Two groomsmen came into the living room to escort their partners out the front door and around to the backyard. In the backyard, rows of white wooden chairs lined up, creating a center aisle. Onyx and Pastor Harris stood before a wooden arch decorated with various sizes and shades of cream and white paper roses. The chairs next to the aisle had a jumbo paper rose attached to it. Leroy Hutson's "So In Love With You," played as bridesmaids and groomsmen walked down the aisle. Lottie was the last to walk down. She smiled and held on to her young man. She swayed as she took a step, counted to one, and took another step. When she got to the spot where she was to release her partner, he held onto her until she shook her head that it was okay to let her go. Tamar held her breath, hoping Miss Lottie wouldn't stumble or, worse yet, fall. Lottie made it to the place next to Zari without incident, and Tamar released her breath. The pastor asked everyone to stand for the bride. Tamar rose as everyone else did and smiled while waiting for the bride to appear. She clutched her pearl necklace when she recognized the sultry sound of Leroy Hutson's "Getting It On" being played. She remembered what she was usually doing when that song played. She gasped when she saw Indigo swaying her hips as she danced slowly down the aisle. She looked at her son to see what he thought of this shenanigan. He was smiling and bobbing his head up and down. When Indigo neared Onyx, he held out his hand, and she stopped dancing and placed her hand in his. They faced each other and held hands as the pastor performed the ceremony. Tamar had not realized that Lottie was seated beside her until she leaned in and whispered, "*Close your mouth, dear.*"

The reception was just as unorthodox as the wedding. There was no first dance, no throwing of the bouquet. Instead, Onyx and Indigo treated it like they would any other party. They laughed, danced, and enjoyed themselves. It was almost 1 am, and the party was now composed of mostly family and close friends hanging on to the feelings that came with having a good time. Lottie was asleep in her bed. Onyx had walked her home that evening around ten. The DJ had left at midnight, but Onyx was playing albums on his stereo system.

"What do you know about Leroy Hutson?" asked his mother playfully.

"What you know about Leroy?" responded Onyx, smiling at his mother. "I found your album collection when I was in middle school. I stole a few of your albums. You got a bomb collection."

"Those were your father's albums. You can have the rest if you want them," she said, no longer smiling.

"Yeah, I want them." They had almost finished the cha-cha when he asked, "Mom...do you know where he is."

"No." She stopped dancing. "But it won't be hard to find out."

"Can you? I think I'm ready to meet him," he said, standing in the middle of the dance floor.

"Why, because you're going to be a father?"

"Partly, and because Grandpa told me once that one day, when I became a man, maybe I could show my father what it is to be a man. Mom, I get it. Sometimes, I get scared when I think about raising a kid and trying to protect him from all the hate in this world. I have a job, money, and a house, and I wake up terrified that I'm going to be responsible for someone else. So, I can only imagine how he must have felt becoming a father at such a young age."

Tamar hugged her son and wished the man she once loved had been brave enough to have been standing with them here in this moment. "Baby, everybody is afraid when they find out that they're going to be a parent. It's good that you're scared because it means that you're taking your responsibility seriously. Some people become stronger and more determined, and some people crumble. You will not crumble; this baby is already bringing out the best in you. I can see it." She caressed his face. "I'll get your father's information just as soon as I can. I should have done that a long time ago."

Chapter 22

Three weeks after the wedding, Indigo and Onyx moved out of Big Momma's house. Onyx had been outbid on the house where he had first asked Indigo to marry him. Which, in the end, worked out for the best. He was able to buy his grandfather's house. Onyx notified his tenants in Inglewood that their lease would not be renewed. He paid their security deposit on the new rental as a thank-you for moving out early. He had also vetted tenants for both Ambrose and Dinah's houses. Both sets of tenants were moving in on the first of next month. Darius and Smitty, two of the guys from the liquor store parking lot, helped Onyx and Indigo move out of Big Momma's house. Indigo's new furniture was going to Darius and Smithy or their family members. She thought Ambrose would be pleased with that. Big Momma's bedroom set would be stored in Onyx's garage until they bought a bigger house one day. She reminded the guys to put the bedframe on the truck and reiterated that only the mattress in this room was being given away. When Smitty came back into the house, he picked up Big Momma's rocking chair and asked if she wanted it on the curb or in the truck.

"On the truck." Indigo turned to tell him to be careful with the old chair. "Stop!" she yelled.

"What's wrong?" asked Smitty, holding the chair above his head.

"There's something taped on the bottom of it," she said.

"Money!" Smitty lowered the chair and turned it upside down.

Onyx walked into the room from the hallway, carrying a large box. He placed the box next to the chair to see what was happening.

"Well," said Smitty.

"What is it?" asked Onyx.

"It's a letter to me from Big Momma."

"Open it!" said Smitty excitedly. "Maybe it will tell you where the money is!"

"There isn't any money, Smitty!" Indigo popped him on the head with the letter. She put the letter in her back pocket and told him to be careful with her chair. Smitty was walking out the door when Onyx asked if she was going to read it.

"Not now. I'll read it when we get home."

She tried to forget about the letter, but she kept patting her pocket, reassuring herself that it was still there. When the truck was packed, Onyx gave the guys his address and told them they would head out after they did a final walk-through. They walked through their grandparents' home alone. Each of them walked through the empty houses, saying goodbye in their own way without saying a word. Indigo looked out of her grand-mother's kitchen window and saw Onyx in his grandfather's kitchen. He was unaware that she was watching him, and that made her smile. When he wandered out of the room, she looked at Big Momma's garden. The old metal chairs were under the tree, and the rosebushes drooped from the profusion of blooms. No one would have ever guessed that her mother had once laid for decades rotting underneath a bed of roses. Her hand went to her pocket before she could stop herself, then she went back to rubbing her stomach. She turned from the window and walked toward the front of the house and out the front door. Onyx was waiting for her next to his car parked in Ambrose's driveway. She walked down the walkway and opened the gate. Lottie's grandsons were outside playing. She waved at them, but they were too busy having fun to pay her any attention. Onyx opened the car door for her and waited for her to get in. On the drive to her new home, Indigo thought about the past year and a half. A horrible year and a half that hadn't been all bad. She was astonished by how much had happened since Big Momma's death. The time she spent with Ambrose and Lottie had been special, and she wished she could have had more time with them. Leaving this neighborhood was like saying a final goodbye to Big Momma, Mr. Ambrose, and her mother. The bittersweet memories of her childhood were wrapped up in a house where happiness had been tainted by an evil act. A home where two spirits were unable to leave because of the violence that had occurred there. The neighborhood she had loved as only a child could was in transition again. There were fewer and fewer people who looked like her, making her an outsider now. Hispanic immigrants were making it their neighborhood now, with only a few Black families remaining. For a year and a half, she had been home and had found the answer to the question that had plagued her most of her life. She had gotten a better understanding of who her mother and grandmother were and hoped to make peace with it one day.

When they got home, she was mentally too tired to read the letter, so she laid it on her nightstand next to the side of the bed she had claimed. After she showered, Onyx rubbed cocoa butter on her stomach. She turned around so he could rub cocoa butter on her back and buttocks. When he smacked her butt, signaling that he was done, Indigo slipped on her gown and got into bed. He looked over at her, waiting for her to say something.

"What?" she asked, feigning ignorance.

"You gonna open that?" He glanced at the letter on her bedside table.

"I'm afraid of what it might say."

"Why would you be afraid when you already know what happened?"

She considered his words for a moment before picking up the letter. She got out of bed and went into the nursery. She sat in Big Momma's rocking chair before she opened the letter.

April 16, 2007

Dear Indigo,

If you're reading this letter, it's because I've gone to be with the Lord. I am writing this letter because I want you to know the truth. I didn't have the guts to tell you the truth when I was alive, and for that, I'm sorry.

Your mother didn't leave you. I stopped her from taking you home. Before I tell you what I did, I need to tell you some things first. I loved your mother; she was my precious baby girl. Your momma was the sweetest baby, a good baby, real easy to take care of. She was a daddy's girl, and he spoiled her something awful. We were happy for so long that I thought that it would always be that way. Big Daddy went to work one day and never came home. He wasn't sick or feeling poorly. He was fine. He left for work before I did, but I liked getting up and fixin' his breakfast and having coffee with him before he went to work. That was our quiet time together before the day got started, and we got too tired to talk to each other. That morning, we talked about maybe driving back home to Louisiana that summer because all the old folks were dying off. Big Daddy kissed me goodbye, and that was the last time I saw him alive. They say he had a massive heart attack and was proba-bly dead before he hit the floor. Maybe I could have handled his death better if he had been sick. Maybe I would have done better by your mother if I had time to get used to the idea. My grief was all-consuming; it almost killed me, and I think some part of me did die. Wanda was a little girl when her daddy died, but when you think about it she was a little girl when she lost both her parents. I wasn't any good to her after her father died. Between grieving and working to keep a roof over our heads, I wasn't a mother. I was tired, just plain tired. So, whatever way Wanda turned out was my fault. I didn't know she was getting high, drinking, and messing with boys until it was too late. I didn't know because I wasn't paying attention. I loved my daughter, but she couldn't possibly know that because I was walking around half-dead, wallowing in my own sadness. When Wanda got pregnant, she didn't know who the father was because she was so lonely that she would give herself to anyone who would have her. She changed when she had you. She stopped getting high and drinking. Our relationship got a little better, but I think it was too late to repair what I had done to her. I think she got the love that I couldn't give her from you. For three years, her focus was only on you. You were the only thing she needed. You loved her like she needed to be loved, and she loved you back. But, like many women struggling to make it on their own, your mother got weary and wanted a man to lean on, so she started dating. Every time a man broke her heart, the more desperate she got. It seemed like she didn't have any standards when it came to them. As you got older, I was afraid that one of those men would do something to you. You were seven years old when I took you from your mother and wouldn't give you back. A man was living with you and your mother. She had moved him in without telling me. I didn't like him from the first time I saw him. I didn't like the way he looked at you. When you told me that he made you sit on his lap and watch TV when your mom was at work, I knew that it was only a matter of time before he hurt you. I brought you home with me and I wouldn't let your mom take you back to that apartment as long as he was there.

I don't know if you remember the night your momma came to get you. I hope not. I tried to get her to let you stay with me, but she wouldn't let you stay. We fought that night, and my own daughter pulled a box cutter on me and threatened to cut me if I didn't let you go home with her. I couldn't let her take you, so I shot and killed my own child.

I'm so sorry that I let you live your entire life thinking that your mother didn't care about you. She loved you with all that she had. Whatever weaknesses or shortcomings she may have had were because of me. I know that you may never be able to forgive me, but I hope you can for your own sake. Hate has a way of corrupting one's soul. Indigo, I pray you have a blessed life. A life full of love and joy.

Know that you are loved from everlasting to everlasting,

Big Momma

Indigo read Big Momma's confession, unaware of the mournful sounds that came from her closed lips. Everything that she knew and believed about her grandmother lay broken at her feet, along with her heart. She already knew that her grandmother had killed her mother, but to see the irrefutable proof written in her grandmother's handwriting shook her deep within her soul. She would never be able to invent a new reality because Big Momma had written it down in black and white. Onyx came into the room and asked if she was okay. She handed him the letter. He helped her up and put her to bed before he read the letter. When he finished, he put the letter back in the envelope and placed it in the filing cabinet in his office. He got into bed and held his wife in his arms until she fell asleep.

The next morning, Indigo stayed in bed. Tears continuously fell from her eyes, so much so that she didn't bother to wipe them away. She cried for the little girl that needed her mother. She cried for the little girl that never knew nor would ever know her father. She cried for the grown woman who needed her grandmother to be who she thought she was. Onyx, unable to comfort her and fearing for his child, called his mother. When Tamar got to the house, he let her read the letter and told her about his and Ambrose's part in the drama. Tamar tapped on the bedroom door and walked into the room. Indigo's eyes were almost closed shut from crying. Tamar was shocked by her daughter-in-law's face. She got on top of the bed and pulled Indigo to her. She rocked Indigo in her arms and began to groan in the spirit. For close to an hour, Tamar spoke in tongues and prayed.

"Moan, baby. Let it out. Cry for everything that you've lost and for everything that you never had. Moan if you can't find the words or don't know what to say. The Holy Spirit will interpret your pain and tell God." Tamar moaned. "What do you think Negro Spirituals are, huh?" She told Indigo how the ancestors survived captivity, the middle passage, the auction block, slavery, Jim Crow, segregation, and race riots. "They cried out to the Lord, and he heard their cries."

Tamar gathered her thoughts before she spoke again because she wanted to make sure she said it just so, "Your grandmother loved you so much that she was willing to tear herself down so that you knew that your mother loved you. I'm going to tell you the truth about being a parent. You're going to make mistakes, lots of them. You're also going to damage the very person that you told yourself that you would never hurt. I know your grandmother meant the world to you. No parent or grandparent wants their child or grandchild to see their nakedness. That's why she couldn't tell you the truth. The fear that the law would find out and take you away and the shame of what she had done was something that she could never burden you with. She told you the truth when she knew you were safe and when she didn't have to see you stop loving her."

Tamar lay the unresponsive Indigo against the pillows and slipped out of the bed. "We all do the best that we know how. Come on, let's get you cleaned up. Then you're going to eat something for the baby."

At the word baby, Indigo looked up.

"That's right, you got to take care of your baby."

Indigo's hand automatically began to caress her stomach.

"Come on," said Tamar again.

She got out of bed with her mother-in-law's help. Onyx, who had been standing in the hall, listening, helped Indigo to the bathroom. He ran a bath for his wife, and Tamar went into the kitchen. Indigo moaned as he washed her body. Her moaning had a melodious quality that he would have sworn was coming from more than her. The washing of her body became a spiritual ritual that promised better days. Tamar heated a can of soup while her son bathed his wife. When they came into the kitchen,

Indigo wore a white cotton gown. Tamar and Onyx watched as she ate her soup and crackers.

"Son, I can go get you something to eat. What do you want?"

Before Onyx could answer, Indigo said she wanted a hamburger, fries, and a root beer float. Tamar looked surprised, and Onyx began to laugh, relieved that his wife was back.

Four days later, Indigo delivered a healthy 8lbs 4oz baby boy, Onesimus Ambrose Linton. Onyx, after prompting by the nurse, cut his son's umbilical cord. The cord that physically bonded Onesimus to his mother spiritually connected him to his father the instant it was cut. After Baby O was examined, weighed, cleaned, and wrapped in a swaddling blanket, he was placed on his mother's chest. Indigo locked eyes with her son, in awe that her baby boy was love personified. Her hand trembled as she caressed his head. She closed her eyes and inhaled deeply. *I understand* she spoke to Big Momma in the darkness of her mind. She opened her eyes and found Onyx looking down at her; a smile flitted across her face before she looked down at her son. *I will protect you with my life... and God forbid...*

Onyx kissed her forehead, and she looked back up at him. For the first time in a long while, she saw a light in his eyes. Indigo thought she smelled roses when she had an epiphany. *Loving someone is like sticking one's foot into a river to test the water, only to be swept away. Love, like a river, is sometimes calm and, at other times, turbulent. It's beautiful and dangerous all at the same time, and before you know it, you're rolling in the deep.*

Indigo puckered her lips, mimicking a goldfish, looking up at Onyx until he bent down and kissed her.

The End

About the Author

Evelyn C. Fortson is a retired Los Angeles Superior Court Judicial Assistant who has worked for over forty years in various litigations, such as criminal, juvenile delinquency, mental health, and probate. Her diverse work experience, love of reading, and listening to the wise words of her elders have given her the tools and imagination to weave creative and relatable stories. She lives with her husband in Victorville, CA.

CONNECT ONLINE
evelyncfortson.com